CHIUN SLIPPED UP TO THE DOOR

He reached up for the door handle and seemed to freeze.

"What is wrong?" Dominique asked.

Remo squeezed her arm to get silence.

As she watched, Dominique realized very slowly that the old Asian was not frozen, as he seemed to be. He was turning the door handle, but doing it so slowly and methodically that he appeared immobile to the casual eye.

"Ah, he is very clever."

Abruptly the door opened and shut almost as quickly. It happened so suddenly it literally took Dominique's breath away. It was as if the door had been the mouth of a mechanical monster that had snatched the old one from sight to gobble him alive.

Nothing happened for a moment.

Then the edges of the door pulsed with the most vivid gray light Dominique had ever seen. And the door flew open like a frightened ghost.

And the awful light poured out.

Created by
WARREN MURPHY
and RICHARD SAPIR

THE

Destroyer™

THE COLOR OF FEAR

A GOLD EAGLE BOOK FROM
WORLDWIDE.®

TORONTO • NEW YORK • LONDON
AMSTERDAM • PARIS • SYDNEY • HAMBURG
STOCKHOLM • ATHENS • TOKYO • MILAN
MADRID • WARSAW • BUDAPEST • AUCKLAND

First edition April 1995

ISBN 0-373-63214-2

Special thanks and acknowledgment to
Will Murray for his contribution to this work.

THE COLOR OF FEAR

Printed in U.S.A.

For Sylvio and Marie-Marthe Maynard Michaud.
And for Paul R. Michaud for jogging past DGSE HQ
and walking us through the cheese.

Not to mention the Glorious House of Sinanju,
P.O. Box 2505, Quincy, MA 02269.
(E-mail: willray@cambridge.village.com)

PROLOGUE

No history book ever recorded it, but the first shot of the Franco-American Conflict of 1995 was fired on a Civil War battlefield outside the city limits of Petersburg, in Virginia.

This time civil war would escalate beyond the shores of the continental United States.

Before it was all over, two long-standing allies would launch punishment raids upon one another's most sacred institutions in a new kind of war, one never before witnessed in human history.

And two men, one famous and one obscure, both of whom the world believed long dead, would collide in mortal combat.

All because Rod Cheatwood misplaced his TV remote control.

History never recorded that fact, either.

1

If Colonel Lester "Rip" Hazard had known as he sped down the Richmond-Virginia Turnpike toward Petersburg that before the sun again rose over his beloved Old Dominion he was destined to fall in what history would call the Second Battle of the Crater, he would have driven even faster.

That was the kind of man he was. Virginia born and bred, he loved the land of his birth, which to Lester "Rip" Hazard meant Virginia first and the good ole U.S.A. second.

It was not that Hazard was no patriot. He had served in Panama and again in the Gulf War. He had fought for his country and he had killed for it. And when he had returned from Kuwait, whole in body but tormented by a nagging cough that forced him to resign from the Virginia National Guard, he swallowed his bitter disappointment in manful silence and devoted himself to software support. A gentleman of the Old South did not complain, and so he did not. His great-great-grandfather, Harlan Hunter Hazard, had died with both legs blown off and his lifeblood oozing into the dark and bloody loam of the land he had loved, and it was passed down through the years that Captain Harlan Hazard had died dry of eye and bereft of regret while humming "Dixie."

That was during the 1864 Battle of the Crater, soon to be renamed by historians the First Battle of the Crater.

If Colonel Hazard could only know, his eyes would have shone with pride, for he loved his heritage far far more than he loved his life.

Instead, he piloted his silver Lexus at high speed while checking in with the caterers by cellular phone.

"Ah'm running a mite late," he told the caterer's office. "Them eatables been trucked in yet?"

A honeyed voice said, "Yes, Colonel Hazard."

"Right dandy. On account of mah boys and me expect a hard siege on the morrow, and they need full bellies and satiated souls to get them through the coming ordeal."

"According to the invoice," the voice continued, "you are getting hardtack, salt pork and red-eye beans sufficient to feed a party of thirty-five."

"That sounds about right, honey."

"No meat?"

"Mah great-great-grandpappy ate no meat unless you count rancid pork for the last six weeks of his God-fearing life. What was good enough for Grandpappy Hazard is right suitable enough for me and mah boys. Let them Yanks come loaded down with pork and beef. We'll whip 'em good and chase 'em clear back to perdition or California—whichever is furthest from Old Dominion."

"Good luck, Colonel. All of Virginia will be with you tomorrow."

"Amen," said Colonel Rip Hazard, his voice choking up. It was not for nothing that the *Richmond News Leader* had taken to calling him "the Hope of Virginia."

At the big brown sign that read Petersburg National Battlefield, he pulled off East Washington Street and followed Crater Road past Napoleon cannon batteries and earthen battlements to the rest area he knew so well. It was dark and so easy to imagine the fortifications as they were when newly erected, back when this was Jerusalem Plank Road.

At the parking area Rip Hazard pulled the Lexus in beside a beat-up '77 Chevy Impala that had been painted over a flat Confederate gray, the stars and bars of the Rebel flag covering the battered hood big as life.

That would be Robins's car. A good boy, that Robins. They were all good boys, but by this time tomorrow, God willing, they would have become men, baptized in bloody hand-to-hand combat with a fearsome and implacable foe.

Hurriedly Rip Hazard opened his trunk and removed the thousand-dollar replica Confederate uniform with blue piping and the gold stars of his rank, a three-hundred-dollar forage cap, yellow buck gauntlets and vintage Spencer repeating rifle. Removing his prescription glasses, he replaced them with 1864 coin-silver spectacles and retreated to the woods to change.

More than a change of outfit came over Colonel Hazard as he donned the regalia of his honored forebears. His dreamy blue eyes turned to flint, his soft face hardened and, leaving the raiment of the twentieth century behind, he strode into the piney woods a true son of Grandfather Harlan Hazard.

He felt as if he were walking back through time. Had he fully understood what lay in store for him, Colonel Hazard would have gone to his maker with a glad smile on his face. He loved the America that had given him his freedom, but he yearned for the South of old and, more importantly, for the South that never was, the victorious Confederate States of America led by wise old President Jefferson Davis.

But he knew none of these things. Only that a great battle impended and the first order of business before him was to break the difficult news to his men. Hazard didn't know how they would take the dire tidings. He couldn't imagine what they would say. But if they were gentlemen and patriots, they would buck up and endure as their forebears had.

As he walked, accoutrements jingling, his campaign saber scabbard slapping his lean blue thigh, Colonel Hazard detected the smell of fresh chicory coffee over the tang of salt pork frying.

Camp food. There was nothing like it on God's green footstool.

Then he heard the familiar harmonica strains.

"God damn those damn-fool pups!" Hazard snapped, breaking into a run.

The harmonica strains begat words, and the first sweet lyrics floated through the pines.

> The years creep slowly by, Lorena,
> The snow is on the grass again.
> The sun's low down the sky, Lorena,
> The frost gleams where the flowers have been.

"Damn them!" Hazard cursed.

His men were bivouacked beyond the crater itself, in the shadow of Cemetery Ridge. Their too-innocent faces burned in the crackling camp fires.

It was Price who worked the harmonica across his mouth, eyes closed, oblivious to all except the rising voices of his fellow volunteers.

> The years creep slowly by, Lorena,
> I'll not call up their shadowy forms.
> I'll say to them "lost years sleep on,"
> Sleep on, nor heed life's pelting storms....

"Turn out! All of you!"

The men jumped to their feet. All except Corporal Price, who sat transported by the strains of his own playing.

Colonel Hazard fell on him like a thunderclap, cuffing the offending instrument from his shocked hands and dragging Price off his stony perch with a strong right arm.

"At attention, you thoughtless cur!" he raged.

"Colonel Hazard! Beggin' your pardon, sir."

"Ah gave you no leave to speak."

Price swallowed. He pulled his fattish body to attention.

"But, sir," another voice quavered, "we were only singing."

Hazard whirled on the speaker. "A song Stonewall himself banned on account its doleful strains set good soldiers hankering for home and hearth. Ah'll have no sloppy sentimentalism in mah ranks. Is that clear to one and all?"

"Yes, sir," a subdued chorus of voices murmured.

"Sing a song Ah care to hear," Hazard snapped.

"Yes, sir!" the men of the Sixth Virginia Recreational Foot shouted in unison.

"That's the kind of refrain suitable for soldiering," Colonel Hazard said, mollified. It cut him deep to upbraid his men so harshly, but war was nigh. Upon the shoulders of the Sixth lay the burden of the future, and there would be no result but total victory if Colonel Rip Hazard had any say in the matter.

"Fetch up some of that coffee and hardtack," he said.

"The hardtack is really hard this time, sir," Price said. "The catering service went a mite overboard, I fear."

"Then fetch up a pan and we'll soften it up in bacon grease," Hazard snapped.

The order was carried out, a dented tin cup of black coffee was proffered and Colonel Rip Hazard hunkered down with his men to sup.

The sun fell, the shadows grew dreary and at length a full moon rose in the southern sky to bless the hallowed soil on which they had bivouacked. The granite obelisk consecrated to the supreme hero of the Crater, Major General William Mahone, became an eternal candle in the night. Somewhere a screech owl gave warning.

Colonel Rip Hazard stared long into his pan of brown bubbling bacon grease as he softened the hardtack to edible consistency, his thoughts roiling. A difficult day loomed before them. Only he knew how difficult it was to be, Hazard ruminated.

In that, he was sore mistaken. Only God knew how terrible the coming day would be. Not only for the Sixth. But for the Union.

Shadows of night filled the grassy cup of the crater where one of the the worst battles of the Civil War had been contested. Whippoorwills called eerily through the pines.

"Favor us with an air appropriate to the occasion, Mr. Price," Hazard said at length.

Price stood up, his uniform already dirty. Tucking instrument to mouth, he rendered a doleful tune everyone recognized as "My Maryland." Eyebrows shot up until Hazard muttered, "Mr. Price's kin hail from Baltimore originally."

Everyone then shrugged in vague acceptance. After all, Maryland was just as southern as Virginia. The eastern part, at any rate.

When the interminable melody finally wound down, Colonel Hazard cleared his throat and said, "Very good, Mr. Price. Mighty fine playing."

Hazard stood up. The others remained sprawled and hunkered around the simmering camp fires.

"Gentlemen," he began, his voice gathering pride and dignity and a kind of mortal thunder with each syllable, "Ah stand here enduring proud to be a son of Virginia. On this spot, six score and eleven years ago, mah honored great-great-granddaddy perished for the cause he believed in. This is hallowed ground to me. This is the very soil that nurtured the first American rebel, George Washington, who, had he enjoyed a longer span, Ah firmly believe would have fought for Davis during the great rebellion."

"Amen," a voice murmured.

"Mah granddaddy gave up his last precious drop of blood to consecrate this battlefield during the Siege of Petersburg, and Ah can do no less."

A chorus of murmured assent came.

"Tomorrow our dread foe will march upon this sacred place, intent upon despoiling it."

A low growl like dogs who are cornered arose.

"As sons of our honored fathers, we cannot allow this travesty to come to pass."

"And we won't!"

"But we are but thirty-five in mortal number, and the legions even now gathering to annihilate us are many."

"We can outshoot 'em," Price piped up.

Hazard raised a quelling hand.

"Well said. But you men do not know war as Ah know war. You have not stood amid its din, inhaled its bitter smoke, heard comrades and foes alike screaming in pain and crying for their God and their mothers so far away and unheeding. Ah have." His voice cracked. "Ah have seen the elephant, as our forefathers so eloquently put it. Accordingly Ah will not lead you brave and willing boys into dismal defeat."

A rebel yell went up, spooking the screech owl to flight and silencing the whippoorwills.

Hazard smiled. This was the spirit of Dixie. Clearing his throat anew, he pressed on with his odious duty.

"As your commanding officer, Ah have taken measures to ensure that come the morrow we will stand victorious against the hated foe."

Another rebel yell howled forth.

"These measures include certain liberties that may be difficult for true men of the South to endure without complaint." He made his voice metallic. "But endure them without complaint you will, for Ah will have obedience and discipline, and in return for these presents, Ah will give you the final victory over the enemy."

This time the men of the Sixth Virginia Recreational Foot grew silent. They could see the emotion in the colonel's face. It was the face a military man wore in defeat, or in the aftermath of defeat. They listened intently.

"At dawn the Yankees will arrive."

"Damn Yankee devils," a man growled.

"I thought the Yanks weren't due till noon?" another asked.

"You're thinking of the *other* damn Yanks. The California Yanks who have come carpetbagging into our preserves."

"Aren't there some Florida Yanks amongst them?" asked Belcher.

Hazard nodded. "You speak God's own truth, soldier," Hazard averred. "But the Yanks who will come at sunup are a different breed, pledged to our cause, not against it."

This pronouncement was met with stony silence and some blinking of fire-dappled eyes.

"As your commanding officer, Ah took the liberty of enlisting the aid of the Forty-fourth Rhode Island Weekend Artillery."

No one spoke. They leaned toward their commanding officer.

"They are, even as we speak, speeding south to succor us in the coming siege. Behind them follow the First Massachusetts Interpretive Cavalry."

"The First Massachusetts!" Belcher blurted. "Didn't we whup their raggety tails once?"

Hazard nodded heavily. "At the Second Manassas Reenactment. They were stout soldiers and true, even if their cause was unjust, but they share our outrage at the thing that is about to be done to this sacred place where good men both gray and blue fell in tumultuous combat."

The silence that followed was brittle. Colonel Hazard surveyed the faces of his men. He was asking them to do a bitter thing in this dark hour, and there was no predicting their mood.

"Ah need not remind you men that on this spot on July 30, in the year of our Lord 1864, Union and Confederate regulars engaged in battle. Tomorrow they will engage in battle once again. But this time they will stand shoulder to shoulder as united Americans to fight a foe more odious to each than they are to one another. Now if these Union boys can lay aside their differences and join cause with us Rebels, how can we fail to do the same in return?"

The longest silence in Colonel Hazard's woefully short life came in the wake of his last wavering plea. On this moment turned the fate of the Petersburg National Battlefield and the honor of the South. Hazard held his breath until his ribs hurt.

"Well, hell," a man said, "if the Yanks care about old Virginny enough to swallow their pride, I guess we can chow down on a little cold crow and accept their help."

"Beats this hardtack and flap-doodle," another barked.

"Not that they'll be much comfort in battle, being New Englanders. Everyone knows New Englanders can't shoot worth a lick."

Colonel Rip Hazard let the hot, pent-up air of Virginia out of his Southern lungs and closed his ears to squeeze back the stinging tears of pride.

"With the North and South reunited against a common foe," he said in a choking voice, "how much chance does the thrice-damned enemy have?"

"... *HOW MUCH CHANCE does the thrice-damned enemy have?*"

At a mobile command post van south of Petersburg, Virginia, a short-sleeved man removed headphones from his ears and snapped a console switch.

"This is Task Force Coordinator Moise," he said into a filament mike suspended before his mouth.

"Go ahead, Task Force Coordinator Moose."

"The Sixth Virginia Recreational Foot has enlisted the Forty-fourth Rhode Island Artillery and the First Mass Cavalry to stand against us."

"Damn good-for-nothing Rebels."

"Advise, please."

"Continue monitoring operations. If fighting breaks out, decamp."

"Roger. Moise out."

AFTER THE VITTLES were consumed and the last of the coarse-grained chicory coffee imbibed, Colonel Rip Hazard ordered his men to turn in for the night. They repaired to their five-hundred-dollar replica pup tents and pulled the coarse wool blankets high to their chins to keep out the evening chill. One by one they dropped off to fitful sleep, knowing that with the dawn the hated Union would return to a place it had not been welcome since the malevolent moles of the Forty-eighth Pennsylvania had tunneled under the Confederate fort and set off eight thousand pounds of black powder, blasting some three hundred Johnny Rebs into eternity while creating the infamous crater lo these one hundred thirty unforgiving years ago.

The enemy did not come with the break of dawn. They skulked in before first light.

Corporal Adam Price had picket duty. He leaned against an oak tree, fortified with camp coffee and listening to his bowels grumble and gurgle as they struggled to move nineteenth-century bacon-grease-softened hardtack through his twentieth-century digestive system.

Somewhere a twig snapped, and he snatched up his custom-made replica Harper's Ferry Minie musket and advanced, calling softly, "W-who goes there?"

A Minie ball came whistling back to shatter his rifle stock and right arm with a single resounding crash.

The explosion of pain in his brain sent him crashing backward, stumbling and crawling blindly. When his vision cleared Corporal Price lay on his stomach.

Through the dense thicket, men in smart blue uniforms with gold shoulder boards and light blue piping advanced purposefully, faces hard and muskets pointed at him. Some wielded the dreaded Sharps carbine.

"You—you men be from the First Massachusetts?" he asked, gulping.

Before an answer could come, a familiar voice called, "Price! Call out, man!"

"Colonel Hazard!" Price screamed. "It's them Yank devils!"

"What?"

"The infernal Yankees! They've a-come early! And they're firing lead ball!"

A volley of Minie balls converged on Corporal Price's head, shattering his thick skull like a ceramic bowl.

And the Second Battle of the Crater was on.

HISTORY WOULD DULY RECORD that the Sixth Virginia Recreational Foot fell defending its ancestral territory from a low-down Northern incursion. Of the thirty-five men in the regiment, all but eleven were lost that day, including Colonel Lester "Rip" Hazard, who would be buried on the spot where he died with the true words "The Hope of Virginia" inscribed on his marble headstone.

Most of the defenders were shot dead in their tents as they stirred at the first dull sounds of skirmish.

Colonel Hazard perished giving a good account of himself after stumbling upon the ruined body of Corporal Adam Price. He had his Spencer repeater up to his shoulder when the Minie balls began arriving in the general vicinity of his head and rib cage, which were promptly shot to kindling. Hazard got off four consecutive point-blank shots before succumbing to his wounds.

History did not record that he fired blanks. Some truths are too painful to endure.

THE NEXT MORNING the ragged survivors of the Sixth Virginia Recreational Foot lay in wait along the Richmond-Petersburg Turnpike outside Petersburg, Virginia, for the Forty-fourth Rhode Island Weekend Artillery.

When the Forty-fourth Rhode Island obligingly came roaring up the road in their chartered buses, pickup trucks bearing Virginia license plates rolled out of concealment, blocking their path.

Elements of the Forty-fourth Rhode Island stepped out of their vehicles in curiosity and confusion. They saw familiar gray uniforms pop up from behind the barricade. Those without rifles in hand reached instinctively for them. Old hatreds die hard.

The Forty-fourth Rhode Island were cut down to the last man by the Sixth Virginia Foot, who this time were not firing blanks.

This engagement was dubbed by the victors the Battle of Redressment and by the losers the Massacre at Colonial Heights.

By the time the motorcycles of the First Mass Cavalry happened along an hour later, the Virginia National Guard had been called out and everyone was packing live ammunition.

The Second American Civil War had commenced. And no one suspected it was only prologue to a wider conflict.

2

His name was Remo and he was on strike.

"No results, no work," he said into the telephone receiver, and promptly hung up. The phone immediately began ringing.

Remo let it ring. As far as he was concerned, it could ring forever and ever.

A squeaky voice called from the floor above. "Why does that noisy device continue to vex us?" the voice asked in a querulous tone.

"It's only Smith," Remo called back.

"He has work?" the squeaky voice demanded.

"Who cares? I'm on strike."

Faster than seemed possible, a wispy figure appeared in the doorway of Remo's sparsely furnished bedroom. "You have struck Smith?" asked Chiun, Reigning Master of Sinanju, in hazel-eyed horror.

"No," Remo explained patiently, "I've gone on strike *against* Smith."

Chiun's almond eyes narrowed to slits. "Explain these white words I cannot fathom."

"Smitty's been stalling. He promised months ago to track down my parents. So far, all I get are lame excuses. He needs motivation. So I'm striking until I get what I want."

"You will do no work?"

Remo folded his bare arms defiantly as the telephone continued to ring. He wore a white T-shirt and tan chinos. "I'm not budging."

"I must find out what Emperor Smith requires of us."

"Be my guest," said Remo, unfolding his arms and plugging his ears with his forefingers. "I just don't want to hear it."

"And you will not," said Chiun, reaching for the telephone. Suddenly he pivoted. A curved fingernail nearly as long as the finger backing it licked out, seeming to brush Remo's forehead slightly.

Remo got his ears unplugged before the paralyzing electricity of the Master of Sinanju's touch shut down his nervous system.

Remo stood frozen while Chiun answered the telephone, an expression of dull shock on his strong, high-cheekboned face. His deep-set dark brown eyes seemed to say "I can't believe I fell for that."

Ignoring him, Chiun spoke into the receiver. "Hail, Emperor Smith, dispenser of gold and welcome assignments. The Master of Sinanju awaits your bidding."

"We have a problem, Master Chiun," said Dr. Harold W. Smith in a voice that sounded the way lemon-scented dishwashing detergent smells.

"Speak, O understanding one."

"Something terrible is going on in Virginia," Smith said breathlessly. "A skirmish has broken out between Civil War reenactors."

"These reactionaries are doomed!"

"Reenactors, not reactionaries."

Chiun wrinkled up his bald head. "I do not know this word."

"Reenactors are people who dress up in the costumes and uniforms of the American Civil War and recreate the major battles."

"They fight a war that has already been decided?"

"They don't use real bullets."

Chiun's forehead puckered. "Then what is the purpose of fighting? For without death, no war can ever be decided."

"It's purely ceremonial," said Smith. "Please listen carefully. It appears a Union regiment bushwhacked a Southern regiment, decimating the latter."

"If they were not dispensing death, why does this matter?"

"This time the Northern shots were real. The survivors in turn ambushed another Union regiment, annihilating them to the last man. When the Virginia National Guard was called in to put down the disturbance, they took the side of the Southern regiment and captured another Northern regiment."

"Then the rebellious ones have won?"

"Not yet. If we don't get to the bottom of this, we may have a second Civil War on our hands. Master Chiun, we must head off further violence."

Chiun shook his aged head. "It is too late."

"What do you mean?"

"Assassins head off wars before they start, not after. You have called us too late, Smith."

"I called as soon as word reached me. But Remo refused to accept my call."

Chiun made a dismissive hand motion that was lost on Smith. "It does not matter. It was too late even then. For once men in uniform begin to fight, they cannot be stopped until one army surrenders to the other. It is a soldier thing."

Smith's voice grew firm. "Master Chiun, I have reports of other reenactors mobilizing in other states. Volunteers are coming out of the woodwork and appear to be converging on a Civil War battlefield at Petersburg, Virginia. There is talk of the Rhode Island National Guard descending upon Virginia to avenge the dead reenactors, some of whom belonged to the Rhode Island National Guard unit."

"It is possible something can be done," Chiun mused, eyeing Remo dubiously.

"Yes?"

"If the general behind this calamity can be found and separated from his head, it may be his army will melt in fear before the swift hand of Sinanju."

"But we don't know that any general is behind this. These men are not true soldiers. They are ordinary citizens who perform on national holidays. It makes no sense."

"It is typically American," said Chiun vaguely. "Would you like to speak with Remo?"

"Er, he is not speaking to me."

"You have not approached him in the proper manner," said Chiun, lifting the receiver to one of Remo's unprotected ears. "You may speak freely now that my pupil's undivided attention is focused on your every syllable."

"Remo, I desperately need your help," Smith said.

Remo stood unmoving as Smith spoke.

"I have been diligently seeking answers to your questions, but you must realize it is difficult. You were orphaned as an infant. There is no backtrail to your parents except the name found on the note on the basket—Remo Williams. Williams, as I have told you a thousand times, is one of the most common surnames in the Western world. Without more to go on, I am at an impasse."

Remo said nothing.

"Remo, are you listening?"

"His wax-laden ears have absorbed your every word, Emperor," Chiun assured Smith.

"And what is his reaction?" Smith asked doubtfully.

"He makes no protest," Chiun said blandly.

"Does that mean what I think it means?" Smith ventured.

"Since you are emperor over this divided land, and your every word law, can your surmises fail to achieve equal perfection?" asked Chiun, and hung up.

Standing before his pupil, Chiun looked up. He was a full foot shorter than his pupil, who stood about six feet tall. The Master of Sinanju was a frail wraith of a man with a mummylike face resembling papyrus that might have soaked up the wrinkles of the passing centuries. He looked old, very old. But there was a wise humor in his eyes that belied the fact that he had been born near the end of the previous century and suggested an inner vitality that would carry him into the next. The years had robbed him of his hair, leaving only a tendril clinging to his tiny chin and a cloudy puff over each ear. The kimono sheathing his frail-seeming body was black and trimmed in scarlet.

"If you wish to continue on strike," he said pleasantly, "I will be happy to leave you in this stricken state."

Remo stood without reacting. A tendril of perspiration trickled out from under his scalp.

"Or," continued Chiun, "I can release you from this state, and you may be allowed to accompany me as my official translator and gofer."

Remo had no reaction.

"I will give you one opportunity to reply. If your reply is not to my liking, I will return you to this unfortunate state and be on my way."

The fingernail touched Remo in the exact center of his forehead, and he snapped alert once more.

"I am not doing any more assignments, Smitty!" Remo barked.

"It is too late," Chiun said lightly. "For I have hung up the telephone, and we are late for our flight to Virginland."

Remo hesitated, one eye on the fingernail hovering just before his chin. The other flicked to the open door, and he calculated his chances of getting out of the room before the Master of Sinanju, who had taught him everything he knew of value, could react. Remo decided his chances were about equal to his sprouting wings.

"I want proof of Smith's good faith before day's end," said Remo.

"And I wish to see evidence that the wisdom I have poured into your thick white head has not leaked out through some hitherto unsuspected hole. Never in the past would you have succumbed to my paralyzing stroke so easily, Remo. For shame. Your head is full of useless dreams and longings, and they have befogged your brain to the point of its former round-eyed denseness. Next you will be consuming burned cow patties once more. O, that I lived to see you sink to this low state," Chiun moaned, throwing back his head and resting the back of an ivory hand against his smooth forehead. He held that pose until Remo spoke again.

"Knock it off. This is important to me."

"Yes, of course. Your roots. You must find your roots. O, that you had only been born a tree so that they would always be at your unmoving feet, where you could admire them. But you were born a man. You have no roots. You have feet." Chiun looked down at Remo's feet, which were encased in hand-made Italian loafers. "Large, ugly, club knobs, but still recognizable as feet. You have no roots. Have I not told you so a thousand times?"

"Somebody gave birth to me," said Remo.

"Possibly," Chiun said thinly.

"Someone else fathered me."

"This, too, is within the realm of the possible," admitted Chiun.

"I want to find out who they are and why they left me on that orphanage doorstep."

"Why do you need to know this trivia? Is is not enough to know that you were abandoned? If you had hitched a ride in an automobile and the driver abruptly stopped to leave you by the side of the road, would you dedicate your adult life to discovering this cretin's life story?"

"It's not the same thing."

"But it is. Those who brought you into the world cast you away like a broken toy. Is there not a more ungrateful and callous act imaginable?"

"I need to know why. Everything that's happened to me in life happened because of it. If I had not grown up in an orphanage, I probably wouldn't have ended up a cop or joined the Marines and gone to Nam. Without Nam, I wouldn't have met Mac-

Cleary, who fingered me so Smith could frame me for that killing. Because I was an orphan and had no family, Smith figured I was the perfect candidate for CURE. Think how my life would have gone if I'd never met Smith."

"You would never have met me." And because the bond between them was strong, the Master of Sinanju looked up into his pupil's angry face with expectant eyes.

Remo hesitated. "All I wanted was a normal life."

"Instead, you got an extraordinary life. No white person has ever been so blessed as you. Since the first Master emerged from the caves of mist, only my ancestors were considered worthy of learning the art of Sinanju, the sun source of all fighting arts, and only the best of them. Only Koreans, the most perfect creatures to tread the earth. No whites. Until you. And you are not happy."

"I never wanted to be an assassin."

In the act of pirouetting about the room, Chiun abruptly whirled to fix his pupil with triumphant eyes.

"And you are not!" he crowed. "You are a Sinanju assassin. The finest of this era or any other."

"I don't want to be an assassin anymore. I want to find myself."

"You do not need to find yourself, Remo Williams. Now that you have been discovered by Sinanju."

"You make it sound like I'm some new specimen."

"You are a white Sinanju Master. My ancestors would be proud to know that I have taken a lowly white and raised him up to near-Koreanhood." Chiun caught himself. "After they finished castigating me for squandering my talents on so pointless a task. But times were hard, there were no suitable clients in this modern world and I had to make do with the meager offers that came to me. I have taken a white foundling and made him a Master of Sinanju. O, wonderful me."

"Stuff it. I'm through with CURE. I don't want to be an assassin or a counterassassin."

"Do not speak that horrid white word in my presence."

"I'm finding myself. After that, I'll take what comes."

Chiun fixed Remo with one steely eye. "You have been taking what came to you all your life. Why show initiative now?"

Remo said nothing.

"You will come with me to the Province of Virgins?"

"Virginia," corrected Remo.

"Good. It is settled."

"Wait a minute! I didn't promise anything. I'm on strike. Besides, it's Memorial Day. A national holiday."

This time Remo actually saw the Master of Sinanju's fingernail arrow toward his forehead. He stepped forward as if to offer himself to the paralyzing nail, then slipped down and out of the way so elegantly the Master of Sinanju had to catch himself before he impaled the white-painted wall of Remo's bedroom.

Recovering, Chiun took his wrists in his hands and let the wide sleeves of his kimono close over them. A tinge of pride suffused his aged mummy face.

"Perhaps not all of my training has been a waste after all," he murmured with a hint of fatherly pride.

ON THE PLANE, Chiun was saying, "Listen well. We go to put down a rebellion. It is a difficult thing, being different than a war between nations."

"I don't think a new civil war is breaking out."

The plane sat at the gate at Boston's Logan Airport. Passengers were still coming on board. A pot-bellied man wearing the full sideburns and blue uniform of the Union Army was boarding.

A stewardess stopped him. "Sir, you'll have to check that pistol." She pointed to his gun-belt holster.

"It is only a replica Dragoon," said the man in an exaggerated New England twang that Remo had never heard spoken on the street—only by comedians playing broad-dialect New Englanders. "It's a black-powder weapon. Perfectly legal."

"Nevertheless, it constitutes a firearm, and I'll have ask you to check it."

Reluctantly the faux Union soldier surrendered his pistol, gun belt and all. Glum-faced, he made his way down the narrow aisle to take a seat across from Remo and Chiun, gold buttons straining to contain his paunch.

"Looks like another would-be combatant," Remo undertoned.

"Why does he wear the uniform of Napoleon III?" asked Chiun.

"Huh?"

"That uniform. French soldiers who followed Napoleon III wore such uniforms, according to the scrolls of my ancestors."

"Little Father, that's a Union Civil War uniform."

"It is French."

"Maybe it looks French. But I know an authentic Union uniform when I see it. See the blue piping? That means he's infantry."

"If that man is flying to Virginland to fight a war that his people long ago won, he is infantile, not infantry."

"Whatever," said Remo.

The cabin door was secured and turbines began to spool up. Conversation became difficult. They sat in silence as the plane lumbered to the runway, picked up speed and vaulted into the sky over Boston.

When the 727 had leveled out and was hurtling southward, Chiun resumed his lecture. "A war between nations is always about treasure."

"Treasure?"

"Yes. Sometimes it is a treasure one emperor wishes to wrest from the other. Now, this treasure need not be in gold or jewels or wealth. Helen of Troy was a treasure, even if she was but a white Greekling with a crooked nose."

"Helen of Troy had a crooked nose?"

Chiun nodded. "Today it is called a deviated septum. Paris did not know. He would have spent the rest of his days enduring her insufferable snoring."

"You should talk," said Remo.

Chiun snorted and went on. "Even when wars between emperors are not over treasure, but something insignificant, treasure is still at the heart of all such conflicts. For each emperor requires treasure to sustain war. Soldiers must be fed and weapons secured. No one works for free. Even in a war."

"Gotcha."

"But a civil war is another matter."

"I don't think this is a civil war, Little Father. It's probably just a Memorial Day misunderstanding gone ballistic."

"We will see. For if treasure lurks behind these events, this war will not be what it appears to be."

Remo was looking at the potbellied Union soldier across the aisle. His squashed-down blue service cap grazed the overhead air-conditioning blower. "That uniform doesn't look French to me."

"It is French. I will prove it." Chiun lifted his voice. "Kind sir, what is the name of your cap?"

"It's a keppie."

Chiun allowed himself a self-satisfied smile. "See, Remo? *Kepi* is a French word. It means cap. You white Americans have created nothing new, but have stolen your ideas from all other lands. Your way of government comes from the Greeks, your dream of empire is very Roman. There is hardly a nation on earth you have not looted of ideas, only to call them American."

"What did we take from the Koreans?" asked Remo, genuinely curious.

"The best years of my life," said the Master of Sinanju, lapsing into injured silence while he monitored the wing on his side of the plane for signs that it was about to tear loose.

Except for the stewardess bringing refreshments and an offer to carry Remo's child, the rest of the flight was peaceful.

3

By all rights the Second Civil War should have been snuffed out on the Richmond-Petersburg Turnpike before the embers of misunderstanding could ignite a national conflagration.

The governor of Virginia had ordered in the National Guard. The unit that had responded rolled out of Fort Lee, whose grounds abutted Petersburg National Battlefield. They had been on Memorial Weekend maneuvers. No precious response time would have been lost. Their orders were to quell a disturbance the local police could not handle. Armed with modern M-16 rifles, tanks and other implements of twentieth-century warfare, they were easily equal to the task of suppressing a group of weekend warriors equipped with muzzle-loading black-powder muskets.

Except for the unfortunate fact that the National Guard unit mobilized was descended from the legendary Stonewall Brigade. When Captain Royal Wooten Page called his unit to halt, he was prepared for a scene of civil disobedience, if not riot.

Instead, he came upon a scene that stirred his deep pride in his home state and Dixie.

For there by the side of the road stood encamped a regiment of Confederate infantry, standing guard over a field of captured and bedraggled bluecoats. Their motorcycle steeds lay stacked in a sorry pile.

"Well, Ah swan," he said, thinking of great-great-grand-uncle Beauregard E. Page, who had fought at both the First and Second Manassas. "Rest a spell, men," he said in his native drawl, "whilst Ah investigate further."

Approaching the encampment, Captain Page dropped his gun belt and came forward with upraised hands.

A voice called, "Halt! Friend or foe?"

"Ah am and always will be a friend of the uniform you wear, suh, seeing as how Ah am proud to carry forward into the coming century the proud banner of the Stonewall Brigade. What unit do Ah have the honor of approaching?"

"We be the Sixth Virginia Foot. Recreational."

"Then you would know Colonel Rip Hazard."

"Ah would. Ah had the sad duty of burying his noble husk this very morning."

"Colonel Hazard is dead?"

"Gunned down by treacherous blueclads."

"Ah served alongside Colonel Hazard in this very unit."

"And Ah served under him in this proud regiment."

Captain Page was allowed to approach. He shook hands with a rangy individual who wore Confederate gray and muttonchop whiskers.

"These the Yanks dastards in question?" Page inquired.

"Nope. We annihilated them early on. These be reinforcements. The First Massachusetts."

"Ah hear they can't shoot."

"Never heard tell of a New Englander that could."

After they had shared a moment of grim laughter, Captain Page asked, "What are you planning on doing with these skulking New England bluebellies?"

"That hasn't been decided. But they're our prisoners."

Page frowned tightly. "Mah orders are to put down this unfortunate uprising."

"That's a right troubling notion, Ah'd say."

"To you and me both, suh."

"Especially what with the true enemy so nigh and all," the Confederate soldier said, looking north to Petersburg with grim mien.

Captain Page gave this dilemma some thought. "What time are them infernal carpetbaggers due?"

"High noon."

"What say we gather up these Yanks and repair to the Crater to await developments?" he asked carefully.

"Will your men follow you?"

"Will yours?" countered Page.

"They be Virginians, as are yours."

"Then let us be about our marching, suh."

Captain Page returned to his waiting tank column and explained the situation. "These fine soldiers were clearly provoked into defending themselves and their honor," he related. "Moreover, they were ambushed while asleep, taking their last rest before meeting the siege army that you all know—if you read your morning paper or watch the TV—is due to descend upon Old Dominion like so many greedy locusts.

"The place where they were cut down is known to one and all, Ah am sure. It is the spot where the malevolent moles under the command of Colonel Henry

Pleasants—an ill-named rogue if ever one was spawned—dug the cowardly tunnel under the finest soldiers of the Confederacy and set a powder keg to light. The resulting blast reverberates to this day, for Ah know personally that some of you men had kinfolk maimed or lost in that unholy blast."

A hateful murmur raced through the unit.

"That awful hour was the darkest of the Siege of Petersburg," Captain Page continued, "and even though the doughty forces of Major General William Mahone repelled the Federal advance that followed, it shall never be forgotten. And now a new siege is about to be laid on that fair and shining city. Ah cannot but assume that the Union devils who wrought this modern calumny were inspired in their villainy, if not in league with, the very foe whose name you all know and which Ah will not sully the pure Virginia air by repeating. To that end, Ah am prepared to pledge this unit in common cause with our grayback brethren."

Utter silence attended this statement.

"Of course, Ah cannot demand that you boys follow me into this new cause. So Ah will give you the opportunity to consider this weighty matter."

When they were done, Captain Page said, "Ah aim to stand by mah fellow Virginians until this matter is understood and the true culprits brought to book. What say you, men?"

There were no objections.

The Union captives, bound and hangdog, were loaded aboard the National Guard trucks and tanks, to which Confederate soldiers clung, waving their service caps and beaming in victory.

"On to the Crater!" shouted Captain Page.

A yipping rebel war whoop drowned out the firing of the engines, and what history would later call the Unified Confederate Disunion Alliance rolled south down the section of Interstate 95 called the Richmond-Petersburg Turnpike entirely unopposed.

When word of this revolt reached the governor of Virginia, he knew exactly what to do. He called the President of the United States.

After he was fully briefed, the President of the United States knew exactly what to do, too. He thanked the governor of Virginia and buzzed his wife, the First Lady.

"There's trouble brewing in Virginia," he said when the First Lady entered.

"I heard. Can't you federalize the Virginia National Guard or something? This is ridiculous."

"I do that, and I'll be lynched the next time I go home to Little Rock." The President was going through his desk drawers. "You seen that T-shirt of mine? The one that says Smith College?"

"Why do you have to go running to that Smith person every time there's a crisis?"

"How many times do I have tell you," the President said testily, "that subject is off limits."

The First Lady glared at the President. "What will you trade for that T-shirt?"

"The golden opportunity to serve out your term as First Lady," the President said glumly. "Because if this nation is facing a new Civil War, we'll both be run out of this office by the Fourth of July."

The First Lady snapped out of her glare as if stung by a hornet. "I'll leak it to the press that you're going for a jog," she said hastily. "That way the cameras will be sure to televise the shirt."

The door to the Oval Office shut behind her as the President stood up to look out the latticed window that faced the South Lawn. It was the same view his predecessors going back to Abraham Lincoln—the most tormented Chief Executive in U.S. history—had enjoyed. Not even the imperfect, object-distorting glass had changed.

But the burden on the man who held the office had. Lincoln had had a young nation to hold together. That was burden enough in the nineteenth century. Here in the twentieth, more often than not the President had a fractious family of nations to watch over, as well as domestic concerns.

But in over one hundred years the essential mission had not changed. Hold the union together. For Lincoln it had been a matter of the North and the South. How simple that seemed today. For while modern America might be unified, it was still fractured along a thousand invisible fault lines. The great Democratic experiment was imperiled by forces that had insinuated themselves into its very cultural and political fabric.

Thirty years before, a great President—destined to be martyred as was Lincoln—had come to a terrible realization. America was doomed. Its laws and leaders were no longer sufficient to hold it together. A tide of lawlessness was sweeping the land. The institutions of government could not hold it in check because the threats all came from within.

Crooked courts and judges and lawyers had all but shredded the Constitution. It was no longer the shield it was intended to be. It was in truth a hindrance to the survival of the greatest nation in human history. Something had to be done. Something drastic.

The long-dead President had considered martial law, repealing the Constitution and sacrificing his own Presidency on the same granite altar of national salvation that had cost Lincoln his life a century before.

Instead, he chose another option.

In secret he created CURE. It was an organization headed by one handpicked man. The letters were no bureaucratic acronym. CURE was simply a harsh remedy for an ailing nation. Bitter medicine, true. But if it worked, the union might endure to the turn of the century and perhaps beyond.

Officially CURE did not even exist. To admit to the existence of CURE was to admit America didn't work. Its mandate was to right the ship of state by extraconstitutional means. Domestic spying. Wiretapping. Even framing of criminals outside the law who could not be gotten within it. No option was too extreme. The utter survival of the nation had been at stake.

Over time the mission expanded even as the nation's ills worsened. In time assassination was sanctioned as a means of last resort. Nothing seemed to be enough. But like a keel CURE kept the ship of state from being swamped by domestic storm. The general public never dreamed it existed. Congress never suspected. Successive Presidents came and went, each sworn never to reveal the secret—except to the man who followed him. Each was shown the red hot-line telephone—kept in the Lincoln Bedroom—that connected with the faceless man who headed CURE.

A man named Smith. The same man handpicked so long ago.

As the President gazed out past the magnolia tree planted by old Andrew Jackson and maimed by a suicidal pilot only months before, toward the cold finger of the Washington Monument and the Jefferson Memorial beyond it, he bitterly cursed the still unexplained accident that had severed the hot line to Smith, wherever he was. It had been a hell of a lot easier to just pick up that phone than to put on a Smith College T-shirt and go jogging for the cameras in the hope that Harold Smith would be watching his TV and get the message.

But knowing Dr. Harold W. Smith, the man already had his people on this ruckus in Virginia.

The President just hoped the bodies wouldn't make too high a pile this time. Last time had been a bitch.

4

At Richmond's Byrd International Airport a minor skirmish broke out when Flight 334 from Boston landed and one Franklyn Lowell Fisk deplaned in Union blue.

As it happened, a civil engineer named Orel Ready simultaneously deplaned from a flight from Atlanta, wearing Confederate gray.

They encountered one another at the baggage carousel.

Ready took one look at Fisk and Fisk at him, and pungent characterizations were exchanged with the riddling vehemence of canister fire. A small but intrigued crowd gathered.

It might have blown over except for the regrettable fact that their baggage arrived just then. In the heat of the moment Ready pulled his cavalry saber from his Tourister luggage, and Fisk extracted his fully functioning Third Model Dragoon commemorative pistol with its walnut grips and 24-karat gold trigger guard and back strap from an overnight bag.

They glared at one another for an eternity of dislike.

"Bushwackin' Johnny Reb!" Fisk snarled.

"Back-stabbin' blackguard!" Ready retorted.

History never recorded the name of the instigator of the Byrd International Airport Skirmish. Some witnesses swore that Ready lunged at his opposite while others averred that Fisk let fly with a .44-caliber Minie ball in a cloud of black-powder smoke before the sword point could begin to move toward his heart.

Either way steel flashed and lead flew—but neither man flinched at the specter of incoming death.

Which was just as well, because they were in no immediate danger.

NO ONE NOTICED the wispy little Asian man in black bustle out of the fringes of the gathering crowd. He stood at least three heads shorter than most, and all eyes were fixed on the two combatants. Or on their weapons, rather.

In the blink of an eye something broke the lunging saber in midstroke. During that eye blink—caused by the discharging of the mail-order replica Dragoon—a force no one saw and both antagonists felt deflected the Minie ball from the dark gray breast of Orel Ready.

With a metallic clang, the ball caromed off something and buried itself into a khaki knapsack that just happened to come sliding down the baggage chute.

When the echoing report stopped and eyes flew open, Frank Fisk stood with Orel Ready's saber seemingly buried in his unprotected stomach while the Dragoon muzzle lay smoking over Ready's heart.

Fisk and Ready each sized up his situation at the same time.

"Dear Lord, Ah am undone," Ready howled.

"You have run me through, you rebellious Johnny," Fisk moaned.

Then both men promptly fainted dead away. Ready still held on to his saber, which—when it came away from Fisk's chest—was shown to have been sheered off to a blunt end like a broken butterknife. There was no smoking hole over Ready's heart, either. Nor any exit wound. No blood, either.

The crowd gathered closer to inspect the honored fallen of the Byrd International Airport Skirmish. An insurance agent from Savannah was the one who found the broken saber tip lying under the men, and held it up so the round dent in the fine-tempered steel could be seen by one and all.

"Day-am!" he said. "'Pears to me the ball broke the tip off this frog-sticker and saved both their lives."

WALKING AWAY from the altercation, Remo said to the Master of Sinanju, "Nice move, Little Father. You avoided a major battle back there."

"You could have helped," sniffed Chiun.

"I'm on strike."

"Does this mean that you are a union sympathizer?"

"I'm an Ex-Marine. That means I'm in sympathy with nobody who puts on a uniform they haven't earned. Why do you ask?"

"Union sympathizers are always going on strike in this mad nation."

"This isn't that kind of union," said Remo.

"What kind is it?" asked Chiun.

Noticing fistfights breaking out all over the airport, Remo grumbled, "A weak one if you ask me."

"All republics are destined to collapse from within."

As they passed knots of belligerents, Chiun took the opportunity to drift up to some of the more hot-headed and surreptitiously inserted a long fingernail into the fray.

The nail flicked in and out so swiftly that when those stung by it finished yelping and examining themselves for puncture wounds, they never connected the insult with a tiny little man in black who glided past, a serene and unconcerned expression on his wrinkled countenance.

Very quickly the airport was evacuated and bee catchers were called in to deal with what airport officials insisted were "a swahm of teeny-tiny killer bees."

But no infestation of bees was ever found.

Thus ended the Skirmish of Byrd International Airport, about which songs would one day be sung.

THE AIRPORT car-rental agent looked Remo and Chiun over with a critical eye. "North or South?" he asked.

"North," said Chiun.

"That's not the north he means," Remo told Chiun.

"What north do you mean?" demanded the rental agent in a suspicious tone.

"He thinks you mean North Korea," said Remo.

"That where he hails from?"

"Yes," said Chiun. "I am hailed in North Korea."

"One north is as bad as another, carpetbaggers," the agent snapped. "Ah ain't renting you no car." He pronounced it "cah."

"That your last word on the subject?" inquired Remo in a cool voice.

"Cross mah heart and hope to die humming 'Dixie.'"

As it turned out, these were the last words the stubborn rental agent ever spoke. For the rest of his life, he hummed. Doctors could find no explanation for his voice-box paralysis. Many articles were written, and medical texts were revised to include the condition, but no similar case ever again surfaced.

All the agent knew was that a thick-wristed hand reached for his face, and while his eyes were fixed on that looming hand, a thumb came out of his left peripheral field of vision and did something sudden and unpleasant to his Adam's apple.

After that, all he could do was hum. And glumly surrender the car keys to the outstretched hand.

Remo drove south. It seemed pleasant country, very green and picturesque. Farms predominated, but there were low-lying swamps, too. Every mile or so signs dotted the land proclaiming this colonial site or that preserved attraction. At first it was interesting. After a while the signs blurred past in unending and mind-numbing numbers.

The surviving chimneys of homes that had been burned flat by the Federal Army of the Potomac during the Siege of Petersburg were carefully maintained like precious scars in the lush countryside. Wherever a Confederate officer, horse or camp dog had fallen, the site was commemorated by a carefully painted and maintained sign or marker. There were Confederate cemeteries galore. Once, the highway actually cut through a large burial ground whose flag-decorated tombstones lined the shoulder of the road.

"Why do these people flaunt the shame of their many defeats?" Chiun asked.

"Search me," said Remo, paying attention to his driving. "Maybe they like to complain, like some other people we both know," he added.

Chiun maintained an injured silence.

After a while Remo remembered something. "I thought Paris was killed during the Trojan War, before he could run off with Helen of Troy."

"Gossip," Chiun said dismissively.

"So what's the real poop?"

"Paris feigned his death and they eloped to Egypt in secret. Some claim that King Proteus slew Paris to win fair Helen, but in truth Paris, driven to distraction by his bride's unendurable snores, committed suicide. Any anti-Korean slander to the contrary is baseless and untrue."

"Wait a minute! Did the House ever work for King Proteus?"

Chiun gazed out the window, his face a parchment mask. "I do not recall," he said thinly.

"My butt!" Remo was silent a moment. "At least we didn't do Helen of Troy."

"Not that there were not offers," said Chiun. "Low ones."

They skirted Petersburg without incident, and all seemed calm, except for the helicopters overhead. Remo spotted state-police helicopters, a few Marine and Army ships, as well as those belonging to various news organizations, all headed in the same direction they were.

"So much for our going in unsuspected," complained Remo.

"What do you mean, we?" sniffed Chiun. "You are a guide and badger only."

"You mean gofer, don't you?"

"Just remember your place, burrowing one."

A mile before the entrance to the Petersburg National Battlefield off Interstate 95, there was a roadblock. Virginia State Troopers were stopping traffic. They were respectful to vehicles bearing Virginia license plates, as well as those belonging to North Carolina and adjacent Southern states. Vehicles with Northern plates were being turned back and in some instances detained.

At first they were polite when it was Remo's turn to pull up to the checkpoint. A solitary trooper in a gray Stetson sauntered up to Remo's side of the car.

"From around here?" he asked Remo. His uniform, Remo wasn't surprised to see, was Confederate gray with black trim.

Remo decided to bluff his way through.

"Why, shore," he said, hoping Virginians sounded like Andy Griffith, the first Southern voice that popped into his head.

"That's good to hear. We're conducting a little roadside eye test. Take but a minute." He held up a flash card. It read Portsmouth.

"Now, what's that say?" the trooper asked Remo.

"Portsmouth," said Remo.

"Nope. It's Porch Mouth," said the trooper.

"It says Portsmouth, not Porch Mouth."

"Try this next one, won't yew?"

"Isle of Wight," said Remo, reading the next card.

"Nope. It's Isle of White."

"It says Wight."

"It's pronounced white," said the trooper without humor.

"I don't see any *h*," Remo said.

"It's a Virginia *h*. Only Virginians can see it."

"Ah'm from Tennessee," said Remo, guessing at Andy Griffith's home state.

"Let's try one more, shall we?"

The trooper held up a card that clearly said Roanoke.

"Roan-oke," said Remo, pronouncing it the way it was spelled because that was the way Sister Mary Margaret used to pronounce it during American-history lessons back at the orphanage.

"Nope. Ro-noke."

"There's an *a* after the *o*," Remo pointed out.

"And there's a bluebelly in the woodpile," the trooper retorted. He gestured to a nearby trooper. "Hey, Earl, we got us another carpetbagger come to make trouble here."

Two more troopers came up to join him, hands on side arms.

In the passenger seat the Master of Sinanju said, "Remo, I must not be delayed if I am to bind this nation together once more."

"What do you want me to do about it?" Remo asked out of the side of his mouth.

"I must save my strength, for I have a great task before me."

Remo sighed. "Oh, all right."

"Kindly step out of that car," the trooper with the flash cards said before the pain signals from his knees informed his brain that they had been ambushed by a suddenly opening car door.

The trooper let out a creditable rebel yell and doubled over to grab his throbbing kneecaps. While he was bent over, Remo removed his Stetson and threw it at the approaching Virginia troopers like a Frisbee.

It whizzed over their heads, spun in place and came back like a boomerang to slap the running troopers about their faces with the whipping chin strap.

Momentarily distracted, they failed to see Remo descend upon them. By the time they realized there was a problem, their fingers had been squeezed together in groups of five and expertly dislocated.

Remo stepped back as the troopers stood about shaking their numb but limp digits, which hung like fat, dead worms off their unfeeling hands.

"What'd yew do to us?" asked the flash-card trooper in a stupefied voice.

"It's called the Sinanju handshake," said Remo pleasantly. "It goes away if you hurry home and make love to your wife."

"What if we don't?"

"Your peckers fall off by sunset at the latest."

"Ah don't believe that for a goldurn moment."

"It's your pecker," said Remo, climbing back into his rental car and driving around the roadblock.

In the rearview mirror the stunned state troopers could be seen imploring motorists to drive them back to the city.

"I have never heard of this Sinanju handshake," sniffed Chiun, rearranging his kimono skirts.

"It's a new wrinkle. Invented it myself."

"I do not like these new wrinkles of yours."

"Then don't use them," said Remo.

"Rest assured, I will not."

WHEN THEY REACHED the entrance to the Petersburg National Battlefield, a bus came rolling up from the other direction. It veered off the road and came to a stop blocking Crater Road. When the doors opened, out poured two dozen fighting men wearing red fezzes, short blue jackets, baggy red pantaloons and carrying antique muskets.

They set themselves in a skirmish line, and a color banner went up.

"Which side are *they* on?" Remo wondered aloud.

"I do not know," admitted the Master of Sinanju. "Let us inquire."

They approached with open faces and empty hands, the better to put a potential enemy off guard.

A group of muskets swung in their direction, fixing them in their sights.

"Halt!" a man shouted. He might have been an officer. Then again, he might not. His colorful costume was no more or less ornate than anyone else's.

Remo and Chiun kept coming.

"We're unarmed," Remo called out.

"Which army?"

"Neither."

"You sound like a Northerner."

Remo and Chiun kept walking. Remo read the legend on the banner. It said Louisiana Costume Zouaves.

"Louisiana sided with the South," Remo undertoned to Chiun. "But what a Zouave is, I don't know."

"It is a French word," hissed Chiun.

"Big deal. So is *soufflé*. Maybe they're the Louisiana Soufflé Brigade, come up to feed the Confederate troops."

"It is French for *clown soldier*," said Chiun.

"Guess that makes them the Bozo Brigade."

"I say again, halt and identify yourself," one of the Louisiana Zouaves ordered.

"Press," said Remo, reaching for his wallet, where he kept cover ID cards for all occasions.

"Then ya'll are spies!" a harsh voice snarled. "Shoot the damn Yank spies!"

And six muskets boomed forth lead balls and clouds of black-powder smoke.

Remo had been trained and trained by the Master of Sinanju until he had unlocked every cell in his brain. Modern science had always claimed that twentieth-century man had never learned to access his whole brain, only about ten percent of it. Scientists speculated that within that untapped ninety percent lay vast potential, powers man might command should he ever fully evolve, as well as skills he had long ago lost when he dropped down from the trees to walk upright and forage the savanna for food.

Centuries ago the Masters of Sinanju began to harness these powers. Their first halting steps planted the seeds for all the Eastern martial arts from defensive kung fu to paralyzing jujitsu. It fell to Wang the Greater, in the darkest hour in the history of the House of Sinanju—which served the thrones of antiquity—to achieve full perfection in mind and body. The Sinanju Master who had trained Wang died before Wang could be taught the accumulated knowledge and wisdom of those who had come before.

It should have been the end of the House of Sinanju. But Wang went out into the wilderness to fast, subsisting on rice hulls and grass, meditating on the fate of the village of Sinanju on the rock-bound coast of West Korea Bay, which for generations had survived only because the cream of its manhood went out into a hostile world to ply the trade of assassin and protector of thrones.

One night a ring of fire appeared in the sky before Wang and spoke in a clear voice.

"Men do not use their minds and their bodies as they should," said the voice of the ring of fire to the Great Wang. "They waste their spirit and their strength."

And in a single burst a flame, the ring of fire imparted the ultimate knowledge that came to be known as the art of Sinanju, then vanished forever.

What Wang had learned he passed down to Ung, and Ung to Gi and on until in the midtwentieth century the last pure Master of Sinanju, Chiun, passed it on to Remo Williams. Remo dismissed ninety percent of the colorful stories and legends that accompanied the teaching of Chiun—especially the ring of fire, which sounded like a medieval UFO sighting—but emerged from his training breathing with his entire body, which in turn awakened his entire brain and unlocked the limitless potential of his body.

Among these abilities were increased reflexes, heightened senses and near-absolute control over his body. It had long ago ceased to be a conscious thing. It had become ingrained. Second nature. Remo no longer had to think about the simple tricks like climbing sheer walls, sensing enemies and dodging what the first Master who encountered them had called "flying teeth" and today are known as bullets. Remo's body performed those maneuvers automatically.

Remo heard the sound of the black-powder explosions before the first lead musket balls whistled toward him. That much was unexpected, because modern rounds fly at supersonic speed and usually reached his vicinity before his ears heard the shot.

Remo had been trained to never wait for gunfire. Instead, the click of a falling hammer or the jacking of a round into a chamber was the trigger for the bullet-dodging reflexes to come into play. There were many techniques. Remo liked to let the bullets come at him, tracking their trajectories until the last possible moment and then casually sidestepping out of their deadly path and back into place so it seemed to a gunman that the bullet had passed harmlessly through his target.

It was easy. Remo's ears might not be able to hear the shot because even supersensitive ears had to await the arrival of the sound, but the eyes read threatening motion as fast as light. So Remo tracked bullets as they came and got out of their way.

These lead balls were to a modern round what a Ping-Pong ball was to an arrow. There was no comparison. His reflexes, accustomed to the supersonic speed of approaching death, hardly stirred.

One ball came toward his side. Remo didn't even have to dodge it. He just leaned to the right slightly, placing his left hand on his hip.

The musket ball obligingly whistled through the open space between his rib cage and his bent left elbow.

Another ball arced toward his head.

Remo bent his knees. The ball grazed the top of his dark hair. Normally that would have been bad form and cause for a severe rebuke from Chiun, but the big lead ball was so clumsy and unthreatening that Remo experienced a playful urge, as if someone had tossed a big blue beach ball in his direction. It was more fun to let it touch hair than do a full evade.

A third ball, probably because it hadn't been rammed down the musket barrel with enough force, dropped desultorily toward his shoe. Remo kicked it back like a golf ball, and it dropped a Zouave, who went down clutching his crotch.

Grinning, Remo turned toward Chiun, and his jaw dropped.

A second volley had been fired at the Master of Sinanju. Remo hadn't been aware of the fate of the first. Only that if he could so easily dodge lead musket balls, so could Chiun.

Four balls came at the Master of Sinanju so slowly they all but announced their arrival.

The Master of Sinanju simply stood there. Remo's grin widened. Chiun was playing, too. But as the balls converged on his frail black-clad form, the old Korean did not move.

Remo's smile froze.

Then Remo was moving in on an interior line—an attack line. Something was wrong. Seriously wrong. The Master of Sinanju was not defending himself.

Remo would have to intercept those suddenly deadly spheres himself. Intercept and deflect—even if it cost him his hands.

5

Remo Williams had both arms extended, with hands open to their fullest, to capture the hurtling lead balls before they could impact upon the sweetly wrinkled features of the unmoving Master of Sinanju. Then Remo felt a stinging sensation in the center of his chest that knocked his legs out from under him, along with the wind from his powerful lungs.

I'm hit, he thought wildly, even as his brain told him that was impossible. No slow-moving lead ball could strike a full Master of Sinanju without warning.

But his body told him he was in great pain.

Flat on his back, through the pain, Remo stared up in surprise.

And beheld the Master of Sinanju withdraw the extended arm that had struck Remo in the chest to calmly bat the musket balls back at those who had the effrontery to hurl them at his awesome presence.

Chiun used the heels of his palms. He had formed the kind of half fists most often used for striking short blows, fingers curled high and tight against themselves so that the palm flesh lay exposed.

With quick, sharp motions, Chiun struck glancing blows at the unmoving balls. Two blows per hand, four balls in all.

Caroming off his palms with meaty smacks, they careered back toward the muskets that had loosed them. Not with quite the velocity of the black-powder explosions that had sent them winging out of their musket barrels, but still with enough energy to sting mightily when they struck flesh.

A smoking musket shattered along its barrel. A man was thrown back from the bone-breaking impact of a lead ball hitting his shoulder. Another went down with a shattered kneecap. The fourth received his ball back square in the breastbone and flew backward as if mule-kicked.

"That was how Kang fended off the flying teeth when boom-sticks were first inflicted on civilization," said Chiun as Remo climbed to his feet.

"Fine," Remo said tightly. "But that doesn't mean you had to knock me flat."

"You were about to throw away your thick-fingered hands for nothing, thick one. Observe and you, too, will be able to duplicate a feat infant masters in training achieve in their first week. Korean masters in training, of course."

"Bull," said Remo, who nevertheless watched closely as a third volley came whistling toward the Master of Sinanju.

Chiun pressed his hands together before his face in an attitude of prayer. Two balls made for his face. Remo had to hold himself back, because Chiun stood completely immobile, with no body vibration warning that he was prepared to dodge or strike back.

Instead, when the lead balls were a scant three inches before his unblinking eyes, the Master of Sinanju made his hands fly apart, knocking the balls away at right angles with dull smacks. They flew toward two other musketeers who were aiming their weapons at them.

The pair yelped and stumbled to the ground, severely chastised.

"Let me try it," said Remo as another small volley was loosed.

He had to restrain himself from moving in to meet the spinning balls. They were just too slow in coming. But when they did arrive, Remo used the heels of his hands to redirect them.

Technically, flesh never touched hot ball. Instead, Remo drove a cushion of compressed air ahead of his fast-moving hands. The balls struck the air pillows, made hard as steel by the blinding speed of his hands, and rebounded off so that he felt their heat but not their impact.

Remo's redirection technique was good, but the return arc was off. Both attackers went down after each took a ball in the top of his head. They might not wake up for another day or three. But they would wake up.

Until he had a handle on what the hell was really going on, Remo didn't feel like taking anyone out permanently.

"Let's address the troops," he told Chiun.

As they approached, the still-standing Louisiana Costume Zouaves were busily ramming lead balls down their musket barrels. It looked like hard work. Most were sweating.

One soldier had the ramrod jammed down the gun barrel and set the muzzle against an oak tree. He kept trying to force the musket into the tree so the ramrod would go in. Instead, the ramrod snapped clean in two.

"I broke it," he sobbed as Remo tapped him on his blue silk shoulder.

"You won't be needing it."

"But it cost me a month's pay."

"That's the biz," said Remo, extracting the musket from the man's unresisting hand and plunging the barrel into the ground until he hit hard stone. Remo pulled the trigger, and the musket barrel split from sight to stock. Then he threw the foully smoking pieces away.

The man screamed in horror.

"It's only a rifle," Remo pointed out.

"It's my hobby."

"Let me get this straight," said Remo. "You came all the way from Louisiana to fight the Yankees because it's your freaking hobby?"

"That ain't it at all," he said. "I ain't come to fight Yanks."

"Then who?"

"I come to battle the First Virginia Recreational Foot."

"Aren't they from the South, too?"

"They are," the Zouave soldier admitted.

"Then they're on your side, aren't they?"

"Not in this sacred conflict!"

"You're siding with the North?"

"Never! My heart belongs to Dixie."

"And your brain belongs in the Smithsonian," snapped Remo. "If you're not with the North, who are you with?"

The soldier drew himself up proudly. He had to catch his tilting fez with both hands. "I came here to take a stand for palpable history."

"I don't follow."

"That is because you are trying to communicate with an idiot," said the Master of Sinanju, drifting up. "You! Cretin. What have the French to do with this outrage?"

"Nothin'. Except our uniforms are copied from a French-Algerian drill team that passed through the nation in the early 1860s."

"Huh?" said Remo.

"It's true," the Zouave said. "At the beginning of the Civil War both sides took their uniform design from the French. Heck, it wasn't until the second year of the war that they got the uniforms standardized. Me and my troupe prefer the Zouave outfit. It kinda sets us apart from the common herd."

"Do tell," said Remo, eyeing the man's outlandish costume with a skeptical eye.

"And do tell us what lies behind this madness," said Chiun.

The Zouave soldier opened his mouth to speak. Musket fire crackled well back in the open area that was Petersburg National Battlefield.

Remo and Chiun looked west. Puffs of smoke were visible some distance away. They rose and mingled as volley after volley followed.

"What are they shooting at?" asked Remo.

"They are shooting up," Chiun decided.

Remo shaded his eyes with both hands. "Nothing's up there but news and Army helicopters."

"They are firing at the Federals perhaps," the Zouave soldier suggested.

"Could be they're firing at the press," Remo speculated.

It was impossible to tell. The choppers scattered like so many clattering, frightened birds. And the volleys kept coming.

"Maybe someone's trying to rescue those captured Union guys," said Remo. "Let's move in and see what we can see."

"What about these clowns?" said Chiun, indicating the cowed Zouave troupe.

"You wreck their muskets?"

"Better. I broke their ramrods, without which they cannot fire their foul-smelling blunderbusses."

"Fair enough. They're out of the fight for now."

"You bunch better stay out of trouble until we get back," Remo warned the others who stood about looking dejected.

The Zouaves said nothing.

Remo and Chiun entered the park.

"Wait till the press conference," the Zouave soldier shouted after them. "That's where the real battle will begin."

"Did he say press conference?" Remo asked Chiun.

"He is an idiot and speaks idiocy," scoffed the Master of Sinanju.

There were pickets set up at various points, watching the main approach, Crater Road. All wore Confederate gray with the squashed-down forage caps that Remo knew were also favored by the Union, except they wore blue versions.

The sentries were easily avoided, never suspecting that two of the most dangerous human beings on the face of the earth were slipping through their lines like drifting mist.

Remo and Chiun soon came to an open area where they saw the Crater itself.

It lay in open field, backed by a high hill. The hill was covered with grass, and the Crater, in the century or more since it had been blown in the earth, had healed over in a depressed scar of grass. It looked to be about one hundred fifty feet long, fifty feet wide and perhaps fifteen feet deep. Remo had expected something round like an impact crater from a meteor, but this was more along the lines of a gash. It was ringed by Confederate sentries, who guarded it while their comrades-in-arms methodically reloaded their muskets and pistols and poured enfilade fire into the sky.

After the helicopters had withdrawn to a respectful distance, the firing abated.

"That sure scared 'em off," a soldier chortled.

"You sure it was them?"

"I tell you, I saw the rodent's ears. Painted on the side of that contraption as big as all outdoors."

"I didn't see no rodent ears," another man grumbled.

"Maybe so, but they was there."

"They wouldn't have sent him in by helicopter. They wouldn't dare."

"Well, they don't dare send him in now. Them TV helicopters captured all the fuss on film."

"What are they talking about?" Remo asked Chiun.

"I do not know, but I aim to find out."

And tucking hands into the sleeves of his red-trimmed black kimono, the Master of Sinanju advanced upon the Confederate lines.

THE FIRST TO SPY the tiny little man in black was Captain Royal Wooten Page of the Stonewall Detachment of the Virginia National Guard.

He looked harmless. He looked very harmless. Captain Page knew his Civil War history, as should a true native of Virginia, which meant he knew it very well indeed. Virginia had been the heart of the antebellum South. Richmond was the proud capital of the Confederate States of America. The Virginia theater had been the largest and most important theater in the arduous and bloody conflict. Page knew that in the early months of the war, before both sides had mustered true armies, the matter of uniform was left largely to each man. The blue and the gray of the later war years had not been established. Men went into battle wearing any old thing, uniform or not. Some wore turbans and fezzes. A few even marched off in their kilts.

Captain Page, who had appropriated a Confederate slouch hat to replace his National Guard helmet, did not quite recognize the uniform of the approaching man. It was not exactly in the Zouave style, which both sides had affected for a time. Nor was it a Garibaldi Guard uniform. But there was one thing Page did recognize. The red piping.

When the little man drew near, Page asked, "Artillery, suh?"

"I spit upon artillery."

Page flinched as if stung. "That is no way for a son of the South to talk."

"I am from the North."

For the first time Captain Page saw the little old man's almond eyes clearly.

"Well, Ah declare. You look more Eastern to me, at that."

"You command this legion?"

"It has fallen upon mah care-worn shoulders. Ah am Captain Page, at your service, suh."

"And I am Chiun, Reigning Master."

"Ah do not know that rank, suh."

"I am at the service of the emperor of this land, who has sent me to this province to discuss terms."

Page blinked. "Terms of surrender?"

"Yes."

"Isn't it a mite early in the day to surrender? The true battle for these blood-blessed grounds has not yet been waged."

A voice off to Captain Page's right said, "The battle's over, pal. You just haven't got the word yet."

Captain Page started. Just behind him stood a Yankee completely out of uniform. Unless a T-shirt and pants could constitute a uniform, but to Captain Page they did not.

"And whom do Ah have the pleasure of addressing?"

"Remo."

"First name or last?"

"Isn't that a National Guard uniform?" Remo asked.

"It is."

"What kind of hat is that?"

"Mah ancestors called it a chapeau."

"That is French for *hat*," whispered Chiun.

"Hold the phone," Remo shot back. "What are you doing with these weekend warriors?" he asked Captain Page.

"Commanding them, suh. By what right do you challenge mah authority?"

"Washington wants to know what the heck's going on down here."

"Why, the South is rising again. Ain't you got eyes?"

"I have a brain, too, and as near as I can tell, this whole thing started over a scuffle between Civil War reenactors."

"In that, you are sorely mistaken. This is a fight for the honor of Virginia in which traitorous reenactors have elected to take the wrong side. The enemy is due at high noon, and we will not surrender this hallowed ground which our ancestors defended so mightily."

"What enemy?"

"Ah will not profane this discussion by mentioning his cursed name."

"Better rethink that attitude," warned Remo. "Uncle Sam doesn't take no for an answer."

"Ya'll are with Uncle Sam?"

"Didn't I say Washington sent me?"

"It is hardly the same thing, suh."

Remo frowned. "Since when?"

"Since Uncle Sam has vowed to pillage this fine state, just as he looted the treasury of Old Dominion."

"I told you treasure was involved," said Chiun.

Remo lifted his hands. "Hold the phone. Something's not right here. Who looted the state treasury?"

"The godless forces of Uncle Sam."

"The your-country-needs-you Uncle Sam?"

"Hardly."

Remo and Chiun exchanged glances.

"Are you thinking what I'm thinking?" Remo asked Chiun.

"You never think," spat Chiun.

Remo turned to Captain Page and asked a seemingly unrelated question. "You got a phone around here I can borrow?"

"Why do you ask?"

Before Remo could answer the question with a hard, angry squeeze of the captain's neck, a black helicopter rattled overhead.

All eyes naturally went to it. It circled once and slowed, hovering over the Crater itself.

Something large and spherical and the color of stainless steel swung from the undercarriage, between the skids.

"What in tarnation is that?" Captain Page asked.

"It looks like a bomb," said Chiun thinly.

"I never saw a bomb like that," said Remo. "It's got lenses all over it."

It was true. The object resembled an old-fashioned steel bathysphere, except instead of portholes, it was pocked with great round lenses, every one a dull, glassy yellow.

"Looks to me kinda like a traffic light," muttered Captain Page.

"Traffic lights are red, green and yellow. That thing has only yellow lights."

Just then, the lights flared into life, warming to a mellow yellow.

"Yellow naturally indicates caution, does it not?" asked Captain Page.

"On a traffic light, yeah," said Remo. "But that isn't a traffic light, so I don't know what it means."

"It is a bomb," repeated Chiun, stroking his wispy beard uneasily.

"Bombs don't light up," Remo said. "They detonate."

The yellow-lit sphere continued to hang off the hovering helicopter, swinging less and less as the seconds ticked by.

"Do they not also fall?" wondered Chiun.

"Sure. Old-fashioned aerial bombs. But that's not a bomb. Looks more like an Easter egg, or maybe a Christmas-tree ornament."

Then, with the sharp snap of a parting cable, the stainless-steel object dropped free.

Captain Page shouted, "Take cover, men! We are under attack! Take cover!" And he threw himself flat.

Remo grabbed him up and tucked him under one arm, then followed the Master of Sinanju as he ran with ungainly speed as far away from ground zero as possible in the few seconds left before impact.

Behind them everything turned as yellow as an exploding sun.

6

There was no explosion. That is, no sound accompanied the powerful detonation. The sky turned sunflower yellow as far as the eye could see. The green grass turned momentarily blue. Trees changed color, too. But not a leaf shook. There was no shock wave, no screaming chunks of superheated shrapnel, no shrieks of wounded or dying men.

Except for the overwhelming sunburst of yellow, nothing much happened.

Until men began pouring out of the Crater.

They were running for their lives, faces twisted and full of horror. Unarmed, they wore the Union blue of the captive First Massachusetts Interpretive Cavalry. Clearly the object that had fallen in the grassy pit among them had spooked them so much they all but trampled their erstwhile captors in their mad rush to escape.

It didn't exactly hurt their chances that the Confederate troops were flat on their stomachs, heads cradled in their hands, awaiting an explosion that had already taken place. They had no reaction time. Their prisoners were well on their way to freedom by the time the Rebels lifted their faces with expressions that could only be interpreted as asking, "When's the explosion coming?"

Remo paused to drop Captain Page to the greensward and called ahead to Chiun, "Looks like a dud, Little Father."

"We do not know this," Chiun shot back. "Do not stop!"

A ragged line of bluecoats surged in Remo's direction, eyes wide as saucers, faces ghost white.

Remo stepped in their path. "What's the rush? It didn't go off."

Like frightened Boy Scouts, the men in blue charged past. They wore the expressions of men chased by angry wasps.

Casually Remo reached out and snared one by the arm. He lifted him over so quickly the man ran on air until his feet scuffed grass again.

"Talk to me," said Remo.

"I—I'm scared."

"Take it easy. It's over. They can't hurt you. They're still crouched down."

"It's not the Johnnys I fear," the man said in a fear-distorted voice. "It's that damn thing that fell into the pit."

"What about it?"

"It turned yellow."

"Yeah?"

"It was the most yellow thing I ever saw in my life. It scared the living bejesus out of me."

"Anyone in the pit hurt?" asked Remo.

"No. I—I think we all got out."

"So what's the problem?"

"I tell you, it was yellow. It was the most hideous yellow I ever saw. It was an unearthly yellow. Nothing should be that yellow. Nothing sane."

"I take it yellow isn't exactly your favorite color."

The bluecoat wiped his sweaty brow. "I always liked yellow. Until today. I don't ever wanna see anything so yellow for the rest of my life." The soldier cast fearful eyes back toward the Crater and started struggling.

"I think you've been sitting in the sun too long," said Remo, not relinquishing his grip.

"Don't mention the sun to me. It's yellow, too."

The soldier continued struggling to break Remo's grip. He might as well have been trying to break the clutch of a steam shovel, but seeing the abject fear in his face, Remo decided to let him go. The Union reenactor ran off like a scared rabbit.

Another bluecoat came close enough for Remo to snare him without too much trouble, so he did.

"Calm down," Remo told him. "It's all over. You've been liberated."

"It was yellow," the man quavered.

"So I hear."

"It was an awful yellow. An evil, twisted yellow. It was so yellow I don't think it was really yellow."

"Yellow's a nice color," Remo suggested. "Buttercups are yellow. And daisies."

"So's fire. This was a fiery, burning, horrible yellow." He tried to look up at his own forehead. "Is my brain on fire?"

"Does it feel like it's on fire?" Remo asked.

The man clutched his head as if afflicted with a migraine. "I can't get the yellow out of my brain. My brain feels yellow."

Captain Page was on his feet, examining his ripped chapeau forlornly. "Ah never thought Ah'd see a Yank with such a yella streak in him," he said in a disgusted voice. He addressed the Union man. "Suh,

Ah would advise you to get a grip on yourself. You are babbling something fierce.''

The Union soldier's nervous eyes moved wildly in their orbits. ''The yellow got into my brain through my eyes. Are they okay?''

''They look scared,'' Remo told him.

''They *are* scared. I'm scared. My—my eyes aren't yellow, are they?''

''No. Why?''

''If they turned yellow, I think I'd have to gouge them out. Otherwise, I couldn't stand to look into a mirror ever again.''

''Aren't you taking this antiyellow thing a little too far?'' said Remo.

''Can I go now? I have a long walk back to Massachusetts.''

''Why not fly home?''

''I would, but I'd have to ride to the airport in a taxi. It might be yellow.''

''Have a nice stroll,'' said Remo, turning his attention elsewhere as the bluecoat ran off.

The puzzled Confederate soldiers were up on their feet now. Some had crawled gingerly to the edge of the Crater and were looking down into it.

The Master of Sinanju approached Remo cautiously. ''You are unhurt?'' he asked.

''I'm fine.''

''You are very active for one who is on strike,'' Chiun said thinly.

''I got interested in things,'' Remo said distractedly. ''So sue me.''

''What was wrong with those men?'' Chiun asked.

''They were yella,'' said Captain Page, spitting out his disgust.

"Get off it," said Remo. "They were just scared by the thing that landed in the Crater."

"It was a bomb," said Chiun. "As I warned you, Remo."

"A dud."

"A dud bomb."

"A miss is as good as a mile," said Remo carelessly. "Let's check the thing out." Remo motioned for Captain Page to accompany them and, when the good captain balked, Remo swept a hand out and took hold of him by the back of the neck and started off.

Captain Page told his brain to make his body resist. He knew his brain got the message because his mental thoughts were perfectly clear and understandable. Unfortunately, somewhere in the neural net of his brain a dendrite must have been down or something because his legs obligingly carried him along at the same pace as the civilian named Remo.

It was very strange. When Remo slowed, Page's legs slowed, too. When Remo topped a rise, Page's legs knew exactly what to do even though all during the hike to the Crater, Captain Page was firmly informing his brain that he did not want to go near the damn Crater.

Page felt exactly like a docile puppet. He wondered if it had something to do with the way Remo manipulated his spine during the walk, tapping vertebrae to hurry him up and squeezing when he wanted Page to slow down.

When they reached the Crater, the Confederates had gotten themselves organized. Seeing Captain Page a prisoner, they leveled their muskets. Others went to work with their ramrods.

"Anyone who wants to walk around for the next month with a ramrod shoved up his backside," Remo said casually, "has my permission to fire."

There were three takers. They let go and then used their hands to bat away the thick black-powder smoke to see how badly their target had been hit.

When the smoke thinned, there was no sign of the skinny man with the thick wrists and dead-looking eyes.

Reflexively they reached for their belted ramrods. And encountered emptiness.

"Oof! Oof! Oof!" the three said several seconds apart. Then a firm hand guided their hands to the missing ramrods.

They found that the missing implements were stubbornly stuck in something and, when they turned around to look, they saw that they were somehow stuck in the seats of their Confederate gray trousers.

The trio formed a daisy chain and tried to help one another out of their rectal predicaments.

After that, the Confederate troops decided it was high time for a long coffee break and set to boiling chicory in their battered tin field cups over open fires. One man surreptitiously began coaxing his camp coffee along with a Zippo lighter.

Meanwhile, Remo guided Captain Page to the lip of the Crater.

The object had landed off center, gouging a raw brown wound in the grassy gash before it had rolled down to the deepest part of the Crater. Most of the lenses had shattered, leaving dull yellow glass shards lying about.

And next to the object a Union reenactor sat sobbing uncontrollably.

"Looks like we got a casualty here," said Remo, starting into the Crater. Captain Page obligingly followed. Or at least his feet obliged. His face scowled in a very ungentlemanly manner.

"These Yanks are a sorry lot," mumbled Page when they reached the man.

"What do you expect?" said Remo. "It's not like they're professional soldiers."

Remo tapped the Union soldier's dusty boot with a toe. "Lose your musket?" he asked solicitously.

The man looked up, face warped and dust smeared. "It was awful."

"What was?"

"The color of the thing," the Union soldier sobbed.

"Let me guess, it was sunflower-colored. The worst, ugliest, most hideous yellow you ever saw. Right?"

"Yellow? It was blue. A searing, crushing, soul-flattening blue. I just want to die."

"You said blue?"

"Yes."

"Not yellow?"

"No."

"You sure about that?"

"I know my colors," the man spat.

Remo let that go. "The blue make you afraid?"

"No, it made me depressed. I feel like the world's come to an end. First we get captured by the people who we come south to succor, then they drop some kind of depression bomb smack on us."

"The other guys ran away."

"I wish I could. I don't even feel equal to standing up."

"Let me give you a hand, soldier," said Remo, offering a thick-wristed hand.

The Union soldier simply sat there dejectedly, his head hanging so low his chin was buried in his chest. His shoulders looked like a wire coat hanger that had been bent down at each wing.

"This is a very unhappy man," said Chiun.

"This is a guy who doesn't know his yellows from his blues," said Remo.

"I have never seen a more unhappy man."

"I'll give you that," said Remo.

"He is a disgrace to his uniform," declared Captain Royal Wooten Page.

Remo gave Page a scornful look. He was now wearing a plumed Confederate officer's bicorne hat that looked as if it had been taken off a dead French admiral circa 1853. "You should talk."

"Ah am a proud son of the South, suh."

"Who deserted his unit to join a bunch of weekend warriors playing at war."

"This is a right serious matter," Captain Page said stiffly. "The state treasury has been looted, the governor co-opted and the legislature is about to sell out the land of their fathers for mere gold."

"Gold is not mere," sniffed Chiun. "It is gold. Therefore, it is perfection."

"These guys probably have some excuses," Remo went on. "They're probably all 4-F's. But you're a real soldier. What got into you?"

"Virginia."

"Huh?"

"Virginia is in mah blood. Ah make no bones about it, suh. Ah would die for the soil that nurtured me." And throwing his head back, Captain Page burst into mournful song:

Take me back to the place where Ah first saw
the light,
To mah sweet sunny South, take me home.
O'er the graves of mah loved ones Ah long for
to weep,
Oh, why was Ah tempted to roam?

Remo reached around for the back of the captain's neck, intending to deaden the man's speech centers when from somewhere inside the broken stainless-steel bomb, a siren began wailing.

"What the hell is that?" he said.

"The bomb is about to explode," Chiun said. "Quickly, Remo, we must escape."

"Bombs don't make sounds like fire engines."

Chiun got behind Remo and began pushing urgently. "Hurry, clod-footed one."

Remo scooped up Captain Page and the Union soldier, one under each arm, and started out of the Crater. The siren sound swelled and grew in pitch like an angry ghost following them.

When it was screaming at its most urgent, and the entire battlefield was thumping with Confederate soldiers running from the Crater, the explosion occurred.

This explosion wasn't yellow. Or even blue. It was on the order of a *thoom*. Not a big, earthshaking *thoom*, but a substantial *thoom* nonetheless. A pillar of blackish smoke crawled out of the Crater, seeking the climbing sun.

After that the Crater hissed like grease in a giant frying pan.

"Hold up, Little Father," said Remo as the hissing reached his ears. He stopped.

Chiun hesitated. "The smoke may be dangerous, Remo."

"Maybe. But I still don't think that was a bomb."

They stood and watched the black smoke coil and twist up from the great Crater to be picked apart by an intermittent southwesterly breeze.

When nothing else happened for five more minutes, Remo walked back to the Crater rim.

"Mind setting us down, suh?" a voice requested.

Remo looked down and saw that he was still carrying the depressed Union soldier and a docile Captain Page under his arms.

"Sorry. Forgot," Remo apologized, dropping the men to the ground.

They hung back at a careful remove while Remo looked down into the Crater.

At the bottom the stainless-steel sphere was a puddle of hot, smoking slag. It bubbled and spread, scorching the grass as it lost its round shape and became flat.

"Guess we won't ever know what it was now," Remo said unhappily.

"I do not mind," said Chiun, "just so long as we do not ever encounter its like again."

"... *JUST SO LONG as we do not ever encounter its like again.*"

At a mobile command-post van a man removed his earphones and snapped a console switch. "Moise reporting."

"Go ahead, Moose."

"According to the field mikes, we hued them good and proper. Opposition forces have abandoned the battlefield."

"That's our read from above. We just sent out the slag command."

"They're talking about it right now. The technology remains secure."

"Roger. Continue monitoring. We may need additional field support come H-hour."

"Standing by. Moise out."

The man in the mobile command post cut his mike and returned the earphones to his head. "I hate being called fucking Moose," he muttered to himself.

7

On the ground overlooking the smoking pit history had dubbed the Crater, Remo searched the sky with his eyes. The black helicopter that had dropped the weird device that was now so much superheated steel slag was gone. It was not among the clustering choppers that hung off in the western sky, well out of musket range.

Captain Page turned to Remo and said, "Earlier, suh, you spoke of surrender terms."

"That's right," said Remo.

"Well, Ah am prepared to offer them."

"Offer? You're going to surrender to us."

Captain Page jutted out his cleft chin with pride. "Never. Ah would sooner die."

Remo flexed his fingers to limber up. "That can be arranged."

Page took a step backward. "Ah will ask you to keep your cotton-picking hands to yourself, if you do not mind."

"No problem," said Remo, folding his lean arms.

Captain Royal Wooten Page relaxed visibly.

"Now you are being reasona—aayaaah!"

Captain Page fancied himself a singer of sorts. Mostly of the soap-and-shower variety. Old-timey tunes were his stock-in-trade. "Lorena." "Rebel Soldier." "Barbara Allen." "Shenandoah." He could manage middle C, especially if the water turned suddenly cold. For the first time in his life, he hit top C. And while he was, technically, singing, lyrics had nothing to do with his impressive performance.

The pain seemed to shoot through his entire body, paralyzing it with shock. It was remarkable pain, far beyond even that time on maneuvers when a half-track had run over the toe of his combat boot. Once, he had experienced something like it. He had been a teenager and gotten some candy cane stuck between two teeth one Christmas morning. For want of a toothpick or dental floss, he had taken some tinsel off the tree and used it to saw the offending particle out from between two back molars.

The pain had been electric and excruciating.

Later he figured out that the aluminum tinsel rubbing between the amalgam molar fillings had generated some kind of primitive electric current. At the time the pain could only be called exquisite.

This pain was anything but exquisite. It was as if his nervous system had been hooked up to a car battery and the juice pumped straight in.

Captain Page dearly wanted to run away, but the pain rooted him. He did manage to jerk his head around because he had the idea the pain was coming from his left. It was, he plainly saw.

The old Oriental gentleman in the black kimono with the red artillery piping had hold of his earlobe. That was all. Just the earlobe. Captain Page wasn't aware of any particular sensitivity in his earlobes. From time to time, in the hot weather, he might develop a pimple in the fleshiest part, but that was it.

The old man was squeezing the lobe between two quite wicked fingernails. Yet they seemed so fragile in their elegantly curved length. Now they were stern, hot needles bringing proud Captain Royal Wooten Page to his quivering knees.

"Now, about that surrender," said Remo.

"Would you prefer total surrender, or would abject surrender suffice?" Captain Page moaned.

"Whatever wraps up this idiocy quickest."

"This idiocy, suh, will never be wrapped up so long as Virginia is threatened from without."

"Who's threatening it?"

"Ah told you. The evil forces of Uncle Sam."

The terrible fingernails withdrew.

"Did you hear, Remo? It is Uncle Sam who is behind this."

"Hold your horses," said Remo. "Let's not get ahead of ourselves. Page, spell it out for me."

"Surely you know of the assault upon our sovereign state of Old Dominion," Page said, getting to his feet.

"I know two groups of idiots are fighting the Civil War all over again."

"It was the Yanks who started it, as Ah have it. Ah was not actually present at the Second Battle of the Crater, you understand."

"I understand exactly nothing."

"The Sixth Virginia Foot had camped out on these very grounds to stand against the would-be plunderers of ole Virginia, Colonel Rip Hazard commanding. He fell when the advance guard of Union troops swooped down upon them in their sleep. It was a slaughter, suh. The Sixth Virginia were not prepared for true combat. Their muskets were tramped down with powder and wadding only. No balls."

"No brains, either," said Remo.

"Ah take violent exception to that."

"Feel free," invited Remo.

"The valiant survivors lay in ambush when the Forty-fourth Rhode Island came along and paid them in their own coin. When the First Massachusetts followed, they were overwhelmed without loss to the Confederate side, Ah am pleased to report."

"Let me guess, no balls, either."

"You have that right." Captain Page frowned. "Ah must admit that portion of the tale has me flummoxed."

"How so?"

"Colonel Hazard had requested the assistance of the Forty-fourth Rhode Island Weekend Artillery and the First Massachusetts Interpretive Cavalry in the coming unpleasantness, and it was his impression that he was betrayed by one or the other. Yet both Northern regiments, when subsequently engaged, were firing paper and powder. They were woefully unprepared for battle."

"Wait a minute. Back up. What coming unpleasantness?"

"Why, the Siege of Petersburg National Battlefield, of course."

"Who's laying siege to this patch of grass?"

"Why, the dreaded Sam Beasley Company, of course. Don't you read the newspapers?"

"Bingo," said Remo.

"The carpetbaggers subverted our state government, extracted millions of taxpayer dollars for road and highway improvements and had the unmitigated gall to think they could erect a so-called Civil War theme park on Virginia soil, despoiling land that has only recently shrugged off the terrible wounds of the late unpleasantness.''

"What late unpleasantness?" asked Remo.

"The War between the States, naturally."

"I wouldn't exactly call the Civil War late," Remo said dryly.

"You are obviously no Virginian, suh. These wounds lie deep, and the scars still fester."

Remo looked around. "I can see that."

"They will never build on this hallowed ground. They failed at the Third Manassas, and they will surely fail here."

"Third Manassas?"

"They desired to build in the vicinity of Manassas National Battlefield Park, but the good people of Manassas chased them away. Their alternative site is just a stone's throw from here. But before God Almighty, we will run them off also or ourselves lie buried in the Crater."

"Third Manassas wasn't a battle, but a public-relations victory, is that it?"

"It is a victory nonetheless." Page thumped his chest once. "Ah only wish Ah had participated personally instead of succumbing to inglorious defeat at your wicked Yankee hands."

"Forget it. We have a beef with Uncle Sam Beasley, too."

"If only he had lived," Page said, wet-eyed. "The kindly old gentleman would never have allowed this vile travesty to be carried out in his name."

"And Colonel Sanders was a friend to chickens," said Remo.

"Suh?"

"Never mind. I want to talk to someone who was at the first ambush."

"My pleasure." Page called over to the men in gray drinking bitter chicory coffee with even more-bitter expressions. "Fetch Mr. Huckabee over here."

"Huckabee has been confined to quarters for dropping character by virtue of being out of period," a sergeant hollered back.

"What was the nature of his offense?"

"Zippoing his coffee, the lazy shirk."

"These men take their soldierly duties quite serious," Captain Page confided to Remo. Remo rolled his eyes.

"Sergeant, you survived the dastardly attack on your fine regiment. This man would appreciate an opportunity to treat with you."

"He won't hurt me, will he?"

"What kind of soldier talk is that?" Captain Page said angrily.

"I'm recreational, sir."

"I only hurt people who keep me waiting," Remo said loudly.

The sergeant cleared thirty yards of clipped grass in jig time.

"Sergeant Dinwiddie reporting as threatened," he said, saluting Remo smartly.

"Here now, you don't salute a civilian," Captain Page said.

"Beggin' your pardon, Captain, but I have been witness to this individual's manhandling skills, and have no wish to enjoy his wrath."

Captain Page rubbed the back of his neck and sighed. "Carry on, then."

Remo addressed the sergeant. "You get a clear look at the unit that attacked you last night?"

"Before God, I did."

"They wore Union blue?"

"They did."

"What color piping?"

"It was light blue."

"Not artillery red?"

"No."

"Not cavalry yellow?"

"Light blue, as I have said."

Remo turned to Captain Page.

"Light blue piping is infantry, right?"

"It is indeed," Captain Page said slowly. "Ah declare, Ah was unaware of a Union infantry reenactment regiment on maneuvers in these parts."

Sergeant Dinwiddie spoke up. "There was none, Cap'n. Just the Forty-fourth Rhode Island Weekend Artillery and the First Mass. Interpretive."

"Great," growled Remo. "You were set up and you fell for it."

"It was dark, sir," the sergeant said apologetically. "And we lost our beloved Colonel Hazard in the first engagement. He would have set us straight had he lived. I am plumb sure of it."

Remo said to Captain Page, "I asked for a phone a while back. You have one?"

"No, suh. Ah ordered the field phones destroyed."

"Why?"

"So headquarters would not recall us before the press conference. Or worse yet, federalize us under the command of Washington and set us against our fellow Virginians." Captain Page visibly shuddered at the thought.

"The Beasley people are coming here?"

"At high noon." Captain Page sank to one knee. "Suh, Ah beg of you. Let me and mah brave boys stand against the Yank devils."

"Only if you behave yourselves. No shooting. No taking prisoners. And if your unit commander orders you to pull out, you'll obey orders."

"Who are you to talk of duty?"

"I was a Marine. I learned to obey my commander."

"We had a senatorial candidate in these parts who was a Marine and did not let orders stand in his way."

"He win or lose?"

"Lost."

"That should tell you something," said Remo, walking away.

The Master of Sinanju followed him, sere of face, his hands tucked into his kimono sleeves. He looked like an angry monk. "Uncle Sam has shown his steely hand at last, Remo."

"Looks that way to me."

"We will have to deal with him, for it is Smith's highest instructions to vanquish the fiend once and for all."

Remo frowned. "It's not going to be easy."

"It was your task to find him."

"Look," Remo said angrily, "I ran my tail off. Sam Beasley World. Beasleyland. Euro Beasley. Beasleyland Tokyo." He held two fingers so they nearly touched. "I was this close to nailing him in Florida, but he flew the coop in a helicopter."

Chiun's frown deepened, making his wrinkles gullies. "It was a helicopter that dropped that bomb," he said, stroking his wispy beard thoughtfully.

"That helicopter was black. The one I chased down in Florida was red and green."

"Are you still on strike?"

"Not where Beasley is concerned. He got us embroiled in a war that first time when he invaded Cuba and tried to turn it into a theme park."

"That was when you should have dispatched him."

"Not me. I grew up watching his cartoons. The best place for him was in a Folcroft rubber room."

"Until he escaped."

"Not our fault," said Remo.

They reached the entrance to the park. The road was filled with white news trucks sporting microwave dishes. The trucks were being held at bay by newly arrived Confederate troops with muskets leveled. The Zouaves were nowhere to be seen.

"Let's take the low road," suggested Remo.

Moving low to the ground, they slipped around the Confederate lines and across the highway, which they crossed unseen, finally coming to an outlying news van that was parked a discreet distance from the rest. Like the others, it was white. The blue letters on the side said Europe 1. The *o* in Europe was either a plum or a blue apple.

"Behold, Remo—proof of French intrigue."

The Master of Sinanju was pointing to a blond woman in a fashionable blue slip dress who wore a black beret.

"She's wearing a beret. Big deal. Anybody can wear a beret. That doesn't make her French."

"She smells French."

"How do French women smell?" said Remo.

"Like cheese."

Remo sniffed the air. "I smell wine."

"Some French women smell like cheese and wine," Chiun admitted.

"Nice try, but this is a Sam Beasley operation all the way. The French have nothing to do with it."

"Let us prove it to your satisfaction by asking the sinister Frenchwoman for the use of her telephone."

"Fair enough," said Remo, changing direction.

The woman in the beret failed to notice Remo's approach, but so would a tiger, a hawk or any other wild creature possessing preternatural senses.

Remo moved with an easy harmony of bones and muscles and tendons that left no spoor for a predator to follow. His natural scent clung to his lean form like an aura instead of trailing betraying odor molecules after him. His feet made no impression in the dirt, and when he passed over grass, the blades sprang back like springs instead of lying crushed and exuding telltale juice.

So when Remo drew up behind the woman in the beret, he had scoped her out completely before she first became aware of his nearness.

She was blond with short-cut hair, limber limbs and a modest chest. Not Remo's type at all. He willed his sex-attractant pheromones to stop producing and let his body slouch slightly. With luck she wouldn't be attracted to him. It was a continual problem. Masters of Sinanju were trained to be masters of their bodies, and the result was not exactly lost on the opposite sex.

"Can I borrow your phone?" he asked quietly.

The woman whirled, green eyes sparking with anger and surprise.

"Who are you to sneak upon me, you—you American clod?" She pronounced "American," "Americain."

Remo frowned. "Take it easy. My car broke down a ways back. I need to call AAA."

"I do not know zis AAA."

"Doesn't matter. I'm a motorist in distress."

"And I am a journalist on a story. Ze line must be kept clear to my producer."

"French?"

"What is it to you?"

"Unusual to see a French reporter on a story like this."

"Zis is a major international story. If you rootless fools are going to tear your nation asunder, it is of concern to ze people of France. After all, you are an ally. Of sorts."

"Thanks for the vote of confidence. Next time Paris falls, remind me to quote you to my congressman."

"If you expect gratitude for somezing zat 'appen' an impossibly long time in the past, you are very much mistaken. Now, if you will excuse me, I 'ave a story to cover."

"You're welcome," said Remo, returning to Chiun.

"You were right," he said. "She's French. Typical winning personality, too."

"They were no more pleasant when the Romans first discovered them living in hovels along the Seine and named them Gauls."

"That one sure had a lot of gall," Remo grumbled.

"I am surprised you did not employ your masculine charms to convince her of the errors of her ways."

"Not my type."

"My," Chiun clucked, "how you have grown. There was a time when all white cows were your type."

"Knock it off. We gotta call this in to Smith."

"Agreed," said Chiun.

A man whom Remo recognized as a national correspondent for a major network was pacing before a microwave van, a cellular phone jammed against one ear, saying, "What's going on? Where are our helicopters? What's going on at the battlefield?"

"It's over," Remo told him.

The man stopped pacing and said, "What?"

"It's over."

"It's over?"

Remo nodded. "Over."

"Who won?"

"America."

"That's not a victory."

"If you're American, it is."

"I'm from Washington."

"Maybe you'll be allowed to join the rest of us if you behave. In the meantime I need to borrow that phone."

"I'm talking to Washington."

"You should be talking to America." Remo told him, and removed the cellular handset from his hand before his fingers could tighten defensively.

"Only be a minute," said Remo, walking off. An excited voice was chattering in his ear when he brought the handset to his head.

"What's going on? The helicopter feed is down."

"The South surrendered," Remo told the voice from Washington.

"Already? This story's only six hours old. Damn. We just preempted 'As the Planet Revolves.' We can't interrupt a bulletin and say it was all a misunderstanding.''

"That's the biz, sweetheart," said Remo, hitting the switch hook. When he got a dial tone, he thumbed the 1 button and held it down. A continuous 1 tone was the foolproof telephone code that would connect him with Dr. Harold W. Smith at Folcroft Sanitarium in Rye, New York. Folcroft was the cover for CURE.

Smith picked up the phone before the first ring sounded on Remo's end.

"Guess you've been standing by the phone, huh, Smitty?''

"Remo. How bad is it in Petersburg?''

"Not bad at all," Remo said amiably. "We have clear skies, a nice breeze and, except for the network news vans, not a cloud in sight. How about you?''

"The Rhode Island National Guard has been stopped at the Virginia border. It's a standoff. The Ninety-ninth Vermont Holiday Sharpshooters is mustering its entire force. The Stonewall Thespian Brigade is being reformed and is moving on Petersburg.''

Smith paused. "Strange. Stonewall was a Southern unit. These men are out of New York City.'' Smith went on. "On a layover in Austin, a commercial flight carrying the Texas Juneteenth Rifles has been detained on the ground by armed and unreconstructed Texas Rangers.''

"Texas-what Rifles?''

"Juneteenth. They are an all-black regiment who take their name from the date when the Negro slaves were freed. I believe the actual date was June 19.''

"They stopped being called Negroes a long time ago, Smitty.''

"They were called that when they were freed.''

"Point taken."

Smith's voice became more urgent. "Remo, we are witnessing the dawn of a second Civil War. It must be stopped. The President went for a jog two hours ago wearing a Smith College T-shirt. When reporters asked him to comment on the situation in Virginia, he said he hoped to find a *cure* for this new kind of divisiveness."

"Oops."

"I sent him an E-mail message assuring him we were on the matter, and warning never to use the word *cure* in public again. Now we must have results. It is unbelievable how quickly the situation is escalating. One moment."

The line hummed. Remo listened for the familiar plasticky clicking of a computer key and, when he didn't hear anything, suddenly remembered that Smith had upgraded to a noiseless keyboard.

"Remo, my computers have just picked up a story moving on the wire. *Old Ironsides* has sailed out of Charleston naval yard. An air unit of the Georgia National Guard have deserted in their helicopters and are moving north to the area. A group calling itself the Thirteenth Illinois Improvisational Engineers has hijacked a Chicago-to-Dayton flight and is demanding to be flown to Richmond. What in God's name has gotten into people?"

"Get a grip, Smitty. We have the situation in hand."

"Say again?"

"We liberated the First Massachusetts, and the Sixth Virginia Foot have laid down their arms."

"Then it's over?"

"Unless all those other idiots get here and stir the hornet's nest back up."

"I will see that they are intercepted if they have to be destroyed."

"Let's try and remember we're all one nation under God."

Smith's lemony voice became flinty. "If a second Civil War comes to pass, Remo, we will all have to choose up sides. This nation is already divided enough as it is. Imagine a Civil War today. Instead of North versus South, it might be east against west. Midwest versus Northwest. Any combination is possible. And that is without foreign nations taking sides."

"Well, the French are already here," Remo said.

Chiun spoke up. "It is true, Emperor. The untrustworthy French have already arrived."

"He means a French news team," explained Remo. "Apple 1 or something."

"Odd."

"I thought so."

"This story is only a few hours old. How could a French news agency have people in place already?"

"Maybe they were in the country doing a story on Memorial Day. They owe us big for Normandy."

"I have not noticed a great deal of gratitude of late," Smith said in a chilly voice. He had served in the OSS during World War II, in his pre-CIA days.

"I hear that," said Remo, looking in the direction of the French newswoman, who was now atop her van scanning the battlefield with a pair of binoculars.

"Listen, Smitty. We have good news and bad."

"I would prefer to hear the bad news first."

"I knew you would. Here goes, according to the Confederate side, they had called down two Northern regiments to help them. But they were bushwhacked by a unit from the North firing real ammo. That's why they attacked the units from Rhode Island and Massachusetts."

"Who were these bushwhackers?"

"They thought it was one of the two New England units."

"How can that be if they intercepted them traveling south as reports have it? It is not logical."

"Logic doesn't fly very high down in these parts, Smitty. When I asked around, these clowns admitted that it was an infantry unit that attacked them. But the New England units were artillery and cavalry."

"Some hitherto unknown reenactment unit goaded them into a fight," Smith said slowly.

"But here's the important part. This whole thing started because reenactors from both sides decided to take a stand here against a common enemy."

"Who?"

"The Sam Beasley Company."

There was silence on the line. And then a groan—long, low and heartfelt.

"Tell me this is not another Sam Beasley scheme."

"They want to build a Civil War theme park around here," said Remo.

"This was triggered by a theme park?"

"Hey, the Trojan War was over a girl who snored."

Smith's voice darkened. "Remo, I want Uncle Sam Beasley found, captured and terminated."

"Wait, Smitty. Think about this a minute. This is Uncle Sam Beasley. We can't just kill him."

"Kill him," Smith said in a brittle voice. "He dragged us into an incipient war with Cuba just to expand his global entertainment empire. Now this. I thought confining him to Folcroft until the end of his days would solve the problem, but I was wrong. Beasley is a menace to the American way."

"Some people think he *is* the American way."

"Find him and destroy him."

"I'm on strike."

"He is not!" Chiun cried out. "He told me so himself."

"If you cannot execute this mission, Remo, have Chiun do it," said Smith.

"I would no more kill the beloved Uncle Sam than I would harm a kitten," Chiun said loudly.

"Then bring him here alive, and I will put a bullet through his brain myself," Harold Smith said tightly. "Do you understand, Remo?"

"Got it. There's a press conference scheduled for noon. We'll let it play itself out, grab a Beasley vice president or something and work our way back to the big cheese."

"Report as necessary," said Harold Smith, who then hung up.

Remo snapped the antenna shut and told the Master of Sinanju, "We have our marching orders."

"I will harm no hair on his venerable head."

"We'll see if it comes to that."

They tossed the cellular back at the network correspondent and started back to the battlefield.

"You did not tell Smith about the bomb that brought terror," Chiun said pointedly.

"He hung up before I got to that part."

As they approached the park entrance, a line of cars roared up the road. They were all a flat primer gray, their chrome trim painted canary yellow.

"What are those?" asked Chiun.

"From the color of the piping, Confederate cavalry," said Remo.

The cars turned up Crater Road. They were waved in by cheering Confederate sentries, who threw their slouch hats and forage caps into the air with raucous whoops of joy.

"We'd better shake a leg. Looks like reinforcements. If they stir up Southern passions, we'll have to put down the rebellion all over again."

8

Mickey Weisinger was the second-highest-paid CEO in human history. He had a stock-option plan that enabled him—virtually on whim—to buy company stock at five dollars a share and resell it at market value. Typically he doubled his thirty-minute investment.

But he was not happy. He was never happy. He would never be happy.

Not until he was the highest-paid CEO in human history.

For the man who ran the company that made all of America and most of the industrialized world smile, Mickey Weisinger lived as if existence was a constant struggle against the piercing paper cuts of life.

Nothing was ever enough. No success could fulfill him.

Yet the successes kept coming and coming. All through the eighties and nineties, under President Mickey Weisinger the Sam Beasley Corporation could do no wrong. Under Mickey Weisinger the Beasley culture expanded, was packaged and exported to other countries.

It began with Beasley Tokyo. Everyone knew the Japanese loved all things American—and what was more American than Mongo Mouse, Mucky Moose and Silly Goose? The Japanese lapped it up, but when the quarterly financial reports came in, Mickey Weisinger saw only failure.

"We thought too small," Mickey lamented.

"The park is raking it in."

"We gave them too damn many concessions. We licensed the damn thing. We should have built it ourselves. We should own Beasley Tokyo lock, stock and castle moat."

"But if it had flopped," he was reminded, "it would have dragged Beasley stock right into the tank."

"Beasley never fails," Mickey Weisinger railed, pointing to the portrait of founder Uncle Sam Beasley, at that time dead for two decades despite persistent rumors he was being kept in cryogenic suspended animation until medical science could discover a cure for his damaged heart, and shouted, "Beasley is America. We are America and next time we're going to own it all."

And they did. They geared up their licensing operation, computerized their animation department, tripled theatrical releases and flooded the planet with Beasely products until they had a gross national product equal to the smaller European countries.

But it still wasn't enough for Mickey Weisinger.

"I want more!" he raged. "More! Find me revenue. Create more toy lines. I want a product stream equal to U.S. military production in World War II. If anyone puts out a coloring book, cartoon or film that even smacks of Beasley, I want the ears sued off the bastards. It's not enough to bury the enemy in product, we gotta crush him before he can get his own product line established. From now on we're like sharks. If you don't keep swimming forward, cruising for fresh red meat, you're on the bottom spilling blood for our enemies to sniff out and devour."

So the word went out, and Beasley exported itself, expanding and conquering. With the untimely death of Beasley CEO Eider Drake, Mickey Weisinger was promoted to chief executive officer.

When it was time to establish a beachhead in Europe, Mickey Weisinger personally oversaw negotiations. He handpicked a site outside Paris in rural Averoigne and, when negotiations were in the final stages, he turned around and made the same offer to the government of Spain.

Pitting the two nations against one another, Mickey succeeded in extracting concessions from the French until they were literally salivating to break ground at Euro Beasley.

Buffeted by the worst recession and coldest European winters in living memory, Euro Beasley underperformed with crushing losses, and Mickey Weisinger watched his stock—both personal and professional—plummet.

"We're pulling out of Euro Beasley," he told the board of directors one chilly morning at the corporate headquarters in Vanaheim, California, pounding the conference-room table emphatically.

"We can't! We own nearly fifty percent."

"Not if we default. Then the banks and the French government will be left holding the bag."

"We can't do that. It'll make the Beasley name mud."

"I don't care about the Beasley name. I care about my name!" roared Mickey Weisinger, who, like so many CEOs in the late twentieth century, cared more about his résumé than the stockholders or the business he was charged to captain.

"If we pull out of France, we might as well surrender Europe to rival theme parks," complained Chairman Bob Beasley, the nephew of Sam and the only Beasley family member left on the board. "Already the Lego people have an outpost in Switzerland. And Banana-Berry Studios are looking at Berlin."

"I don't care. Let Lego have Europe. We'll concentrate on Asia and South America. We're too exposed in Europe."

"That wouldn't have happened if we'd have licensed the damn thing," a voice grumbled.

"Who said that?"

No one raised his hand.

"That sounded like a vice president's voice," Mickey Weisinger said suspiciously, patrolling the room. "Which vice president?"

No one volunteered.

So Mickey Weisinger fired all the VPs on the spot.

At the next meeting a flock of newly installed VPs voted to a man to pull out of France.

Until Bob Beasley quietly objected.

Mickey Weisinger hesitated. No one bucked Bob Beasley. He was considered all but the proxy of the dear departed spirit of Uncle Sam Beasley.

"I think we should lay this before a higher authority," he drawled, scratching at the trademark family mustache.

"Uncle Sam?"

"Uncle Sam."

Weisinger sighed. "What'll it be this time? Tarot? Ouija board? I Ching? Or do you want me to dim the lights while you try to channel him?"

It was New Age bullcrap, Mickey Weisinger privately thought, but this was southern California, where people took their poodles to shrinks at five hundred bucks an hour and arranged their furniture according to two-thousand-year-old Chinese superstition.

"I think we should pay Utiliduck a little visit," Bob suggested. "We have that new command-and-control wing down there. You know, the one we built in the event of thermonuclear exchange."

Mickey scowled. "The cold war's over. The wall fell. Hell, Moscow has been faxing us feelers on a Russo Beasley project, but we'll never bite. If French winters are this rough these days, Russia's bound to be an iceberg."

"Take a walk with me, Mickey," said Bob Beasley in his folksy voice, clapping an arm over Mickey Weisinger's broad shoulders and steering him out of the conference room.

They took the monorail over Beasleyland, walked through the park, and for a moment Mickey Weisinger's sour mood lightened. Even he was not immune to the spell of Beasleyland under a glorious California sun. Everyone seemed to be having a great time. Except the park employees—the only slice of the American public the Sam Beasley Corporation treated with naked disdain.

Mickey's good mood lasted until Screwball Squirrel minced up, bushy tail quivering, and stuck the cold steel muzzle of a MAC-11 into his back.

"What the hell is this?" Mickey growled.

"Just come along quietly, Mickey," said Bob Beasley in a new tone. One completely without respect.

"What is this, a furschlugginer coup?"

"Not exactly," said Beasley as Mickey was escorted to a turn-of-the-century apothecary shop on Main Street, U.S.A., and into an open elevator.

Down in Utiliduck, where the trash was processed and the rides and attractions were controlled by massive mainframes, Mickey Weisinger walked along stainless-steel corridors to the hardened wing of Utiliduck.

A door emblazoned with the three overlapping black circles representing the silhouette of Mongo Mouse's round-eared head lifted like a dull guillotine, and he was pushed through.

A pleasant plastic sign featuring Mongo wearing a policeman's uniform and lifting a white-gloved hand traffic-cop style greeted them. The sign said Unauthorized Persons Not Allowed Beyond This Point. Intruders Will Be Shot.

"Isn't that a little extreme?" said Mickey Weisinger.

"Not down here," said Bob Beasley. "You've never been to this wing, have you?"

"No," said Mickey in a very small voice because he felt like a Brooklyn hood being taken for a ride in the trunk of a Buick.

The room Mickey Weisinger was taken to was as warm as a steam bath. He started sweating immediately. It was a control room, he saw. Grid after grid of wall video monitors showed every cranny of Beasleyland above, including, he saw with shock, his private office.

At the far end a man sat at a chair, punching buttons.

"Uncle, he's here."

"Give me a fucking minute," a grumpy voice said.

Then the chair turned, and Mickey Weisinger found himself staring at the man whose place in the Beasley corporate structure he had usurped.

"Uncle Sam?" he blurted.

"You were expecting Tinker-fucking-belle?"

It was Uncle Sam Beasley, all right. Not much older than on the day he had been buried three decades ago. His mustache was whiter, almost like hairs of frost. One eye looked glassy. The other was protected by a white eyepatch emblazoned with the corporate logo— Mongo Mouse's black silhouette. And where his right hand should be was a gauntlet of articulated steel.

"Wait a minute, you're radio-animatronic," Mickey blurted.

"That's right," said Uncle Sam Beasley.

Mickey breathed a hot sigh of relief. "Whew. For a minute I thought you—you, you know—" Mickey swallowed "—were back."

"I am."

"This is a joke."

"No, you're the joke."

"Hey, I won't have a robot talk to me like that."

"I'm not a robot, you bagel-munching moron."

"You can't talk to me." Mickey turned to the others. "Who programmed this anti-Semitic hunk of junk?"

Then the hunk of junk lifted itself out of his chair and walked across the room.

Mickey Weisinger stared. He knew the science of radio-animatronics. The concepteers at the Sam Beasley R&D unit had pioneered the science of free-standing radio-animatronic marionettes. They could move, after a fashion, simulate motion and voice and the semblance of life well enough to make Buccaneers of the Bahamas the most popular attraction in any and all theme parks the world over.

But one thing they had never learned to do was walk.

Mickey Weisinger felt a chill climb his spine under his three-thousand-dollar raw silk Versace suit as the thing that should not walk came striding toward him.

"Somebody turn this thing off," Weisinger commanded.

"You can't," said Bob Beasley in an affable voice.

"Then shoot it."

"I couldn't do that," Beasley said. "Not to my Uncle Sam."

And before he could react, the thing that looked shudderingly like Uncle Sam Beasley reincarnate took Mickey's soft, fleshy hand in his steel grip and pumped it with hydraulic force.

Through his own screaming, Mickey Weisinger heard the famous voice of Uncle Sam Beasley croak, "Aren't you going to welcome me back into the fold, Mickey my boy?"

"Yahhh!" said Mickey Weisinger as the room turned a dull optic red before irising down into a smoldering blackness.

WHEN HE AWOKE, Mickey Weisinger lay on his back, blinking up at the hideous face of Uncle Sam Beasley.

"They tell me you're the fuck-wit who's been running things in my absence."

"That's true."

"When people used to come to work for me, I would tell them straight out. You're here to promote the good name of Sam Beasley. If you buckle down and work your tail off for me, we'll get along fine. If not, you can haul your ass out of my office."

"I tell my people the same thing, only more nicely."

"You've been running my corporation like it was your private fiefdom!" Uncle Sam roared.

"But—"

"But it's not," Uncle Sam snapped. "It's *my* private fiefdom. Where do you get the nerve to run it into the ground?"

"It's expanded wonderfully."

"You built a fucking cold-climate theme park with my name on it. We're been hemorrhaging dollars over there."

"Euro Beasley's turned around lately," Mickey pointed out.

"Yes. No thanks to you. It's a good thing I escaped from that damned loony bin."

"What damned loony bin?"

"Never mind. I'm back and, since I was on ice when you climbed aboard the good ship Beasley, let me dispense with the usual pep talk."

Mickey Weisinger was wondering if "on ice" meant what he thought it meant when Uncle Sam's face came up to his own and turned ferocious.

"You work for me, asshole, and you dedicate yourself to the advancement of the name Sam Beasley. If there's any other agenda, you can leave now."

"Can—can I think about it?"

"Go ahead. But this isn't like the old days. You know I'm alive. Can't have it getting out. The government's trying to commit me. The only way you're leaving Sam Beasley is in a pine box."

"This isn't the Mafia."

"True. The Mafia is built on loyalty. There'll be none of that sentimental guinea crap here. I pay you, I own you. It's that simple."

"Did Bob tell you about the park in Virginia?"

"Tell me? It was *my* fucking idea."

"I thought Bob came up with it."

"My idea. He was just the mouthpiece. Old Bob's been feeding you my ideas for months now."

"Exactly how long have you been back, Uncle Sam?"

"Remember that time Sam Beasley World disappeared into a Florida sinkhole a couple years back?"

"Yeah ..."

"I was around then. Then I had a little problem and had to drop out of sight for a while."

"You've been out of sight since the sixties," Mickey pointed out.

"There's different ways of dropping out of sight. Never mind. I'm back and I'm running the show again. You've been screwing up. First this Euro Beasley and now Beasley U.S.A."

"We have the state legislature of Virginia on our side. The governor's practically in our pocket."

"And you got us chased out of Manassas. From now on we're digging in for a knock-down, drag-out battle. We break ground on Beasley U.S.A. by next year, or I break ground on *you.*"

Mickey Weisinger gulped.

"You're going to Virginia."

"Anything you say, Uncle Sam."

Mickey Weisinger's teeth clashed as a steel hand patted him on top of his head with brute affection. "That's my boy. I have a plan to break all resistance to Beasley U.S.A. But I need someone to whip up local passions."

"I'm a great corporate cheerleader. You should review the commercials I've been doing."

"I have. You have the smile of a shark."

"I'll get my teeth fixed."

"Keep 'em. I need a shark for this. I want a guy out there people hate. I want you to be at your most insincere."

"I'm not an actor."

"Just act natural. If my plan backfires and people look ready to lynch you, I'll step in and save the project."

"And me, too, right?"

"If it's not inconvenient. Remember, I own you."

"But I'm the second-highest-paid CEO ever," Mickey insisted.

"A Beasley serf is a Beasley serf," said Uncle Sam Beasley as he clumped over to his control console and punched up different camera angles on his empire.

9

Narvel Boggs never celebrated Independence Day. Never. Instead, he wore a black armband every July Fourth. What was there to celebrate when the nation into which he had been born, the late lamented Confederate States of America, had been cruelly vanquished a century before he had been born into this sorry world?

Narvel had once celebrated Memorial Day. Proudly. Back when it was a proud Southern holiday known rightfully as Confederate Memorial Day. Then a few years back Washington federalized an obscure Yankee holiday called Decoration Day, renamed it Memorial Day and killed Confederate Memorial Day for good and longer.

It was one of the last aftershocks of the War Between the States, and the fact that it had taken place in 1971 hadn't made it sting any less to an unreconstructed Southerner like Narvel Boggs.

Probably no one was more unreconstructed than Narvel Boggs of Savannah, Georgia.

As boys, some fantasized of pitching for the Braves, circling the earth as astronauts or, if their imaginations were particularly unfettered, crashing around the universe as Superman.

Narvel's youthful fantasies had been especially un-fettered. When he was eight years old, he began to imagine himself as Colonel Dixie, Scourge of the South, wearing a smart gray leotard and a cape pat-terned after the glorious Stars and Bars. Colonel Dixie's mission in life was to change history. Southern History.

In his imagination Narvel Boggs had been a lowly Confederate corporal who, when the cruel tides of history threatened to swamp the grand forces of Gen-eral Robert E. Lee's Army of Northern Virginia, re-versed his uniform, pulled on the very colors he carried into battle and launched into action as Colo-nel Dixie, superhero.

Narvel saved the day at both Manassas, Antietam and Cold Harbor. He salvaged Jeb Stuart's life with a transfusion of his own supercharged blood and, in his favorite fantasy, single-handedly stemmed the repulse of Pickett's Charge at Gettysburg, thus saving the Confederacy, which, no longer held back by Yankee foot-dragging, ultimately put an Atlanta boy on the moon in 1948.

As he'd grown, the character of Narvel's fantasies naturally altered. It became harder and harder to sus-tain a Confederate victory even in daydreams when you opened your eyes and there was the cold concrete of the hateful Union. So Narvel contented himself with rescuing old Jeff Davis from his Union prison at Fort Monroe, rebuilding scorched Atlanta, flying an astonished and trembling Abraham Lincoln to odious exile in faraway Liberia and once in a while leading a twentieth-century uprising to restore the Confederacy.

When puberty had hit, Colonel Dixie flew less and less often through the landscape of Narvel Boggs's imagination. And when he'd settled down and married Eliese Calkins, Narvel Bogg's invincible alter ego stowed away his battle-flag cape for good. A man had to raise a family, even if he didn't breathe quite free in his home state.

Years passed as Narvel drifted from job to job. Eliese lost her easy Southern-belle smile and moved out. And of late Colonel Dixie had begun to peer out of the closet door of Narvel's interior life more and more, wondering if there was a place for him in the world. Once in a while Narvel let him fly around for an hour or so. After all, it was all transpiring inside his head. Who would know any different?

So when the radio crackled the news that there was new Confederate skirmishing up Petersburg way, Narvel Boggs climbed down off the roof he was shingling, piled into his primer gray Plymouth Fury and lit out for a piece of the action.

If the South was about to rise again, Narvel was going to be in the thick of it. Civil war came along only once a century, after all.

On the drive to Petersburg, Narvel got on the CB and, using his Colonel Dixie handle, recruited some like-minded souls until a line of primer gray cars occupied an entire lane of Interstate 95 and no one dared stop him. The entourage stopped only for beer and guns and the necessary roadside piss.

At one stop Narvel bought a Confederate uniform and flag. He put it on, tied the Stars and Bars around his collar, then turned around until the breeze sent it skimming smartly off his shoulders.

"What are you supposed to be?" a good ole boy named Hoyt asked from around a plug of chewing tobacco.

"Just call me Colonel Dixie," Narvel said proudly.

When no one laughed, Narvel got into his Dixie-mobile and sent it roaring toward Petersburg, hope in his Southern heart.

BY THE TIME cheering pickets waved Colonel Dixie's Raiders onto the grounds of Petersburg National Battlefield, Narvel Boggs saw himself a man of destiny. Who needed superpowers when he had a cause both good and true?

When the Crater came in sight, he put a yellow-gauntleted hand out the window and called, *"Cavalrrryyy—halt!"*

The convoy of gray cars screeched and slid to a halt with only two or three crumpled fenders.

Narvel stepped out, throwing back his Confederate cape so the wind caught it good and said, "Colonel Dixie's Raiders reporting for action."

"You're too late," said a man in a uniform that combined the Confederate cavalry and the Virginia National Guard.

"Who or what the hell are you?" Narvel demanded.

The man threw a salute. "Captain Royal Wooten Page, at your service, suh. Stonewall Detachment of the Virginia National Guard."

Narvel hesitated. Did a superhero colonel salute a lowly military captain? He decided what the hell and returned the salute.

"Colonel Dixie, savior of the Confederacy." A freshening wind flung his cape across his face with a slap.

"Ah fear you are a mite late with your messianic favors, Colonel. We have agreed to lay down our arms."

"You done surrendered?"

"We are obliged to cease all rebellious operations until such a time as the dread foe is met and sent whirling back to the lower regions from whence he came."

"What dread foe be that?" demanded Narvel, falling easily into the speech patterns of his ancestors. After that PBS special a few years back, it had begun to catch on with the more unreconstructed among them.

"The vile forces of Uncle Sam Beasley, naturally."

"What about them durn Billy Yanks?"

"It appears some form of misunderstanding has been perpetrated upon us."

"Day-am!" said Narvel, fighting to keep his whipping cape out of his eyes. "My raiders didn't come all this way to protest that idiot theme park. We come to lift up the South and deliver it from durance vile. We come to shoot bluebellies." Colonel Dixie turned, thumped his gray chest manfully and said, "Ain't that right, boys!"

"Day-am right!" chorused his raiders, brandishing an assortment of shotguns, squirrel guns and semilegal machine pistols.

A lieutenant in the uniform of the old Army of Northern Virginia stepped up and said, "We can't allow you men to go about toting them things."

"What in hell's wrong with them?" Narvel bellowed.

"They're not in period."

"In what?"

"Period. They're post-Reconstruction, except for them old squirrel guns. They're maybe okay, depending on what ammo you're using."

Narvel Boggs stared in stupefied amazement.

"And you'll have to get them newfangled cars off the battlefield, too."

Narvel Boggs couldn't believe the words he was hearing. "Ain't you fellas been listening to the damn radio?" hc barked.

"Radios are twentieth century. Not permissible."

"There's an angry regiment of the Ninth Pennsylvania Memorial Day Sappers barrel-assing this way, according to the radio."

"If they come in peace, Ah imagine we'll give them a right passable welcome," said Captain Page.

"The Rhode Island National Guard has sworn bloody vengeance and is camped out on the Washington side of the Potomac. If they ever ford the river, it'll bc a plumb shooting bee."

"Imagine they've calmed down a mite by now," Captain Page allowed.

"And up in New York City they've organized their own Stonewall Brigade."

"How can that be, suh? Ah am proud to lead the only descendant of that mighty band."

"They ain't exactly forming up no sons of Stonewall Jackson, if you take my meaning."

"What other Stonewall is there?"

"The Stonewall Riots kinda Stonewall. It's a, you know, fairy kind of brigade. Call themselves the

Stonewall Thespian Company. By that I figure they got some hairy-chested women littering their ranks."

Captain Page paled noticeably. "They have usurped our good name?"

"Usurped, besmirched and appear hell-bent on dragging it through mud and muck and mire and doubtless worse."

"This is a most grievous insult," said Captain Royal Wooten Page in a harsh voice.

"No telling what their unmanly antics will do to the good name of the true Stonewall Brigade."

"If they come," vowed Captain Royal Wooten Page, raising a trembling fist to the pure blue sky of Old Dominion, "we must smite them to the last man."

"Or whatever," added Narvel Boggs, a.k.a. Colonel Dixie, who then turned to his waiting raiders and announced, "We came to fight and we fight to stay!"

A fiendish rebel yell leaped from every lip.

THREE MILES AWAY the war whoop was reproduced in a set of headphones clamped around the head of Mickey Weisinger, CEO of the Sam Beasley Corporation.

"These fucking yokels sound serious," he said thickly.

"They are," said Bob Beasley in an utterly unconcerned voice.

"I can't just drop in there and make a speech. They'll tear me limb from fucking limb."

"There are worse things."

"Name one."

"Oh," said Bob, ticking off items on his fingers, "pissing off my Uncle Sam, betraying my Uncle Sam and finding your balls clutched tightly in my Uncle Sam's hydraulic right hand."

In the mobile communications van, parked in a thicket of piney Virginia woods, Mickey Weisinger crossed his legs protectively and croaked, "When do I go in?"

"After the shooting starts," said Bob Beasley, snapping a microphone on.

"Shooting? What shooting? Who's going to shoot who?"

"Everybody."

"Huh?"

"Everybody's going to shoot everybody else once the California Summer Vacation Musketeers break through Rebel lines."

"Whose side was California on during the Civil War?"

"*Our* side," said Bob Beasley. He brought his lips close to the mike and said, "Musketeers, it's your day to howl."

Mickey Weisinger wiped his moist brow with a silk handkerchief. "I just hope it isn't my day to die."

10

The line of primer gray cars disappeared up Crater Road in a dusty cloud. The trailing car, windshield smeared with dirt, fell more than five car-lengths behind the others. It was a four-door sedan, Remo noticed.

"Quicker to ride than to walk," Remo suggested.

"Agreed," returned the Master of Sinanju.

They started off, moving with an easy grace that oddly enough seemed to slow the faster they ran. The great worm of brown dust that had all but consumed the trailing Confederate car swallowed them up, too.

Coming up on the sedan, Remo broke left while the Master of Sinanju veered to the right-hand side. Their hands snagged the rear door handles, popped them, and with a skipping hop they bounced into the backseat cushions. The doors closed with a perfectly synchronized double thunk.

Ensconced in the rear, they rolled past the Confederate pickets who guarded the entrance to Petersburg Battlefield Park. Remo saw that they wore no boots. No shoes or socks, either.

He and Chiun exchanged puzzled glances and settled down for the short ride back to the Crater. They sat perfectly still, knowing that the human eye was sensitive to sudden movement, and if they kept still the driver was unlikely to notice them in his rearview mirror.

They would have probably ridden all the way to the Crater undetected except for the fact that a front tire hit a chuckhole and let go with a pop and a low hiss. The left forward corner of the car began to settle, and the driver tapped the brakes and banged his steering wheel with a hammy fist.

He turned in his seat to reach for the tire iron that sat on the drive shaft hump. A helpful hand attached to a thick wrist obligingly handed it to him.

The driver recoiled as if brushed by a stinging jellyfish.

"Who the hay-ell are you two!" he thundered.

"Passengers," said Chiun in a voice as bland as his papery expression.

"Passengers in a hurry," clarified Remo.

"Get the *hell* out of my car!"

"When we have reached our destination," said Chiun.

"And not before," added Remo.

The driver threw open the door, cupped his hands over his mouth and set his elbows on the car roof. "Hey, you Johnnys! Lend a hand here. I just caught me two Yank spies!"

The slapping of bare feet came up the road. Confederate troops surrounded the car on all sides. They began shoving musket muzzles in through the driver's window, some with their ramrods still jammed in.

"Who are you boys?" a quavering voice demanded. It belonged to a cadaverous blond man with the double bars of a Confederate first lieutenant on his collar. His droopy mustache puffed out with every syllable.

"I was just about to ask you the same question," said Remo in a cool, unconcerned voice.

"We be the Kentucky Bootless Bluegrass Band."

"Is that a military unit or a musical group?"

"Well, we do a little pickin' and grinnin' now and again," the lieutenant admitted. "But just 'cause we prefer the banjo to the bullet don't meant we can't scrap when we get a mind to."

"Do tell," said Remo.

"Now, are you gonna come out or do we perforate your skulking Yank breadbaskets?"

"Open your window, Little Father," said Remo to the Master of Sinanju.

"Gladly," said Chiun.

The windows came rolling down, and more muskets intruded into the car interior, vying for a clear bead on the captured Union spies.

"Are you a-comin' or are you a-dyin'?"

"Neither," said Remo, snatching the lieutenant's musket from his unresisting fingers, along with a clump of adjoining weapons.

He laid them at his feet. They clattered atop the bunch the Master of Sinanju had already harvested.

"Hey! That ain't fair. You give us back our ordnance, hear?"

"No," said Chiun.

"Not until you change that front tire," said Remo.

The lieutenant took a step back and raised his voice to a bellow. "Men! Commence firin'!"

More musket muzzles crowded in through the windows—only to be clapped flat as they were met by the hands of the Master of Sinanju and his pupil. They withdrew as if sprained.

"Reinforcements!" the first lieutenant cried in a harried voice. "We be needin' reinforcements hereabouts."

Additional knots of rifles angled in through the three open windows and were as quickly confiscated to form a knee-high pile on the floorboards.

After that no more muskets intruded.

The first lieutenant tried to bluff it out. "You are surrounded. And must come out," he said firmly.

"Not a chance," said Remo, slapping away a stealthy hand that tried to slip in and recover a weapon.

"There is no escape. We are not a-gonna go away."

"Fine."

"We are prepared to starve you out," the first lieutenant warned earnestly.

"Go whistle 'Trixie,'" sniffed Chiun.

"That's 'Dixie,'" Remo reminded.

"Please," begged the first lieutenant, "this be my first real fuss, and Ah don't wanna go home to my pappy with my honor all in tatters."

"Fix the tire and we'll think about it," Remo told him carelessly. And during the hesitant pause that followed, he lifted a filigreed musket from the pile and began taking it apart with steel-boned fingers.

An anguished wail near the trunk became a semiarticulate "That's my great-great-great-great grandpappy's 1861 Springfield. He shot it from Chickahominy clear to Spotsylvania! It's a prized family heirloom!"

Remo wrenched the firing lever loose and tossed it out the window, saying, "Bet I can fieldstrip this antique before you guys can get that tire changed."

Remo lost that bet, but not by much. A jack came out of the trunk, the car cranked up, lugs spun off, a fresh tire swapped for the flat and the sedan dropped back on four good wheels before Remo could separate the barrel from its mounting.

"Nice time," said Remo as the sedan finished rocking on its springs.

"I was a pit-crew chief at Talladega six years runnin'," an eager voice told him, adding, "Can I have grandpappy's Springfield back now?"

"After you drive us to the Crater," said Remo.

"We will have to accompany you, a-course," the first lieutenant said sternly.

"Why don't you drive?" suggested Remo.

"A singular suggestion," said the first lieutenant, ducking behind the wheel. He started the engine, then called out to his troops. "You men form a double column behind this redoubtable war wagon and follow smartly. Ah will drive at a suitable trot."

Driving at a trot was the first lieutenant's sincere plan, but once the car began bouncing along the road, his foot became exceedingly heavy on the gas. He started to wonder if his barefoot state had something to do with the problem when he felt the steely fingers clamping the back of his neck and realized they had been there some minutes.

"What are you doing, you confounded Northern spy?" he demanded.

"Steering," said Remo, giving the first lieutenant's head a sharp twist to the left. The First Lieutenant's hands on the wheel obligingly steered to the left, taking the coming turn at very high speed. He had nothing to say about the matter, he was astonished to discover. In the rearview mirror the Kentucky Bootless Bluegrass Band, straining to catch up, broke into a dead run.

"We are putting my band behind."

"They'll catch up," Remo assured him.

As they approached the loop in the road before the Crater, the first lieutenant noticed the olive drab tanks parked here and there among the Confederate gray cars.

"Whose tanks be these?" he asked.

"Stonewall Brigade."

"Sure they ain't Sheridan's?"

"Search me," said Remo. "Keep your shoulder down. I need to see to steer."

A finger came off one of the first lieutenant's neck vertebrae and tapped another. The lieutenant's foot came off the gas and tapped the brake more smartly than if he had had something to say about it. The gray sedan eased to a stop, and the rear doors fell open.

The first lieutenant grabbed for the door handle when a thick-wristed hand reached in through the open window and snapped the steel lever clean off, then threw it away.

"Why don't you set a spell?" Remo told him.

"Ah can get out the other door, you know."

"Barefoot boys have crunchy toes," Remo pointed out, shattering a stone under the heel of one shoe.

"Reckon Ah'll await my men," said the first lieutenant, tucking his precious toes under him where they would be safe from the Yankee devil spies. After all, he was a picker, not a fighter.

THE MASTER of Sinanju following, Remo walked over to a knot of good ole boys brandishing assorted shotguns and modern rifles.

A man in some sort of gray buttoned tunic, the Stars and Bars of the late Confederacy whipping from his broad shoulders, turned at their approach. He had a wide, beefy face and thick black hair piled high on his head in a lustrous Elvis pompadour.

"What manner of soldier is that one?" asked Chiun.

"Looks like a Confederate Captain Marvel."

"Nonsense, Remo. He is at least a general. Behold the many golden stars upon his proud shoulders. As ranking Master, it is my duty to treat with him and accept his abject surrender."

"Ranking Master?" said Remo, but Chiun had already hurried ahead. Remo didn't bother picking up his pace. If there was going to be trouble, Chiun could handle it. After all, Remo had driven the car.

NARVEL BOGGS, a.k.a. Colonel Dixie, Scourge of the South, saw the tiny little man approach. His eyes went past him to the fruity white guy who brought up the rear.

"Looks to me like an advance guard of them New York Stonewalls," one of his trusty raiders muttered.

"He does have that look about him. Not exactly swishy, but them's certainly faggy garments."

"'ppears to be a chore for Colonel Dixie," said Narvel Boggs, hitching up his golden sash and striding forth to meet the walking insult, the good ground of Virginia quaking with his tread, his black eyes striking intimidating sparks like twin meteors streaking toward his foemen.

On the way he passed the impossibly old Asian, who greeted him. "Hail, O illustrious general of the South."

"One side, slope," growled Colonel Dixie, who threw his protective cloak around the fair flower of Southern womanhood and the cream of Dixie manhood, but no other persons.

In that moment Colonel Dixie, the Meteor of the Second Civil War, stood poised on the brink of eternity. And never dreamed it. The face that launched a thousand comic books, TV cartoons, lunch boxes, coloring books and CD-ROM games stood a hairbreadth away from being peeled from its skull by a flurry of exceptionally long fingernails, when from a screen of trees just west of the Crater came a bloodcurdling battle cry.

"HURRRAAAH!"

And out of the pines came a wave of blue uniforms pushing shot and smoke and the stirring storm of battle ahead of it.

The deadly fingernails withdrew.

And the Third Battle of the Crater was under way.

11

The California Summer Vacation Musketeers poured out of the trees, screaming like banshees, fully two hundred strong. They wore Union blue, with light blue infantry piping, and wielded assorted muskets, including Maynard rifles, Brown Bess shotguns and Sharps carbines.

For a frozen moment the Unified Confederate Disunion Alliance stood rooted, the Sixth Virginia Foot, Stonewall Detachment of the Virginia National Guard and Colonel Dixie's Raiders alike. Down Crater Road the Kentucky Bootless Bluegrass Band skidded to a callused stop, hesitated and then came pounding up, venting a whooping rebel yell that froze the blood.

Over the din a lone voice called, "Prepare for action, men!"

It was the ringing clarion voice of Captain Royal Wooten Page, CSA. He clambered atop a tank and spearing his plumed bicorne hat on a cavalry saber, leaped fearlessly into the fray, waving it aloft for all to see. "Follow me!" he cried.

He got about a dozen feet before the dashing figure of Colonel Dixie swept in, tripped him and appropriated his saber.

"For God and Dixie!" Colonel Dixie bellowed, slashing at the sky with the saber-speared hat. "Not necessarily in that order!"

All along the Union line officers followed suit, lifting their chapeaus high on their swords.

Drawn inexorably by ancient enmities their ancestors had believed laid to rest in a courthouse surrender at Appomattox, two opposing waves of men surged toward one another, collided and ran together like oil and water mixing.

At first the overwhelming Union numbers stood to take the day. But the Kentucky Bootless Bluegrass Band, recovering their muskets from the back seat of the car where they had been stashed, made a flanking maneuver and opened up with a withering enfilading fire that cut many a man down.

Unfortunately, due to the confused disposition of the opposing forces, they struck down nearly as many Confederate brethren as Union foes. History recorded it as a brilliant if desperate stroke, but of course the unwritten truth was that it was an equal mix of panic and sheer idiocy.

From other quarters reinforcements put in their appearance.

The First Massachusetts Interpretive Cavalry, which had been hiding in the easternmost reaches of Petersburg National Battlefield, came slipping up to see what all the commotion was about. When they grasped the enormity of what their startled eyes beheld, they picked up stones and sticks and waded in.

The Louisiana Costume Zouaves also poured into Crater Field. They took one look and after some hesitation took the Union side of the engagement. Confusion ensued.

Confusion became a close-quarters tumult, and tumult gave way to a ferocious frenzy of clubbing and fisticuffs as the nearness of friend and foe alike precluded reloading of muzzle-loading rifles.

"BEHOLD, REMO," proclaimed the Master of Sinanju. "Your long-lost roots."

"Looks like a giant barroom brawl," Remo Williams remarked from the high ground of Cemetery Ridge.

Chiun narrowed his eyes to imperious knife slits. "Once begun, the madness of war cannot be halted."

"You saying there's nothing we can do?"

"The madness must be allowed to run its course."

"I'm for stepping in and stepping on toes."

"What will that accomplish?"

"You can fight or you can hop. But you can't hop and fight at the same time."

"True, but an army possesses toes in multitude. You have only two feet to stamp with."

"We can't let this go on all day."

"They are doing no more killing. See? The vultures have realized this and even now circle hungrily."

Remo looked up. TV news helicopters were beating near, camera lenses angling around like the electronic orbs of robotic voyeurs.

"Vultures is right," said Remo, picking up a rock and letting it fly. The stone whizzed skyward and bounced off a Plexiglas chopper cockpit. The cockpit spiderwebbed, turning white as snow. The pilot wrestled his ship to an open patch of turf. The other ships withdrew out of what they assumed to be the range of stray musket balls.

"I can't just watch," Remo said, starting down off the ridge.

"You can if you are on strike," Chiun pointed out.

"I'll strike in another way," Remo said, and moved into the fray.

"And I will help you, if only to hasten you along in your folly," sighed Chiun, following reluctantly.

MICKEY WEISINGER HEARD the not very distant thud and jostle of battle from the open clearing where Beasley technicians were laying great colorful swatches of silk on the grass as the hot-air engines began firing.

He said, "I think the shooting's died down."

"Our musketeers are under strict instructions to close with the enemy as quickly as possible so things don't get too bloody," Bob Beasley said affably. "After all, this is a media event."

"The radio says it's practically civil war."

"Think of it as a sort of a made-for-TV movie with light casualties."

The first balloon began to take shape. It was pink. They were all pink. Even the wicker baskets were painted a creamy pink. As the fabric filled, the smiling face of Monongahela Mouse, world-famous mascot of the Sam Beasley entertainment empire, swelled into merry life.

"That's your car," Bob Beasley said, guiding Mickey to the waiting basket. Beasley concepteers were fitting giant pink disks to each side of the basket, from which trailed insulated wires.

"What the hell are these things?" Mickey wanted to know.

"Mongo's ears."

"Mongo's ears are black. These are pink. Hot pink."

Bob Beasley chuckled. "You don't know how right you are."

"Huh?"

"Just climb in."

Mickey clambered in, finding himself standing amid a profusion of wiring and stacked car batteries.

Other balloons filled with hot air, revealing the faces of Dingbat Duck, Mucky Moose and other famous Beasley characters. All were smiling the identical vacant grin that, market researchers informed Mickey Weisinger when he'd first ordered them redesigned, people interpreted according to their own moods. And since they reflected each person's mood exactly, they could not be improved on.

Every basket was fitted with four pink Mongo Mouse ears, like lollipops made from frozen pink lemonade, so no matter what angle they were viewed from, the famous mouse ears jutted unmistakably. As he looked closely, Mickey realized that they were transparent plastic, like lenses. Inside each ear networks of filaments and semiconductors formed electronic webs.

"Do these things light up?" he asked.

"Do they ever," Bob Beasley grinned as he climbed aboard.

"Huh?"

"You'll catch on. In time."

"If I fucking live," muttered Mickey Weisinger.

The ground crews released the anchor ropes, and before his fear of heights could kick in, Mickey Weisinger was high in the sky over the peaceful Virginia countryside. Only then did he notice who rode the other balloons.

They were the concepteers, wearing official Beasley greeters costumes. One basket contained Gumpy Dog, wearing a Confederate soldier's trappings. Dingbat Duck also wore gray, as did Mucky Moose, Screwball Squirrel and others. Missy Mouse was dressed in the hoop skirt of a Southern belle.

In the second balloon, grinning like the idiot he was and waving inanely, stood Mongo Mouse. In Union blue of course.

"This isn't so bad," Mickey Weisinger said, relief in his voice. "This is kinda like an observation balloon, isn't it? We're going to observe the battle from a safe height, aren't we?"

"No," said Bob Beasley. "We're going to land smack dab in the thick of it."

"Meshugga schmucks," muttered Mickey Weisinger, clutching one of the guy ropes for support.

REMO WAS COLLECTING keppies. It was the Master of Sinanju's idea. As they moved into the fray, Chiun pointed out how the battle surged like tidal pools, with waves and streamlets of men following the officers who swirled about with a mad frenzy of their own. In the thick of battle, all men blended into a riot of milling uniforms. But the officers could be picked out from the rest by their upraised sabers holding keppies aloft.

It was just a matter of getting to the officers.

Chiun, being short, simply ducked low and flitted between combatants until he got within range. A stabbing fingernail to an elbow brought a Confederate saber and forage cap into his hands. He moved on.

Remo stood taller than most of the soldiers. The bulk of the fighting was being done with musket stocks, heavy stones and the stray bowie knife. Remo weaved out of the way of them all, his exposed skin functioning like an enveloping sensor array. He felt the body heat of attackers, shifted wide, and sensing the advancing shock waves of muskets aimed at his skull, artfully evaded all until he zeroed in on an officer.

Harvesting the keppies was simple enough. The officers fired off their Dragoon pistols, but since their free hand was occupied with their keppie banners, they couldn't reload. So they contented themselves with waving saber and pistol and accomplished nothing more useful than to shout themselves hoarse leading their men. Mostly about in circles.

Remo grabbed Union saber wrists, bent them against the natural flex and the sabres dropped obligingly into his waiting hand.

"Much obliged," Remo made a point of saying before moving on.

When they had collected every officer's saber on the battlefield, Remo and Chiun broke all but two and threw the others away. Remo went one way and the Master of Sinanju went the other, holding up opposing headgear.

It was a good plan. Perhaps brilliant strategy. The opposing forces, thinking most of their officers were down and needing leadership to carry them through the fog of war, began moving in opposite directions. Fighting began to break off.

That was the point when the balloons appeared.

They were hard to miss, hanging in the sky like great pink clusters of grapes, but amid the din no one noticed them arrive. Except the news helicopters, which hastened to get out of the way lest their rotor wash cause an aerial catastrophe.

When they were almost directly overhead, the pink mouse ears began to glow.

The sky turned pink. The entire battlefield was bathed in a hot pink glow.

All eyes were drawn to the source of the radiance.

And the magic began.

WHEN THE FIRST CHRONICLES of the Second American Civil War were penned, it was set down that the Third Battle of the Crater was halted by an angelic light streaming down from heaven. And when the forces of the two Americas looked up toward heaven, their anger was smitten by the smiling faces of familiar creatures who reminded them of their shared culture, their common heritage and their deep and abiding love of cartoon characters.

At least that was the way the Sam Beasley Corporation press release represented the event.

ON THE GROUND battle-sweaty men turned, faces lifting then slowly softening, curious eyes filling with a blazing pink radiance.

"Day-am! That be the pinkest pink I ever did behold!"

"Never had much truck with the hue myself, but I purely like that particular shade."

"It's a powerful shade of pink, all right."

"Right purty."

All across the battlefield hands that a moment before had been turned against other men because of the color of their uniforms or the queerness of their accents fell quiet. Arms hung slack in unthinking hands, all faces turned to heaven as the bright pink lights drew closer and closer.

"Ah do believe Ah spy the famous ears of Mongo Mouse," said Captain Royal Wooten Page, spanking dust off his hybrid uniform.

"Could be. But seems I recollect that mouse sports ebony ears."

"There's no mistakin' them hearin' appendages. Must mean Mongo Mouse hisself is a-comin'."

And as the hovering balloons began venting hot air, dropping them toward the Crater in a silent string, the unmistakable figure of Mongo Mouse, waving from the lead balloon, became visible to all.

Forage caps and chapeaus were pulled off heads and clutched to chests both blue and gray in worshipful respect.

"It's that day-am mouse, all right."

"Gotta admit, it brings a catch to my heart to see his grinnin' ole puss."

"Shouldn't we be shooting that varmint?" Colonel Dixie asked in a wary tone.

"You wouldn't ventilate ole Mongo, now, would you?"

"He's come to despoil Old Dominion, ain't he?"

A man spit on the ground. "That mouse never harmed a fly."

"What about that other guy?" Colonel Dixie said unhappily, pointing to the strained white face in the second balloon. "Ain't that that Weisinger scamp who's pushing Beasley U.S.A. down our throats?"

"Sure, but we can hear him out."

"Yeah. Besides, he's with the mouse. Anybody with Mongo is all right with me until I see different."

Colonel Dixie's broad, slab-of-beef shoulders drooped. "What's got into ya'll? That be the high enemy comin'."

But not a hand was raised as the balloons dropped into the Crater, pink bags collapsing.

The combatants, fingers well away from triggers, crowded close to the long gash that was the infamous Crater.

The roar of trucks came up Crater Road, and the few heads that could tear their gazes away from the angelic pink radiance spilling up from the Crater saw that they were TV satellite trucks.

No one moved to stop them.

Then, as camera crews leaped out and began recording events at a safe distance, a white flag bearing the three welded-together black circles that emblematized the most famous mouse that ever lived came out of the Crater and fluttered in the wind. When it was not shot to rags, the pear-shaped figure of Monongahela Mouse himself came out and planted his flag into the good rich soil of Old Dominion, as if daring a thousand muskets to cut him down.

But no one fired a shot. Faces impassive to the point of tranquillity, the soldiers simply leaned on their rifles, awaiting developments.

Then Mickey Weisinger stumbled up from the pit, escorted by polyurethane cartoon animals wearing Confederate gray.

"WHO IS THAT ONE, Remo?" the Master of Sinanju said with quiet interest. "I do not remember him from any cartoon."

"That's Mickey Weisinger."

"Who is Mickey Weisinger?"

"CEO of Sam Beasley Corp.," said Remo without concern.

"No doubt he is the perpetrator of this madness."

"The big cheese, without a doubt."

Chiun looked to his pupil. "Are you not going to seize this big cheese as planned?"

"Not now. I'm on strike again." Remo looked down. "How about you?"

"I feel a strike coming on, as well."

Remo nodded. "That's a nice shade of pink."

"A most excellent shade," Chiun agreed.

"Peaceful," said Remo. "I'm not big on pink, but the guy who came up with that shade knew what he was doing. I haven't felt this relaxed in years."

The Master of Sinanju lifted his bearded chin. "He may be a vassal of wicked overseers, but Mongo Mouse is a great mouse."

"The greatest," said Remo.

As they watched, the cartoon figures upended a wicker basket for Mickey Weisinger to climb atop.

He was greeted with a polite ripple of applause, which he acknowledged with a Richard Nixon-like raising of arms.

"Gentlemen, gentlemen," he began, "I have come in peace."

More applause. Smiles.

"On this glorious Memorial Day weekend, I offer a truce to the people of Virginia. I know we've had our past differences, but I think they can be worked out."

The smiles grew broad in faces washed with a warm pink glow.

"I have come not to exploit history, but to enhance it. The Sam Beasley Corporation is willing to work not only with the gentle people of Virginia, but with its noble reenactors. Those who desire them will have jobs."

Sustained applause.

"You hear that? He's offering us jobs!"

"He's been offering you'uns jobs for months," Colonel Dixie barked. "I thought you folks said never."

"He didn't offer it to us face-to-face like that."

"Yeah. He comes across right sincere in person."

"Sincere and in the pink."

"Pink?" said Colonel Dixie.

"Can't you see the honest pinkness of his words?"

"Search me. I got me a spell of color confusion."

"What say?"

"I don't see my colors right. Get my reds and greens kinda mixed up. Pink might as well be purple to me."

"You're missing out on one of the great pleasures of life if you can't see the color pink."

"You don't say?" said Narvel Boggs, wondering what had gotten into folks.

"And because we respect the sentiments of Virginians and other Southerners," Mickey Weisinger went on, "when we build Beasley U.S.A. we will have an If the South Had Triumphed Pavilion."

A rebel cheer went up.

"And virtual-reality games in which the South always wins."

A greater cheer. Even the Union reenactors cheered.

"You *will* know what it was like to have been a slave!"

An even greater cheer.

"Of course," Mickey added, "we will also serve history by reflecting the true denouement of the events of the—"

Mickey Weisinger replaced the earphone that had popped out of his ear.

"War Between the States, you jackass," came the crusty voice of Uncle Sam from the earphone.

"War Between the States," said Mickey Weisinger to the cheering of the Union reenactors. The Southerners also cheered. They cheered as if the outcome of the Civil War was a cause for great jubilation and always had been.

"Before all these cameras," Mickey went on, "I would like to close ranks with you men, bury the hatchet and ask for your support in this great project."

Reenactors surged forward with such suddenness that Mickey Weisinger hastily jumped off the wicker basket and would have sought the safety of the Crater except that Gumpy Dog and Mucky Moose grabbed him and pushed him back atop his wicker-basket soapbox.

Outstretched hands reached eagerly for his. Mickey shook them as fast as they came.

Then, with a crack and flutter, like canvas in the wind, a gray-and-scarlet figure surged through the crowd to lay a choke hold on Mickey Weisinger's thick neck.

"Urrk!" said Mickey.

"Maybe all the rest of you have turned milk-liver," thundered Colonel Dixie, "but Ah ain't! Ah aim to break this Jew Yankee's neck."

"No, no, don't."

"Please don't, Colonel Dixie."

"He's Mongo's pal. He don't mean no harm."

"Urrk!" said Mickey Weisinger as the world and Virginia turned dark all around him and a roar like a distant ocean began in his ear canals.

Over the roar a harsh voice said, "I can see every-thing that's happening. Promise him—"

"I can make you rich," Mickey Weisinger said in a squeezed voice, repeating the words in his ear.

"Colonel Dixie don't need wealth. His heart is pure as Georgia rain."

"I can offer something better than wealth. I can make you an official Beasley licensee."

"Huh? How's that again?"

"You'll join the honored family of Beasley characters."

The hands slackened their strong, choking grip.

"You mean pal around with Mongo?"

"Tell him, Mongo."

"Sure," Mongo squeaked from off to the right, gesturing with his yellow-gauntleted hands. "We'll have tons of neat adventures together."

"Will I get my own comic book?" Narvel asked his captive.

"Comics, cartoon shows, video games and all the personal appearances you want. We'll make you Beasley U.S.A.'s official mascot."

"It's a damn deal," said Narvel Boggs, who had shingled his last home and because of the events this day would ultimately be worth a quarter-billion dollars by the turn of the century.

Mickey Weisinger hacked and coughed as the red went out of his face and his lungs resumed normal functions.

"MAYBE THIS WAS ALL a misunderstanding," Remo was remarking to the Master of Sinanju as Mickey Weisinger and Colonel Dixie were lifted on the shoulders of the cheering throng.

"Wars are always fought over treasure. This land is the treasure, and now those who contested it have reached a truce. The war is over."

"Guess we can go home now," said Remo. His head suddenly turned as he tracked a moving figure.

"What is it, Remo?"

"There's that French reporter."

The woman in the beret and blue slip dress was creeping around the periphery of the Crater, which was jammed with fighting men turned peaceful. She had a satellite phone up to her face and was talking into it with obvious vehemence.

"What's she saying?" Remo asked. "I don't understand French."

"She is saying that the battle is over."

"It sure is," agreed Remo.

"But she cannot discover why."

Remo shrugged. "She'll figure it out."

But she didn't. She hung well back of the mob, moving back and forth like a wary tiger. Eventually she backed toward Remo and Chiun, unawares.

"J'essaie de constater cela," she was muttering. "I am trying to ascertain this."

"Boo!" said Remo.

She whirled, face a stark white. "You again!"

"Yep. Me."

She straightened and the spooked light went out of her eyes. She smoothed her skirt with a nervous gesture. "Perhaps you can 'elp me."

"If we can," Remo said agreeably.

"I did not see what 'as 'appen' here. Ze fighting 'as ended. Can you not tell me why?"

"They saw the balloons."

"*Oui.* I saw ze ugly balloons descended, as well. But why would zey stop fighting? Were zey not against ze Beasley people?"

"I wouldn't call them ugly."

"Zey 'ave giant uncouth cartoon faces on zem."

"Watch what you say about an American original," said Remo. "Besides, you have to admit the light show was spectacular."

"I saw only zat it was very bright."

"Struck me as more soothing than bright."

"What is soothing about bright white light?"

"White? It's pink."

"Oh. I am, how you say, *daltonienne?*"

"Say what?"

"Color-blind."

"Must be nice," said Remo.

She looked at him questioningly. "Was ze bright object zat fell from ze black 'elicopter also pink?"

"How do you know it was black if you're color-blind?"

"Answer my question, *s'il vous plaît.*"

"No. It was yellow. Petrified the guys it landed on, too."

"You say yellow?"

"Yes."

"But now pink?"

"Yeah."

"Ze yellow scared some men, and now when ze pink light comes zey all lay down zeir arms and cease fighting?"

"I don't know if there's a connection, but sure, it might be that way." Remo looked at the girl under the beret more closely. "Anyone ever tell you you have a nice accent?"

"Yes," Chiun chimed in, "you have a very nice accent for a Frankish wench."

The girl glowered at them.

"What's your name?" asked Remo.

"Avril Mai."

"Nice name."

"Yes, you have a very nice name for a lying Frank," said Chiun.

Remo and the girl looked at the Master of Sinanju.

"She has just told you her name is April May," Remo told Chiun.

"Must be a Taurus. Are you a Taurus?"

"I am a Cartesian."

"It is an impossible name for a Frank," said Chiun without rancor. His hazel eyes swept back to the warm pink shine coming up out of the Crater.

The girl began backing away. "I must be going," she said quickly. "I 'ave a story I must phone in."

"Good luck," said Remo.

"Au revoir," said Chiun, waving her away with a graceful flutter of fingernails.

As she walked away, she began hissing words into satellite phones intently.

"What's she saying?" asked Remo.

"'*La charade se perpètre avec lumières de très brillantes couleurs. Les lumières de très brillantes couleurs sont la clef,*'" Chiun repeated.

"In English, I mean."

"'The charade is being perpetrated with very bright colored lights. The bright colored lights are the key.'"

"What charade?"

"I do not know," said the Master of Sinanju, who had caught the eye of Mongo Mouse and exchanged friendly waves with the upright rodent. "And I care even less."

12

Dr. Harold W. Smith was tracking the progress of the Second American Civil War on his office computer when he got the call.

On an amber map of the continental United States he was carefully plotting the position and movement of the converging forces.

The rogue Rhode Island National Guard unit was still camped out on the District of Columbia side of the Potomac, just above Arlington, under the watchful eye of D.C. Capitol Police while elsewhere other units were on the move.

It was an astonishing sight. On the screen, which was buried under the black tempered glass of his desktop where only Smith could see it, it looked as if mighty armies were on the march to Petersburg, Virginia.

Smith had assigned tags to each unit. The Confederate regiments were represented by amber numbers while the Union troops were assigned letters. These were keyed to a list of regimental names that kept scrolling by on the left-hand side of the screen like marching soldiers.

That they went by designations like the 13th North Carolina Unreconstructed Signal Corps, 5th Tennessee Butternut Guerrillas or the 501st Motorized Michigan Touring Teamsters did not detract from the deadly earnestness of the situation.

Bands of men with guns were converging on Virginia, armed and intent upon fighting the Civil War all over again. Passions had been inflamed. In many states, both North and South, law-enforcement agencies, unable to put aside their sympathies, refused to intercept or put down these rogue units of weekend warriors.

And from Petersburg National Battlefield was coming the first sketchy reports of a pitched battle under way.

It was high noon. Memorial Day, 1995. Perhaps the last Memorial Day in U.S. history if the tides of battle were not quickly reversed.

When the blue contact telephone began ringing, Harold Smith was so intent he didn't register the sound at first. It took three rings before his aged hand reached out and brought the receiver to his pinched gray face.

Harold Smith was a New England Yankee, but his colors were Confederate gray. He wore a gray three-piece suit enlivened only by his Darmouth college tie, which was hunter green. His eyes were gray behind rimless glasses. His sparse hair was a grayish dusting on his head. Even his dry skin had a grayish cast, the manifestation of a congenital heart defect.

When he spoke, his voice was as flinty as the granite hills that had birthed him.

"Yes?"

"Hey, Smitty," said Remo in a bright voice.

"Remo, I have reports of a battle going on at Petersburg National Battlefield."

"Guess that's why they call it a battlefield, right?"

"Remo, this is serious!"

"No," corrected Remo, "this is over."

"Over?"

"Over. As in the boys can start going home now."

"But I have reports of other reenactment units moving on Virginia."

"Well, when they get here they can move right out again. The Blue and the Gray have patched things up."

"What happened?"

"Mongo Mouse dropped by, and everybody came to their senses."

"Remo, you are babbling."

A squeaky voice piped up. "No, Emperor, everything Remo says is true. Mongo came, along with Dingbat and others of his gallant company."

"They dropped down in balloons," Remo added.

"Balloons, Remo?"

"Big pink ones. Lit up like bottles of calamine lotion with light bulbs inside."

"Remo, you are not yourself."

"Hey, I just had a pleasant afternoon. Don't spoil it with your ulcerous crabbing."

"Ulcerous crabbing? For the first time in over a century we have civil war!"

"I told you," Remo said patiently. "It's over. It was a great big misunderstanding. When the balloons showed up, everyone simmered right down. Mickey Weisinger made a big reconciliation speech and won 'em all over. They've laid down their muskets, and there won't be any more trouble. Chiun and I hardly had to do anything. Isn't that great?"

There was a pause on the line.

"Remo," Smith said in a cautious voice, "I have some bad news for you."

"Shoot."

"I have hit another stone wall in the search for your parents."

"Aw. Too bad. But I know you'll keep trying, Smitty."

"That is just it," pressed Smith. "I have reached an absolute dead end. There is no other avenue to search."

"Gee, that's disappointing," said Remo.

"I am calling off the search. Do not ever raise this subject again."

Remo's voice diminished as he turned from the telephone and said, "Chiun, he's calling off the search for my parents."

"At least he tried," said Chiun without concern.

Remo's voice came back to the telephone receiver. "I know you tried, Smitty. Appreciate it. Really."

"Remo, you are not talking or acting like yourself."

"Who else would I talk and act like? Daniel Boone?"

"You are too calm, too relaxed, too accepting."

"I told you I feel pretty mellow."

"Remo, what happened out there today?"

"Told you. The war's over. Hallelujah."

"Remo, did anything unusual happen out in the park?"

"Well, lemme see," Remo said slowly. "I can't think of anything except the yellow bomb."

"What yellow bomb?"

"You hung up before I could mention it last time. A black helicopter buzzed the Crater, dropped this thing that looked like a traffic light except all the lights were yellow and when it hit, everything turned *really* yellow."

"What do you mean—everything turned really yellow?"

"We were running away because we thought it was a bomb."

"It was," inserted Chiun calmly.

"It didn't explode. But there was flash, I guess. The sky turned yellow. So did the grass and trees and everything. Then the Union prisoners started pouring out of the pit, and were they scared. Every one of them babbling about the yellow light."

"Then what happened?"

"Chiun and I went to investigate and when we got to the Crater, the bomb or whatever it was started screaming and melting into a puddle of slag."

"In other words, it self-destructed?"

"Now that you put it that way, yeah. Sure."

Chiun's thin voice added, "You forgot about the man in the pit, Remo. Tell Emperor Smith about him."

"Oh, right," said Remo. "Before the bomb melted. We found a Union guy in the pit. He wasn't like the others, who were scared. He was kinda down."

"Down? Do you mean depressed?"

"Yeah, and he claimed after the yellow light exploded in his face, everything turned blue. That part doesn't make much sense, I know."

"Actually it does," said Smith.

"It does?"

"Yes, it was a phenomenon of color where if one stares at a certain color for a long time, then looks away, he will see the complementary color as an afterimage in his retina."

"Blue complements yellow?"

"I believe it does," said Smith, saving his U.S. map file and bringing up another file.

"Then I guess red insults green, huh?" Remo chuckled.

"Describe this yellow light," Smith said without humor.

"It was very very bright. But we didn't look directly into it."

"But you say it frightened those who did?"

"Scared the living beans out of them," said Remo.

"Now, this pink light. Describe it."

"Pink. Nice. Pleasant."

"Bright pink?"

"Happy pink," said Remo.

"Very happy pink," said Chiun.

"The happiest," added Remo in a happy voice.

"But it was intense?" Smith prompted.

"I wouldn't call it hot pink, although it sure wasn't cool."

"Where did the pink light come from?"

"The mouse's ears. Didn't I mention that?"

"What mouse's ears?"

"You know how a hot-air balloon supports a wicker basket?"

"Yes."

"The ears were fixed to the baskets. Fours sides, four ears. When the balloons showed up, they started to glow."

"The basket or the ears?" asked Smith.

"The ears. Then everything turned pink."

"And nice," added Chiun.

"I see," said Smith. After a pause he asked, "Was there anything else unusual?"

"Except for the mini-Civil War?"

"Yes, except for that."

"I don't think so."

"Tell Smith about the French woman," prompted Chiun.

"Oh, yeah. There was the French woman."

"Yes, you mentioned her before."

"After the press trucks charged in, she showed up again, trying to figure out what was going on."

"Did she?"

"She was talking into a cellular phone or something. What was it she told the party on the other end, Little Father?"

"*'La charade se perpètre—'*"

"No, I mean in English."

"'This charade is perpetrated by bright colored lights. Bright colored lights are the key.'"

"You hear that, Smith? She said bright colored lights are the key."

"Did you detain or question her?"

"No. Why?"

"Because she obviously knew something about the phenomenon at work on the battlefield!" Smith said testily.

There was a pause on the line.

"Smitty," Remo said in an abashed voice. "No need to shout, you know."

"Sorry," said Smith, making a fist of frustration with his free hand. "Go on."

"That was it. She took off."

"And Mickey Weisinger?"

"Carried off on the shoulders of a unified and grateful nation," Remo said happily. "Don't you love a happy ending?"

"This has just begun," Smith said bitterly.

"What do you mean?"

"Whatever phenomenon affected those men on the battlefield obviously also affected Chiun and yourself."

"Nothing affected us," Remo retorted. "In fact, we feel great."

"You were supposed to stop the fighting."

"Someone beat us to it."

"And seize a Beasley executive and interrogate him about the whereabouts of Uncle Sam Beasley."

The distant sound of snapping fingers came over the wire. "Oh, right," said Remo. "Damn. We forgot."

"We will not forget again, Emperor," Chiun called out.

"Scout's honor," said Remo, a trace of worry in his voice.

"Can you find that woman again?" Smith asked.

"Maybe."

"Learn what she knows. Clearly she is not a newswoman."

"What makes you say that?"

"A hunch."

"You don't have hunches. They require imagination."

"I do this time," Harold Smith said grimly. "Report when you have something."

Harold Smith hung up and turned his attention to his desk terminal. His fingers floated across the keyless keyboard, the letters flashing silently with each stroke of his age-gnarled fingers.

The first reports of cessation of hostilities at Petersburg National Battlefield were coming across the wire. Smith tapped out the command that converted his terminal to color-TV reception.

A network news anchor was looking abashed.

"We still have no confirmation of what has taken place this Memorial Day in Petersburg, Virginia," he said as a graphic titled Civil War II? floated beside his head. He tapped his earphone. "What's that? We have national correspondent David O'Dull on the line. Go ahead, Dave."

"Peter," a chirpy voice said, "we are having just a swell time here in historic Virginia on this glorious holiday afternoon."

"That's wonderful, but tell us about these reports of a major battle."

"All done," Dave chirped.

"What exactly do you mean by 'all done'?"

"It's a wrap. The Beasley people dropped by, made nice and everything's hunky-dory again."

"Dave, you'll excuse me, but we're not getting many facts from you. Are you all right?"

"Wait a sec. They're breaking out the camp coffee and flap-doodle, and newspeople are invited. Hey, call you back. *Ciao.*"

"Dave? Dave!"

Watching the network anchor grind his teeth in frustration before millions of Americans, Harold W. Smith muttered to himself, "The force has affected the electronic press, as well. But what is it?"

Harold Smith had not long to puzzle over the matter because a red light flashed in one corner of his screen, indicating that the Folcroft basement mainframes, which continually trolled the net in search of mission-related data or news events, had captured something of importance.

Smith tapped a hot-key.

And on-screen appeared a capsulized digest of a story just moving on the wire.

BULLETIN
REUTERS
PARIS, FRANCE. FRENCH AIR ARMY WARPLANES OPERATING OUT OF TAVERNY AIR BASE FLEW SORTIES AGAINST EURO BEASLEY THEME PARK. PARK SUSTAINED SEVERE DAMAGE. ALL PLANES AND PILOTS RETURNED SAFELY TO BASE.

"Oh, my God," croaked Harold W. Smith from his Spartan office overlooking Long Island Sound. "What does it all mean?"

It meant that the Second American Civil War was over, and the Franco-American Conflict of 1995 had just begun.

13

History duly recorded the Second American Civil War and the Franco-American Conflict of 1995 as two entirely separate and unrelated conflicts.

History was wrong. The Second American Civil War ended at exactly 12:22 Eastern Daylight Time, while the opening engagement of the Franco-American Conflict was logged at precisely 5:47 Greenwich Mean Time, less than thirty minutes later.

Because they were to be forever believed separate and unrelated conflicts, historians never suspected that a satellite phone call placed from Petersburg National Battlefield in Virginia triggered the bombing of Euro Beasley.

The call was placed by a secret agent code-named Arlequin to her case officer at the Paris HQ of the Direction Générale de la Sécurité Extérieure, on Boulevard Mortier.

The station chief brought the cryptic report to the head of the DGSE, France's primary espionage service.

"'Bright colored lights are the key,'" repeated Remy Renard, director of the DGSE.

"That is what the agent said."

"You have no other report?"

"None."

"Thank you, you are excused," said Renard.

After the case officer left, Renard steepled his long fingers and frowned deeply. Here was a conundrum. A possibly important fragment of intelligence had come across his desk, and he had two immediate choices: file and forget it or communicate this data to a higher authority.

After a moment's thought his duty appeared with a crystaline clarity. He would not file it. But even that simple choice led inevitably to another conundrum: to which higher authority did he report?

It was the director of the DGSE's duty to report directly to the president of France on matters of national security.

The question stood before him like an uninvited visitor. Was this mere national security or did it impact upon a greater concern? Namely the honor of France herself?

It was difficult, this conundrum, and so DGSE Director Remy Renard leaned back in his seat, closed his deceptively sleepy-looking eyes and meditated at length.

During that quiet meditation the minutes ticked by, and with it dissolved the immediate historical linkage between the new American Civil War and the Franco-American Conflict of 1995.

Finally he reached for his telephone.

WHEN HIS TELEPHONE RANG, French Minister of Culture Maurice Tourette answered it personally. He always answered his telephone personally. It was the culture minister's wish to receive all communications from his beloved citizens directly and free from interpretation. For the minister of culture fervently believed that the citizens of France were *his* citizens.

In other nations the title "minister of culture" was a bland euphemism for espionage chief or a mere honorific. Not in France. And least not after Maurice Tourette acquired the singular honor.

He saw his mission in life to purify France, much as Joan of Arc had in an earlier time with her unflinching sacrifice.

To Maurice Tourette the worst calamity in the proud history of his country was the liberation from Germany. Not for a moment did Maurice consider the German occupation a good thing. No. It had been a travesty. But the Germans in time would have withered and gone home to their heavy beers and their unpalatable bratwursts, and knockwursts and sauerbraten. It would have been possible to wait them out. And when they finally left, they would have been gone for good.

The liberators, on the other hand, had left their many stains on the proud soil they had supposedly liberated.

Maurice Tourette had grown up in post-liberation Paris and watched, helpless and impotent, over the decades as the foul and corruptive gangrene of Americanism crept across his beloved city of lights.

First it was the Ford cars, then the McDonald's hamburger kiosks with their hideous golden arches. American movies with their shallow emptiness of spirit began crowding Clavie and Depardieu and the treasure of France, Deneuve, from the cinemas. While Parisians laughed at the brilliant crudities of Jerry Lewis—as they should—they had let down their defenses and had embraced such ugly coinages as *le marketing, le cash flow* and that impossible neologism, *le cheeseburger.*

By the time the threat had made itself manifest, and Pompidou had created the High Committee for the Defense and Expansion of the French Language, the language had been swamped and the tide was all but irreversible.

And so it seemed when Maurice Tourette had taken over the culture ministry.

In his first public speech as culture minister, he vowed to rid France of junk—junk food and junk words. He went after the fast-food emporiums first, and succeeded in getting most of them closed down.

It was hailed as a magnificent triumph of French culture over Anglo-Saxon barbarism.

For Maurice Tourette saw the spread of American popular culture as nothing less than a dangerous hegemony that, unlike Nazism, would envelop the world and France in a cultural dark age from which it might never emerge.

After that first triumph, Maurice went after the advertising billboards that littered the Champs-Elysées with crude slogans such as Always Coca-Cola and Just Do It and the worst offender, *Ford Vous Offre L'Airbag.*

He coined a name for the horrid words that mangled French articles with Anglo-Saxon nouns. This, he told the press, was the abominination of abominations, Franglais. He drew up a list and called for such words to be outlawed.

A bill was put before parliament. It passed after much rancorous debate. Henceforth, foreign words were forbidden on television, radio, billboards, public signs and announcements. No work contract or advertisement could be written in anything but pure French, or the offender faced severe fines and six months in jail.

Oh, the multinational companies fought back, but their cause was already lost. Maurice Tourette himself composed a long list of acceptable alternatives to the hated Franglais. No more *l'airbag* or *le video clip* or the unpronounceable *data processing*. Instead, the linguistically acceptable *sac gonfable, bande promo,* and *informantique* were the law of the land.

Maurice Tourette felt justifiably proud of what Parisians called La Loi Tourette. He had begun the long battle to reclaim his nation from the hated liberators. It was only a matter of time before all who wished to enjoy the benefits of living in La Belle France learned to speak the lingua franca—or be summarily deported.

When his desk telephone in the culture ministry rang, Maurice Tourette picked it up and said, *"Allô?"*

"I have most distressing news."

"I am steeled."

"The Blot. We may have an understanding of it."

"Tell me of this understanding," the culture minister invited.

"We have an agent in Ameri—"

The culture minister pinched the bridge of his nose painfully. "Do not enunciate that horrid name, please."

"The Uncouth Nation, I should say."

"Very good. Proceed."

"The agent code-named Arlequin."

"Ah, yes. An excellent lover. You have had her, I presume?"

"I daresay I have not."

"Pity. Go on."

"She reported the following—'The charade is perpetrated with bright colored lights.'"

"Bright colored lights?"

"'Bright colored lights are the key,' was her last transmission. Then all communications ceased."

"Was she compromised?"

"In what way?"

"Why, in any way."

"I do not know."

"Advise me if you learn her fate, will you? I should hate to think that her charms should be denied us in the future."

"Of course. Now, as to this other matter."

"Ah, yes. 'Bright colored lights are the key.' What can that mean?"

"You are, of course, aware of our difficulty penetrating the Blot?"

"Pah! It is just a matter of time."

"Agents go in. They come out. They report nothing. Nothing."

"Brainwashing?"

"I do not think so. They show no evidences of such cunning tamperings, but it is as if once they come under the sway of those cultural interlopers, their powers of resistance and duty are abolished. They speak highly of the experience."

"Just as my poor people are drawn into their colorful web."

"Yes. It is very chilling."

"Have you told anyone else of this?"

"No."

"Not even the president?"

"Should I?"

"I think not. He has shown great reluctance to act on this matter, despite the increasing and undeniable gravity of the threat."

"What can we do?"

"You, you may go back to your duties, all the while keeping me closely informed, while I shall make some discreet calls."

"To whom?"

"To those who share with me a higher sense of duty to La Belle France," said French Culture Minister Maurice Tourette, quietly replacing the receiver.

He next dialed the general of the French Air Army, doing so personally. There must be no record of this call.

"Mon Général," he said after getting through to the private, unlisted number.

"Oui, Monsieur Ministère?"

"The secret of the stain on the honor and dignity of your mother nation is becoming clearer and clearer with each passing hour."

"Oui?"

"I cannot now divulge this, but a brave military man, one who can envision himself as the next de Gaulle, could advance his career most wonderfully were he only to made a bold stab."

"How bold?"

"One so bold it might ripple across a certain ocean and lap at the clay feet of a certain ally of doubtful standing."

"I see...."

"The Blot must be pacified and its secrets wrested from within."

"And after that?"

"After that," said the French minister of culture carefully, "who can say? Poof! It might be bombed flat, salt sown into the very soil it once despoiled so that no trace of it passes into the next century."

"I cannot say what I may or may not do, *Monsieur Ministère.*"

"Nor would I expect you to."

"But if action is to be taken, it will be taken imminently."

The culture minister smiled broadly. "I knew you loved France above all things."

The minister of culture hung up the telephone and turned on the radio. He would pass the tense time to come listening to beautiful music and, if an important bulletin should break, he would be among the first to hear of it.

To his regret all the stations were playing either rock, heavy metal or that abominable cacophony known as rap. The minister of culture endured the unendurable for the sake of his higher duty, reflecting that if he had only known that rap lay around the cultural corner, he would never have moved so ruthlessly to suppress disco.

AT 5:57 PARIS TIME a squadron of six French Mirage 2000Ds rocketed out of Taverny Air Base and dropped BGL laser-guided bombs onto the tiny village called Euro Beasley in the Averoigne suburb of the city.

The bombs, contrary to first reports, packed not high explosives, but a combination of dense black smoke and pepper gas.

As the first stinging clouds broke and wafted across the blue-and-cream towers of the Sorcerer's Chateau,

Euro Beasley patrons, greeters and employees alike broke for the exits.

True, some were trampled to death in the ensuing confusion, so it was not an altogether bloodless engagement. But in less than an hour Fortress Euro Beasley lay naked before any who wished to enter it.

The trouble was finding someone with sufficient personal courage and the political will to do so.

THE PRESIDENT OF FRANCE was considering the problem in America when an aide entered his office unannounced. He did not look up. This was a difficult matter. America had hiccuped. According to the quarter-hourly reports coming across his desk, it was either a highly localized insurrection or the United States of America was poised on the brink of civil war.

If it was a hiccup, it didn't matter. Americans hiccuped several times a year. They were that way. Undoubtedly it was a consequence of their lackluster diet.

But if it was civil war, the president of France would be obliged to choose sides. Perhaps not immediately, and certainly not until a clear victor emerged, or if not a victor, he would wait until an undeniable political opportunity became visible, making either choice advantageous.

In the previous American Civil War—which seemed very recent in France's long history but was only halfway through the lifespan of the United States to date—France had sided with the Confederacy. It was not a good choice, but France had not suffered for it. America was a political nonentity in those lamented days. Unlike today.

Thus, it was politic not to choose a side until at least the second or possibly as late as the third year of the Civil War.

The immediate problem was how to remain neutral during that brief interval. After all, Washington would expect immediate support. The utter infants. But what did one expect from a nation that had occupied a distant corner of the planet for less than five hundred years? They had such growing up to do.

Frowning, the president of France picked up a solid gold Mont Blanc pen and began composing a neutral statement to be issued later in the day. It was very bland. One could read it any way one chose. This was very important, for French attitudes toward the United States were at a crossroads.

On the one hand there was the usual anti-American condescension and distaste always fashionable among the literate elite.

On the other hand the younger generation and even some of the old, their memories of France's liberation from Nazi occupation reawakened by the fiftieth-anniversary celebration of the Normandy invasion a year previous, had developed a renewed, if politically challenging, appreciation of certain things American.

The president of France was scribbling a sentence suggesting a youthful and untested country like the United States of America was bound to experience growing pains when the patient aide standing before his desk cleared his throat.

The president looked up. "Yes? What is it?"

"It appears the insurrection in America has been quelled."

The president of France quirked a salt-and-pepper eyebrow to the vaulted ceiling. "How severe were the casualties?" he asked, crumpling his three-sentence draft speech into a ball and tossing it into a waiting wastepaper basket.

"Light."

"Did the Army put it down?"

"Non, Monsieur Président."

"Local police units, then? I understood they were neutral."

"Non, Monsieur Président."

"Then who? Quickly, speak!"

"The Sam Beasley Company."

The president of France blinked in a kind of stunned stupefaction. "The Sam Beasley Company?"

"They descended from the sky in balloons, and the fighting ceased."

"Were they not the instigators?"

"That is the suspicion of the DGSE."

"How curious," said the president of France. "Then it is over?"

"It is most definitely over."

The president of France sighed. "Perhaps it is just as well. The long-term positive aspects might not outweigh the short-term political embarrassment of remaining neutral while they fought it out among themselves. And we may need their industrial might should the Germans become territorial again."

"Do you wish to make an official statement?"

"I wish to take a nap."

"Oui, Monsieur Président," said the aide, withdrawing discreetly.

The president of France did not take a nap, however. He had barely thirty minutes to digest the lost opportunity of an American Civil War when the same aide who had so quietly entered now reentered with his face like a cooked beet and his eyes resembling cool Concord grapes.

"*Monsieur Président! Monsieur Président!*"

"Calm down! What is it?"

"Euro Beasley. It has been bombed!"

"Bombed? Bombed by whom?"

"Early reports have it air-army Mirages bombed it."

The president of France came out of his leather chair as if hoisted by unseen guy wires.

"On what authority?"

"This is not known."

"Get me the general of the air army! At once!"

But no one could reach the general.

"What is happening?" the president demanded of anybody who proved reachable by telephone. "How severe are the casualties? Are any of our people dead or injured?"

"All pilots returned safely," he was told.

"No! I mean our French citizens on the ground."

But no one had that answer. The event was barely ten minutes old.

Then came the call from Minister of Culture Maurice Tourette.

"*Monsieur Président,* a wonderful opportunity has fallen in our hands."

"Are you mad! We have bombed an American theme park."

"We have bombed French soil. It is our sacred right to bomb French soil."

"We have bombed a symbol of American culture residing on French soil," the president shouted.

"Is this such a bad thing?"

The president swallowed hard and sat down. He lowered his voice, straining to retain his self-control. "I do not wish to get into this argument with you at this moment. This is a very awkward thing. The Americans are supposed to be our friends."

"We own the overwhelming majority of Euro Beasley. The Americans have reneged on many of our understandings. The park has lost over a billion in U.S. dollars over its first three years."

"That has turned around," the French President pointed out.

"Yes, at our expense. We French have been pouring into it at an alarming rate."

"Yes, I saw your confidential figures," said the president of France, who did not think it unusual that the minister of culture tracked French attendance at Euro Beasley. It was not for nothing that the place had been denounced as a cultural Chernobyl when it was first opened. "I understood this was the result of Parisians wishing to experience the cultural abomination once before it closes. Possibly to gloat over the triumph of French cultural resistance to its gaudy blandishments."

"Propaganda. We have reason to believe there is a sinister explanation for Parisian citizenry suddenly flocking to this Blot."

"Blot?"

"It is a blot and a stain upon the bosom of La Belle France."

"I do not disagree with that. Unofficially, of course," said the president of France. "But we can't go around bombing American symbols. This is not the nineteenth century anymore. Perhaps in another generation or two we can spit into their eyes with impunity should we wish to, but not now."

"I have developed intelligence suggesting that Euro Beasley has been exerting a diabolic hypnotic influence upon our citizenry, luring them in and shucking them of their francs and their inborn appreciation of French culture."

"This is a most grave charge."

"Highly serious."

"With international implications. Are you suggesting that Euro Beasley is some sort of espionage platform?"

"Worse."

"Military?"

"Worse still. It is a cultural neutron bomb, dispensing hard, corrupting radiation throughout France."

"Go on."

"I have only limited information, but as we speak, Euro Beasley lies naked, unguarded and undefended. We can take it with minimal difficulties and light-to-negligible casualties."

"Take it? What on earth would we want with it?"

"You must act quickly, *Monsieur Président*. For as you know, this is a difficult predicament, politically speaking. We have bombed an American theme park. Explaining this would be difficult under ordinary conditions."

"Impossible, you mean," the president said bitterly.

"Justifying it is your only option. You must send troops in to secure it and discover its secret."

"What is its secret?"

"Bright colored lights."

"What do you mean by 'bright colored lights'?"

"I am sorry. That is all I have."

"That is not enough to act upon."

"Can you afford to wait for the reaction from Washington? You must act immediately if you are to spare yourself the embarrassment of the hour."

The president of France chewed his moist lower lip until bright specks of blood discolored his incisors. "I must think on this problem."

"Time flees," the culture minister reminded, terminating the connection.

And in his office in the Palais de L'Élysée, the president of France watched the clock tick and click its hands along the dial while he considered which of the few and unimpressive cards he would play this day.

14

When DGSE Intelligence operative Dominique Parillaud had been told that her latest assignment was to go to the United States of America, her first impulse was to faint dead.

Upon being revived, she briefly considered suicide.

"Do not send me to that cultural hellhole," she pleaded with her case officer.

"It is for the good of France," he told her in a stern voice.

"I would do anything for France," Dominique said anxiously. "I would give my very life for France. I would spill my blood for her. I would drink the very blood that I spill just to be privileged to spill even more blood for France. You must know this."

"You are one of our most capable operatives," her case officer assured her in the HQ building called the swimming pool because it had been built over an old municipal pool. "Your bravery is well documented."

"Then do not destroy my career by sending me to America."

"How would that destroy your career? This is a career-advancing assignment."

Dominique took her tawny hair in her long, tapered fingers as if to wrench it out by the roots. Her green eyes rolled around in their sockets as if she were having an epileptic seizure.

"I would lose my mind in America. I would go insane. I beg of you. Send another."

"We have no others."

Dominique Parillaud, code-named Agent Arlequin in the confidential casebooks of the DGSE, got off her trim knees and reclaimed her seat. Her manner became professional in the extreme.

"What do you mean?" she inquired.

"You are aware of the denied area called the Blot?"

"I am aware of the Blot. Who cannot be aware of the Blot? It is a...blot. But I have never heard it called a denied area. For does Euro Beasley not charge admission?"

"We have officially designated it as a denied area. Agents have gone in..." The case officer's voice trailed off, and he made a hopeless gesture with his hands.

"They do not come out?"

"They come out," he admitted. "They come out...changed."

"How changed?"

"Happy."

"Happy. Is this bad?"

The case officer waved his cigarette around his head describing distorted helices of tobacco smoke.

"Happy and unmotivated. They were tasked with penetrating the subterranean chambers called Utilicanard in an attempt to explain the sudden and perverse increase in interest in the Blot."

"I have not heard of this Utilicanard."

"The cover story is that it is where they process their trash and refuse."

Dominique Parillaud barked her next words. "Then they should sink the entire park and process *that!*"

"Agents Papillon, Grillon and Sauterelle, all were sent into the Blot and all returned clutching over-priced Beasley souvenirs and unable to perform their duty to France."

"Because they were made happy?"

"Agent Grillon was made so happy that ever since he has taken great exception to insults leveled at Euro Beasley. But Agent Sauterelle came out quite frightened. He was afraid to go back in. On the other hand Agent Papillon could not stop throwing up for three days."

"What did the poor man see?"

"He could not articulate it beyond the pageantry and bright lights of the Blot. He mentioned a particularly vivid green, as I recall."

Dominique Parillaud shot to her feet. "I hereby volunteer to penetrate the Blot."

The case officer raised his hand.

"No, I must insist. This is obviously a great mystery and must be dealt with." She straightened her spine, chin lifting in defiance. "I will go today. Immediately. I am not afraid. My fierce devotion to my country and my culture make me unafraid."

"You are going to America," insisted her case officer.

Whereupon Dominique Parillaud sank back into her chair and began weeping into a fresh linen handkerchief whose frilly edges were impregnated with cyanide in the event of her capture by hostile forces.

"Your mission will be to monitor all unusual events pertaining to the Sam Beasley Corporation," her case officer explained. "If you can gain employment with them, so much the better."

Dominique Parillaud threw her shoulders forward and plunged her face into the cupped handkerchief.

"You will report daily, and—"

With a cry of anger the case officer lunged across his desk. He threw himself across his best female agent, and the two ended up on the floor, rolling and clawing for possession of the cyanide-laced handkerchief that Dominique Parillaud was desperately holding on to with her strong, stubborn Gallic teeth.

WHEN THE AIR FRANCE flight landed at Furioso International Airport, Dominique Parillaud at first considered hiding in the lavatory and taking the same plane back.

But her duty to her country brought her out of the comfortable seat and out into the humid air of Florida.

It was awful from the first minute, from the very second she deplaned.

The air was hot and sticky. It clung to her perfectly milky skin, dampened her Parisian coiffure into a soggy mass like cornflakes and made her haute clothing chafe and itch like sackcloth.

The people were boorish, their accents rude and bewildering. They actually pronounced their terminal consonants. And as for their attire, the only word to describe their gaudy prêt-à-porter rags was *abominable*.

At the grocery store there was no decent bread to be had. The cheeses were flavorless, and the wine would not pass for swill.

And the food. Lamentable in the extreme. They used no sauces except for *sauce piquante,* which they spelled sometimes *catsup* and sometimes *ketchup.* There was no delicacy in their cooking, no art in their dress. Everything was heavy and oafish, from the food to the men, which Dominique Parillaud also sampled out of sheer need to find some meager comfort in this hot, brutish land.

She found work in Sam Beasley World as an interpreter, but discovered nothing of importance. Except that they treated her—and all other employees—so horribly that she was forced to quit.

It was no better in Vanaheim, California, although the strength-sapping mugginess was replaced by a delicious dry heat that after two months seemed to exert a severely deleterious effect on her motivation, much as the Florida heat had sapped her strength.

At a good Vanaheim restaurant, where a valet parked her car for her, Dominique discovered an item on the menu called French fries. Her eyes lit up and she ordered them eagerly.

"What will you be having with it?" the waiter asked.

"Nothing. Just pile these French fries on a plate and give me your best house chardonnay."

When they came, Dominique saw these fries were neither French nor palatable. If anything, they were fit only for the bland British palate. She toyed with them idly as she consumed an entire bottle of barely passable chardonnay.

On another occasion she came upon French toast on a breakfast menu posted on a diner that she would ordinarily not otherwise enter, the smells coming from within it were so disagreeable.

But Dominique did enter, ordering two portions of French toast. "And your best breakfast Bordeaux," she added.

"No Bourdeaux, sorry."

"Very well. Beaujolais, then."

"We don't have an alcoholic-beverage license, ma'am," the waitress said.

That was another strange thing. It was impossible to obtain beer or wine in many restaurants. Even bad beer or wine, of which the oafs produced in abundance.

"Then give me a pot of coffee. Black."

When the French toast arrived, Dominique saw with brimming eyes and it was not in any respect French, although it vaguely resembled a species of toast.

She drank the entire pot of coffee, which tasted salty from the bitterness of her endless tears.

The cinemas were singularly insufferable. It was all junk, as were the television programs. The only bright spots came twice a year, during the Bastille Day Jerry Lewis movie marathon and again on the American Labor Day when Jerry conducted a telethon. When he sang "You'll Never Walk Alone," Dominique hastily taped it, and it became instantly and forever her favorite song.

She had never known that Jerry could sing.

By the time of the affair of Beasley U.S.A., Dominique Parillaud was a dispirited shell of her former self, who contemplated suicide with whatever was at hand. Her case officer had steadfastly refused to allow her any of the cyanide pills, hollow teeth or death-laced handkerchiefs of her trade.

Thus she carried a tiny aerosol can of Black Flag bug killer. If need be she could swallow the nozzle and

depress the trigger with the very strong and agile
tongue whose talents had enabled her to climb the
clerical ranks of the DSGE. Men appreciated her agile tongue. Or at least Frenchmen did. American men
made disgusting comments about her ability to
French-kiss, then would not—or could not—explain
why such kissing was ascribed to the French above all
others.

She had been in Virginia for three weeks, posing as
a TV reporter for the European TV network, Europe 1, when the Second American Civil War unex-
pectedly broke out. Dominique's had been one of the
first news trucks on the scene.

It was the perfect cover. Apparently all Americans
were obliged to obey the many rules and laws of the
land, but for some reason journalists were exempt.
Even foreign ones.

Upon swooping down, Dominique discovered it was
impossible to infiltrate the Petersburg National Battlefield, and had to content herself with eavesdrop-
ping on other news agencies, some of which had
helicopters to spy on the battle below.

It was an astonishing sight. Their country seemed
poised to rend itself apart, and instead of showing
concern for their future, all that mattered to them was
the all-important story.

Had they been French journalists covering a modern Reign of Terror, they would have been guillotined
without benefit of trial, their treason was so great and
so very apparent.

When the battle finally broke out, the Confederate
pickets withdrew and the press surged in. At first
Dominique thought they were going to take sides
themselves. They did not. Instead, they sought out the

roar of battle, and their bravery before the sharp whistling of the subsonic musket balls would have been admirable had it not been so obviously the product of an utterly congenital foolishness.

Nevertheless, Dominique picked her way through the park with its sticky pines and its idle Napoleon cannon and marveled when she came upon the battle how very much like uniforms of Napoleon III the soldiers' trappings were.

It confirmed to her that Americans gave the world nothing of high culture, but only took from it.

"I cannot tell one side from the other," she complained to an American journalist who was snapping pictures like a tourist at the Eiffel Tower. Wildly and without framing his shots.

"It's simple. The blue versus the gray."

"But they are all gray."

"What are you, color-blind?"

"Yes, I am color-blind."

The handicap turned out to be a blessing when the great balloons of the Beasley Company descended moments later.

Their effect was magical. Men lay down their arms and took up expressions of childlike wonder and awe when the cartoon faces showed themselves.

And everyone spoke of the impossible pink color of it all. Dominique saw only bright light tinged with dull gray. For all colors were shades of gray to her green eyes. In her heart she envied the Americans for their ability to become so childlike at what was after all a blatantly commercial spectacle.

But she had a mission to perform.

The balloons did not drop out of a clear sky, she knew. Someone had to guide them to their landing area. And Dominique Parillaud was determined to discover that someone.

For with the pressing crowd of soldiers in dark gray and light gray, and the outer ring of American TV reporters crowding close, it was impossible to reach the man she most wished to reach, Mickey Weisinger.

AS THEY WALKED BACK into the Petersburg National Battlefield, the Master of Sinanju was saying, "It was very understanding of you to accept Emperor Smith's explanations of his failure."

"I know he tried," Remo said unconcernedly. "Guess I have to give this back."

He pulled from his pocket a coffin-shaped white pill.

Chiun regarded it with quirking brows. "Smith's poison pill?"

"Yeah, remember I confiscated it last time out? Swore I wouldn't give it back until he dug up my past."

"You are very understanding today."

"That time Smitty had to erase his computer data bases when the IRS swooped down on Folcroft probably crippled his ability to do deep background searches like he used to."

"You are undoubtedly correct, my son."

"Thank you, Little Father."

As they walked they came to a place where a screen of trees obscured their view of the pink shine that lay over the battlefield like an angelic aura.

Remo's face abruptly darkened. "That damn Smith!" he said suddenly.

"Remo!"

"He had no intention of finding my folks. Never had."

"Remo, what has come over you?"

"When I see him again, I'm going to shake the lame excuses out of him, and then we'll see how motivated he is."

"You are very childish, you know that?" Chiun fumed. "One minute you are well behaved and then next you are throwing a temper tantrum like a spoiled child."

"You should talk."

"Me? I—"

They passed through the pines and came upon Crater Field again. The pink glow touched their face like an angel's kiss.

"I am sorry I raised my voice to you, Remo," Chiun said, suddenly mollified.

"And I am sorry I got out of line, Little Father. You know I think the world of you."

"And well you should," Chiun purred contentedly.

Remo spotted a figure in a slip dress and beret. "Hey, isn't that April May?"

"Yes, she is sneaking away."

"Smith said to find out what she knows. Why don't we follow her?"

They returned to the screen of pines, their feet not disturbing the brown carpet of needles any more than did the passing daddy longlegs spiders that patrolled the area.

As they blended into the intermittent shadows, becoming hunters again, their faces lost their placid cast and they became hard of eye. But they said nothing.

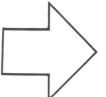

NO COST! NO OBLIGATION TO BUY! NO PURCHASE NECESSARY!

PLAY "LUCKY 7" AND GET FIVE FREE GIFTS!

HOW TO PLAY:

1. With a coin, carefully scratch off the silver area at the right. Then check the claim chart to see what we have for you — FREE BOOKS and a gift — ALL YOURS! ALL FREE!

2. Send back this card and you'll get hot-off-the-press Gold Eagle books, never before published. These books have a total cover price of $16.98. But THEY ARE TOTALLY FREE; even the shipping will be at our expense!

3. There's no catch. You're under no obligation to buy anything. We charge nothing — ZERO — for your first shipment. And you don't have to make any minimum number of purchases — not even one!

4. The fact is thousands of readers enjoy receiving books by mail from the Gold Eagle Reader Service. They like the convenience of home delivery . . . they like getting the best new novels before they're available in stores . . . and they love our discount prices!

5. We hope that after receiving your free books you'll want to remain a subscriber. But the choice is yours — to continue or cancel, anytime at all! So why not take us up on our invitation, with no risk of any kind. You'll be glad you did!

SURPRISE MYSTERY GIFT
IT CAN BE YOURS <u>FREE</u> WHEN
YOU PLAY "LUCKY 7".

GET YOUR FREE GIFTS NOW! MAIL THIS CARD TODAY!

THE GOLD EAGLE READER SERVICE: HERE'S HOW IT WORKS

Accepting free books places you under no obligation to buy anything. You may keep the books and gift and return the shipping statement marked "cancel". If you do not cancel, about a month later we will send you four additional novels, and bill you just $14.80*—that's a saving of 12% off the cover price of all four books! And there's no extra charge for shipping! You may cancel at any time, but if you choose to continue, every other month we'll send you four more books, which you may either purchase at the discount price…or return at our expense and cancel your subscription.

*Terms and prices subject to change without notice. Sales tax applicable in N.Y.

If offer card is missing, write to: Gold Eagle Reader Service, 3010 Walden Ave., P.O. Box 1867, Buffalo, NY 14269-1867

BUSINESS REPLY MAIL
FIRST CLASS MAIL   PERMIT NO. 717   BUFFALO, NY

POSTAGE WILL BE PAID BY ADDRESSEE

GOLD EAGLE READER SERVICE
3010 WALDEN AVE
PO BOX 1867
BUFFALO NY 14240-9952

NO POSTAGE
NECESSARY
IF MAILED
IN THE
UNITED STATES

MARC MOISE couldn't for the life of him figure it out.

As chief communications officer of Operation Crater, it was he who miked the battlefield so that all enemy operations could be monitored. He had planted the mikes personally. Video cameras were not an option. They were too big to hide in the treetops without running the risk of detection.

But when the balloons landed, they carried remote cameras, and Marc was busy monitoring the feeds from those.

That was the worst part. During the balloon launch, he had been preoccupied inside the mobile communications van parked down the highway. After the balloons had been launched, Bob Beasley had entered the van, saying "Carry on" in a gruff tone of voice entirely unlike his usual avuncular one.

But since he was practically Sam Beasley reincarnate, Marc Moise had carried on.

When the first video feeds came in, Marc duly taped them for later analysis and evaluation. They showed Mickey Weisinger giving the performance of his insincere life and winning the crowd over.

It was the lights. Marc didn't know how it was the lights. But he saw the way the crowd had turned—just as the crying faces of children changed for the better when Mongo or Dingbat or any of those other two-dimensional idiot grins flashed their way.

As it happened, the seated figure of Bob Beasley chuckled from the other console. "Give an American kid a choice between the keys to the kingdom of heaven and two free tickets to Beasleyland, and the little bastards will snatch up the tickets nine times out of ten."

The voice didn't sound quite like Bob Beasley's, Marc thought as he struggled to catch every word coming through his earphones.

Then his heart jumped so high in his throat he opened his mouth to let it out.

Bob Beasley emerged from the Crater and gave the cheering soldiers a hearty wave of approval!

"But—" Moise sputtered.

A chill ran down his hunched-over spine. Something was not right here. Bob Beasley couldn't be out at the field. Bob Beasley was seated at his back.

Marc got a grip on himself. This was some fluke, some nutty glitch. Maybe the figure he was seeing was some animatronic robot. Maybe the situation was too dangerous to risk the real Bob Beasley, valuable corporate spokesman that he was, in the field, and that was a double waving to the crowd. Sure. A double. The guy snapping switches behind him was the authentic Bob Beasley. That was it.

But the body language of the man on the field was definitely that of Bob Beasley. No actor was that good. Not when playing to an ignorant audience.

So, while pretending to do his job, Marc Moise turned slowly in his seat to better visualize the man in the console chair.

The face was turned almost away, but the flat cheek and a suggestion of a mustache were visible. It was frosty white. Bob Beasley's mustache was dark brown. It was said he dyed it to seem youthful.

He was talking low and vehemently into his mike, and the words he spoke were repeated by Mickey Weisinger, several miles away.

Then a cold gray eye rolled in Moise's direction, and a frosty voice said, "What the fuck are you looking at, Moose? Get back to work!"

Marc Moise shifted in his seat, trying to keep the contents of his bladder from escaping his body.

The man behind him was not Bob Beasley. That man in the field was. And the voice that had called him by the hated nickname, Moose, made the short hairs at the back of his neck bunch up and squirm.

He knew that voice. It was imprinted on his brain, a part of his earliest childhood experiences. It was the voice that had cheered him up on Sunday nights before a flickering TV screen and assured him that even though school started the next day, all was right with the world.

It was the long-dead yet immortal voice of Uncle Sam Beasley!

15

Bilious black smoke was still rising above the Norman ramparts of the Sorcerer's Chateau of Euro Beasley when the first five-seat Gazelle utility helicopters swarmed over the theme park. They did not land. They merely dropped like clatter-winged dragonflies and moved through the park's airspace, cockpits sealed, pilots heavily goggled and gas-masked as their beating rotors whipped up and dispelled the combination of black camouflage smoke and pepper gas that lay like a pall over the so-called Enchanted Village.

When the helicopters had beat the pungent exhalation into harmless dissipating rags, the SuperPumas came floating in.

They did not land, either. Instead, red-bereted French Foreign Legion paratroopers rappeled down in full combat gear.

When their black boots touched ground, they deployed through the deserted Main Street, U.S.A., encountering no resistance.

Before a grid of video monitors Chief Concepteer Rod Cheatwood groaned and said, "We're screwed. They're onto us."

And he reached for the button marked Supergreen.

A HUNDRED YEARS from 1995 learned historians would convene at Brown University in Providence, Rhode Island, to settle the question of the root cause of the Great Franco-American Conflict.

They would argue and hold rancorous panels for five solid days and still reach no consensus, although there would be a memorable fistfight in the apple orchard adjoining the John Hay Library where one professor would repeatedly crack the forehead of a colleague against the ancient monument dedicated to the illustrious H. P. Lovecraft until he had won his particular point.

One side said it had all started with a mouse. A reasonable argument, since the Sam Beasley Company lay at the heart of the conflict and *it* had started with Mongo Mouse.

Another school of thought held that twentieth-century French cultural chauvenism exacerbated a minor dispute until it erupted into a full-scale international imbroglio.

And a third said U.S. cultural imperialism naturally created the friction. America was as unpopular then as now, the visiting professor from Harvard pointed out.

None of them got it right. It did not start with Sam Beasley's famous mouse, any more than it did with U.S. cultural imperialism or French snobbery.

It started with Rod Cheatwood of Vanaheim, California.

More specifically it started the sunny spring day Rod Cheatwood misplaced his TV remote control for the forty-eighth time.

Rod was a concepteer at Beasleyland in Vanaheim, California. By that it was meant that he was a technician.

Although he worked out of Beasleyland, he was no maintainer of attractions. No designer of rides. Instead, Rod was strictly research and development.

Five years out of Cal Tech, Rod was a specialist in lasers. The downsizing of the defense industry put him on the street. He answered a blind ad and was surprised to see a happy cartoon mouse grinning back from the door when he showed up for the interview.

"Why do you need a laser technician for a theme park?" Rod asked the interviewer, a suit with a blank face. "You can order all the light-show lasers you could ever want."

"We want our own lasers."

"I'm strictly into lasers as a military application."

"You could do that here," the interviewer said, his glassy smile matching his glassy eyes. Did they all become so fatuous working here? Rod wondered.

"I could perfect military lasers working for Sam Beasley?"

"In a manner of speaking. We have a problem at our French base."

"Base?"

"Euro Beasley."

"Never thought of it as a base."

"The French hate us. Won't stand in line in the cold weather. Won't buy our souvenirs. They take day trips so our hotels are practically empty. We've lost billions."

"So close the park."

"You don't understand. We have a great track record in France. Our magazine, *Journal de Mongo,* has been a bestseller since 1934. The French love us. They just haven't warmed up to the park yet."

"Lower your prices."

"We've tried everything," the interviewer went on as if Rod's suggestion was out of the question. "Aroma therapy. Coupons. Nondiscount inducements. We even broke a long-standing rule and allowed beer and wine to be served in our park restaurants. Nothing seems to staunch the hemorrhaging."

"A laser light show won't do it, either."

"We'll give you a lab to work in, a full staff and anything you could want."

Rod stood up. "Sorry. If I'd known this was you Beasley boys, I'd never have come in for the interview. I hear you treat your employees like dirt."

"If you change your mind, give us a call, won't you?" the inteviewer said without taking offense or losing his fixed smile.

Rod Cheatwood did come around in time. There were no defense jobs in California, true. And he was loath to move out of state, also true.

But the real reason—entirely lost to posterity—that Rod came back to the Beasley Corporation was that he lost his TV remote and it was the forty-eighth time by actual count. It was also the last straw.

The UHF band of the TV dial could not be accessed without the remote clicker, and while Rod flung sofa cushions about with wild abandon and raged at the cruel and unjust gods who had turned their faces from his simple wants and desires, he missed the two-part final episode of "Star Trek: the Next Generation."

The next morning Rod was back in the Beasley employment office.

"I'd take the job on one condition," he said.

"We don't do conditions here at Beasley, but I'm willing to listen."

"In my spare time I use your facilities to work on a side research project of my own."

"What kind of project?"

"A TV-remote finder."

"We own all marketing rights outright," the interviewer said quickly.

"Two conditions," said Rod. "I get marketing rights."

After a three-day negotiation involving slamming telephones, harsh words and veiled death threats, Rod Cheatwood agreed to split marketing rights on anything he developed with the Sam Beasley Corporation fifty-fifty.

In his first day they explained color therapy to him.

"Color therapy?"

"It's old. It's very old. The Pythagoreans used it to heal the sick. So did the Greeks and Egyptians. They found that exposing the eyes to different colors produces different psychological effects on the brain. We discovered it works. We just need to make it work on a grander scale."

"With lasers?"

"The brighter the color, the better it works. Lasers are as bright as color gets outside of nature."

"I follow," said Rod Cheatwood, fingering his tufted chin.

"We want you to develop the brightest, most colorful laser light possible."

"We're talking a cold laser here?"

"Yeah. We don't want to burn holes in tourists by accident. It might kill repeat business."

"An eximer laser system is what you need. But I can't guarantee it will do what you want."

"We can prove it to you."

"Go ahead."

"You're still unhappy over our contract negotiation?"

"You people," Rod said bitterly, "probably don't bury your dearly departed dead until you yank the gold fillings from their teeth, sell their bones to make gelatin and remove the fat for tallow."

Surprisingly they took no offense. One even smiled with a quiet inner satisfaction.

"How's your blood pressure these days?"

"My blood pressure has been elevated ten points since I started here," Rod added testily. "And it's only been a day."

"Come with us."

They took him to a sealed chamber in Utiliduck beneath Beasleyland. The door was labeled Pink Room.

The door was not pink, but when it was opened, the room was certainly pink. The walls were a mellow pink. Overhead lights shed a warm pink radiance. Even the recliner chair was pink. And when they closed the door after him, Rod saw the other side of the door was also pink. He was entirely enveloped in a womb of pink.

"Sit down," he was told by intercom.

Rod sat. He reclined in his chair and at first he didn't feel anything. After a few moments he relaxed. Then he really relaxed. His muscles softened. Even his bones seemed to soften.

When they came to take him out fifteen minutes later, he didn't want to go.

"Please let me stay a few minutes," Rod begged.

"Fifteen minutes more. But you have to sign a release."

"Anything," Rod said, signing without reading a sheet of paper thrust under his nose.

After the fifteen minutes were up, he still refused to go. A Beasley doctor was summoned, a blood-pressure cuff was clamped over his exposed bicep and, when the doctor announced that his blood pressure was perfect, Rod was surprised.

"Can I work in there?" he asked.

"No. You won't get anything accomplished."

"I don't mind."

Eventually they had to shut off the lights and leave him alone in the dark room until he begged to be let out of the Pink Room.

"Our research tells us color therapy works through the second visual pathway."

"There's more than one?" Rod muttered, staring at a pink spot on the other man's tie. It brought back calming memories of the Pink Room.

"The first visual pathway goes from the retina to the optic nerve. That's how we see. But there's a second pathway, a more primitive one, that goes from the retina to the hypothalamus, which is in the reptile part of the brain."

"Did you say reptile?"

"Evolution has successively added layers to man's brain structure, sort of like stacking blocks," one of the Beasley boys explained. "The human brain is stacked atop our animal brain, and under that is the most primitive—the so-called reptile brain. That's where the second visual pathway leads. Other than to trigger melanin production, biologists don't know what it's for. But we've determined that strong primary colors follow this evolutionarily abandoned pathway to affect the reptile brain in a very primal way."

"I've always hated green. Hated it with a passion."

"Orange makes me nervous. And bright red can trigger seizures in some epileptics. It's our reptile brains reacting to color stimulation of the retina. As I say, it's an ancient psuedoscience that's still kicking around. They paint prison walls in some penitentiaries pink to calm down the most-violent inmates. Works like a charm, too. In fact, it's the secret behind the success of our Technicolor cartoons. We used only positive hues."

"Okay, you sold me."

"Good. Now, get busy delivering a laser that will pacify a planet."

Rod went to his lab, but he wasn't thinking of pacifying planets. He was thinking of making his TV clicker impossible to lose ever again.

Every TV remote, he knew, operated on the infrared principle. Different wavelengths of infrared light triggered different relays in the TV photocell receptor.

It had been Rod's fantasy to implant a signal beacon in his clicker so that when he lost it, all he had to do was put on a pair of special goggles and hunt around for the constant infrared pulse.

Trouble was, when Rod tended to lose his remote, he *really* lost it. Infrared light could pulse from under the couch, beneath a pile of magazines or from the bathroom. Rod had TV sets all over his house. And because too many remotes were almost as much trouble as no remote, he carried a universal remote whenever he walked through his house so that every set responded to his commands.

There wasn't a form of light known that could pass through solid walls. Therein lay the problem with the infrared beacon.

A new, more intense kind of color might solve that problem, Rod realized. Just as it might solve the Beasley problem. Two problems with a common solution, just like the condom.

Taking apart a universal remote, Rod got down to cases. He hooked it up to a power source and started converting it to an eximer laser.

"I need a pink several orders of magnitude greater than hot pink," he muttered.

Rod experimented with various pink dyes extracted from natural substances, mostly exotic flowers, pink minerals and gemstones.

And he knew he had it when he started feeling good—really good for the first time—since coming to work for the Sam Beasley Corporation.

The feeling passed the minute he shut down the hot-pink pencil of the laser.

When he showed his bosses what he had accomplished, they grinned under the pink radiance, clapped him on the back and told Rod Cheatwood what a wonderfully inventive employee he was, a credit to the Beasley Corporation, yesireebob.

When the laser was shut down, they turned on him.

"Not pink enough," one said.

"We need saturated pink," said another.

"Saturated?" Rod blurted. "I never heard of saturated pink. What is it?"

"We'll know it when we see it."

And they did.

Using a dye laser in which the essence of the pinkest natural substances was diluted in alcohol and beamed out in one huge pulse of light that instantly exhausted the power source, Rod found himself walking his lab in happy circles when the closed door jerked open and a dozen happy faces crowded in.

"You found it!" one Beasley boy crowed.

"It's perfect," exulted another.

"Do it again."

"Can't," said Rod. "It burned out the power source."

"Hook up another."

"Wait a minute," Rod said suddenly. "How could you know what happened? The door was closed."

"The pink pulse came right through the wall, it was so powerful."

"Eureka!" Rod shouted, because he couldn't think of anything more appropriate. "I did it! I did it!"

"He did it! He did it!" the Beasley boys said. "We have our saturated-pink hypercolor laser."

"No, that's not what I meant. You saw the pulse through solid wall. It's my TV-remote finder. I'm going to be rich."

It was close to that moment when the pink pulse aftereffect began to dwindle, and the Beasley boys grew serious of face.

"Actually," one said, "Beasley gets rich. Not you."

"I own half the rights," Rod said.

"You *owned* half the rights."

"You signed them away, remember?"

"When? When?" said Rod. "Show me proof."

And they did. It was a short legal document, iron-clad, and when he saw his more-flowery-than-usual signature at the bottom, Rod Cheatwood wanted to one by one tear out the larynges of the Beasley boys with his angry teeth and swallow hard.

"When did I sign this?"

"It was the release. You wanted fifteen minutes more in the Pink Room."

"I thought it was a medical release," Rod said in horror.

"Did we say medical release?"

"No one ever said medical release."

And the Beasley boys smiled that inner smile of theirs.

"Damn," said Rod.

"Let's have some more pink," one of the boys said.

"Let's renegotiate that contract," countered Rod.

And when the Beasley boys hesitated, Rod knew he had them. Sort of.

In the end Rod settled for ten percent, because truth be known, he ached to bask in the glow of the pink laser, too.

"It's really pink," the Beasley boys said happily.

"The pinkest."

"Hot pink."

"Let's call it Hotpink. One word. That way we can trademark it."

"What's next?" asked Rod.

"More colors."

"Try green."

"Then red."

"What will they do?" asked Rod.

"We'll find out when you generate them."

Because the color-therapy charts they had supplied said that green was a particularly soothing and healing color, Rod built a second dye laser that generated an extreme green pulse from the pigments of tropical lizards. Everyone wanted a sustained glow, but that damn eximer laser ate up power too quickly.

This time the Beasley boys stood around in front of the laser while Rod set a timer and, like a photographer wanting to be in the picture with his subjects, he rushed to join them. They were standing expectantly awaiting the green beam, which filled their eyes with the most vivid, hideous, stomach-churning green ever conceived.

When Rod Cheatwood woke up in the Beasley infirmary three days later, his first question was a strange one.

"What day is it?"

"Sunday."

"The sixth?"

"Yes. You've been under three days."

And tears started welling up in Rod Cheatwood's stricken eyes.

"There, there," the Beasley nurse with the starched white cap adorned with paper mouse ears said soothingly. "We expect you to make a complete recovery."

"I missed it...." Rod blubbered.

"Missed what?"

"The season finale 'Next Generation' episode," he said miserably.

When he was well enough to return to work, Rod told the Beasley boys, "I guess green is out, huh?"

"On the contrary, it's a perfect offensive color."

And they showed him a chart.

Most color charts broke down into complementary colors or contrasting colors. The Beasley chart was divided into offensive colors and defensive colors.

And they had new names. Hotpink. Supergreen. Contrablue. Ultrayellow. Optired. Infraorange. Deepurple.

Over time they cataloged their properties and created various beamers.

"How about we call them phasers?" suggested Rod. "They phase light."

"Can't. Not our trademark."

"Oh, right," said Rod.

When they told him he was being shipped out to Paris to install the first hypercolor beamers in Euro Beasley, Rod Cheatwood was horrified.

"I don't want to go to Paris."

"Why not?"

"They hate us. And they love Jerry Lewis." Rod shuddered.

"You don't have to go to Paris. You can live under Euro Beasley."

"Under? They have a Utiliduck there, too?"

"Utilicanard. It means the same thing."

It was not so bad. There were dorm rooms, with kitchenettes and TVs. And when the new pink lights were installed all over Euro Beasley, attendance shot up almost immediately.

"How about a raise?" Rod asked one day when even the Beasley boys could not disguise the dramatic turnaround.

"What do you need a raise for? You have your ten percent royalty."

"I haven't had time to make my remote finder."

"When you do, that will be your raise."

"Mousefuckers," Rod grumbled.

And so Rod lived for the day his work at Euro Beasley was done.

Unfortunately that day never came. Instead, the French Foreign Legion came rappeling out of hovering helicopters and advanced on one of the many entrances to Utilicanard.

When they were all on the ground, Rod knew what to do. He clapped a pair of solid lead goggles onto his eyes and, with his pounding heart high in his throat, he depressed a console button marked Supergreen.

Even though he was spared the awful green light hitting his retina, he threw up anyway.

16

The unmarked van was parked on U.S. 460, south of Petersburg National Battlefield Park. It was the direction the balloons had come from, so it was reasonable to conceive of a link between the two.

Certainly if it was a TV truck, it would have identifying call letters or a network logo painted on the sides.

That was how Dominique Parillaud perceived it as she drove past the van in her Europe 1 satellite truck before parking it well down the highway and out of sight. After exiting the vehicle, she moved low toward the waiting van. There was no sign of life or activity around the van. No one behind the wheel.

But the nest of electronic array atop the van was very suggestive.

Crouching behind a thicket, Dominique unshipped her 9 mm MAS automatic and started out of the hedges. If the van contained the secret of the bright colored lights that had her countrymen literally agog, and she could acquire it, the Legion of Honor medal—not to mention the adulation of all Frenchmen—would be all but hers.

More importantly she could leave this hellish nation of imbeciles and cretins.

She started forward.

And her beret swallowed her head like a Venus's-flytrap made of cloth.

"Merde!"

Some force took her by the shoulders and spun her around inexorably, but still she retained the presence of mind to jut her MAS snout forward. When she felt it come into contact with her assailant's chest, she pulled the trigger.

The gunshot was not loud. A mere snap of sound. The automatic convulsed once.

"Hah!" she said triumphantly, yanking the beret off her face.

Dominique blinked as the familiar features of the American named Remo stared back at her with a slight smile touching his cruel face.

"But—I could not miss."

"Sure you did."

"Never! I am an expert markswoman."

"Was," said Remo, relieving her of her weapon with a casual twist. He tossed it away.

"You're French, right?"

"Belgian."

"You sound French."

"We Belgians speak French. It is our native tongue."

Remo looked to the tiny Asian gray-beard who stood beside him, hands tucked in his kimono sleeves. "This is true, but this woman speaks the dialect of Paris, not Brussels."

"Caught you. You're French."

"French women do not wear berets," Dominique pointed out.

"Sure they do," said Remo.

"It is an impossibility. How can you be so stupid?"

"Practice," said Remo, handing her back her beret.

"The beret is gauche. Do you know nothing of French customs?"

"As little as possible," Remo admitted.

"I categorically deny French citizenship."

The tiny Asian turned his head, "Behold. Is that not the illustrious Jerry Lewis approaching?"

Dominique whirled.

"Jairy? Jairy is here. Where? I idolize him!"

But there was no one there and when she looked back, the tiny Asian was beaming triumphantly. The man named Remo was saying "tsk-tsk" while making some arcane gesture at her that involved rubbing his forefingers in her direction.

"Caught you again," he said.

"I am a tourist."

"You're a French agent. You have French agent written all over you."

"In French," said the Asian gray-beard.

"I deny everything."

"What's the French interest in this?" asked Remo.

"I refuse to say any more."

"We have ways of making you confess," warned the tiny Asian.

"I am notoriously fearless."

Abruptly the tiny Asian stiffened and said, "Hark!"

Remo stopped.

Dominique listened. "I hear nothing."

"Do you hear it, Remo? The pumping sound."

Dominique frowned. "I hear no pumping."

"Yeah," said Remo. "It's coming from that van."

"Two heartbeats. One human. One not."

"Yeah, and the human one sounds pretty scared."

"Let us investigate."

"Heartbeats. I hear no heartbeats."

"Remo, detain that woman while I investigate."

"Little Father, don't you think we should both—"

"No!"

Remo subsided, Dominique was surprised to see. Was he afraid of the old one? It seemed doubtful.

They watched the old one slip toward the back of the van, Remo holding her in place with steely fingers clamped about her elbow. They felt like blunt knives and, when she reached up to loosen them, they refused to budge.

While his attention was on her fingers, she tried a judo throw that never failed.

It involved the feet. A quick step back, crunch down on the handiest instep and flip the opponent with his own reverse impetus. Dominique had once thrown a two-hundred-kilogram Sumo wrestler in this fashion.

"Watch the shoes," said Remo when she brought her stiletto heel onto his instep. "They're new."

She tried to flip him anyway.

Remo refused to flip. It was as if his feet were set in concrete. He had no discernible center of gravity. None that she could find. Refusing to give up, she twisted and tried to insert her fingers into his nostrils and give them a fierce twist absolutely guaranteed to cause the most stern grip to relinquish.

"Easy. I'm ticklish," said Remo, his nostrils easily evading her darting fingers.

"You are unlike any man I have ever encountered," said Dominique, switching to flattery.

"I hear that a lot."

"I am sure."

"Too much, in fact. I like to be treated like an ordinary guy."

"I would treat you that way if you would allow me."

"You're not my type. Sorry."

"I French-kiss like a sailor," Dominique said, using a line that had been used on her.

"I'm not into sailors. Now stop struggling. I wanna see what Chiun does."

Dominique's head turned toward the van, having no other option once Remo had laid his heavy hand on her head and turned it like a faucet fixture.

Her eye fell upon the old Asian named Chiun as he slipped up to the door and laid a tiny ear to it.

"What is he doing?" Dominique hissed.

"Making sure it's not a trap."

"He can tell by listening?"

"He can tell what time it is by closing his eyes and finding the sun with his face."

"What if it is night?"

"Search me. I never saw him do it in the nighttime."

Dominique glanced at Remo's hard, obdurate fingers. "How can one be so slim and so strong at the same time?"

"Same way Popeye did it."

"How so?"

"Spinach."

"You are making fun of me."

"Tell it to Jairy."

"You insult a great clown."

"Shh."

As they watched, Chiun reached up for the door handle and seemed to freeze.

"What is wrong?" Dominique asked.

Remo squeezed her arm to get silence.

As she watched, Dominique realized very slowly that the old Asian was not frozen, as he appeared to be. He was turning the door handle, but doing it so slowly and methodically that he appeared immobile to the casual eye.

"Ah, he is very clever."

Abruptly the door opened and shut almost as quickly. It happened so suddenly it literally took Dominique's breath away. It was as if the door had been the mouth of a mechanical monster that had snatched the old one from sight to gobble him alive.

Nothing happened for a moment.

Then the edges of the door pulsed with the most vivid gray light Dominique had ever seen. And the door flew open like a frightened ghost.

And the awful light poured out.

REMO SAW THE VAN DOOR outlined in green. It was like a kick in the stomach, that green. Remo had never seen such a green. It was hideous, a violent lizard green. Some Sinanju instinct caused him to begin to turn away, when the door flew open and the Master of Sinanju came fluttering out.

Remo naturally looked back to see what Chiun was doing. What he saw shocked him. Chiun's face was twisted with some terrible strain. His arms and legs pumped as if to outrun the green glow.

The green light stabbed out all around him, and in his last moment of consciousness Remo felt his stomach contract involuntarily and the contents of his stomach erupt from his throat.

His last thought was how much he suddenly hated the color green.

DOMINIQUE PARILLAUD felt Remo's grip suddenly relax, and her professional instincts took over. Just in time, too.

She stepped away and by the narrowest margin avoided being splashed by a jet of hot vomit that seemed composed mostly of rice and small chunks of what seemed to be fish.

A horrible expression on his face, Remo fell face-first into his own vomit.

Dominique spun around and saw the old Korean also pitched forward in midstep, a cloud of milky vomit cascading ahead of him.

When he skidded into the grass, Chiun lay still.

Dominique crouched down, her color-blind eyes on the vivid gray light as she searched the grass for her fallen MAS.

The thing came clumping out of the van while she was preoccupied with her weapon.

Dominique experienced a strange stab of recognition mixed with horror. The horror, she thought at first, was a consequence of watching two formidable American agents—she had no doubt that was what they were—succumb to some force she could not comprehend.

But the horror soon resolved itself when the stab of recognition became awful, unbelievable certainty.

"You are l'Oncle Sam," she blurted as the figure strode toward her.

"Why aren't you lying facedown in your vomit?" the man demanded in a frosty voice.

And as he came on, his left eye began flashing. The livid light. It was coming from his eye somehow. He had an artificial eye. It was like a small strobe light, pulsing and flashing, and he was coming closer and closer. He was aiming it at her as if it were a deadly laser.

And Dominique realized it must be. A laser that did not burn but made strong men give up the contents of their stomachs and pitch unconscious into it.

The realization hit her just as her questing fingers found the cold, reassuring steel of her MAS.

She snapped it up, aimed and pulled the trigger once.

A hand that she saw was fashioned of steel segments clamped over the weapon, pinching her thumb and fingers. Still, she squeezed the trigger.

The weapon refused to discharge, its slide held in place by the hand that then began to whir as hydraulic fingers compressed and compressed with irresistible, inexorable power.

Dominique pulled her fingers free just before the fine-machined steel became a grinding, spitting tangible shriek of steel.

"Mon Dieu!"

"French, eh?"

"Oui."

"I hate the fucking French."

"You are not Oncle Sam Beasley, who loves all mankind."

"I love only money," said the familiar voice as the steel hand swept up and grabbed her by the hair.

"What do you want of me?" Dominique said, squirming.

"There's just one thing I want from you."

"What is that?"

"Give it to me straight. What does that clown Lewis have that my Mongo doesn't?"

17

The first battle-damage-assessment reports from the Blot were most disturbing.

They came in the form of aerial photographs taken by a low-flying Gazelle equipped with a gun-sight camera.

The photographs were laid on the desk of the president of France. "Are these men dead?" he asked.

"We do not know, *Monsieur Président*."

"Is that not blood spilling out from under their still bodies?"

"It is not red."

"Then what can it be?"

"Either piss or vomit. The analysts have yet to determine."

The president of France turned the picture in his hand this way and that. "It is vomit, I think."

"We should leave this to experts, *non?*"

"Piss is more transparent. This is thick."

"Not all. Some appears soupy."

The president shrugged. "Some could have eaten soup and then thrown it up."

"We have experts who understand these matters," the aide said dismissively. "What do we do?"

"We cannot leave them lying about like so many fallen toy soldiers. These are Frenchmen. Oh, to see them with their proud red berets in the dirt."

"It is asphalt."

"Dirt. Asphalt. The outrage knows no name."

"We must act quickly to contain this matter, before the Americans learn of it and lodge a protest."

"Has there been no word from Washington?"

"Not yet. But soon. That is why you must act instantly."

"I should never have listened to that *bouffon*," moaned the president of France.

"What clown?"

"The minister of culture."

"He is not such a clown. He has spearheaded the drive against the detestable Franglais, he has banished—"

"Enough. Enough. Order our Foreign Legionnaires to storm the Bastille."

"You mean the Blot."

"I mean to see this matter ended before that *bouffon* calls to complain," the French president said testily.

"The culture minister?"

"No. The President of the United States."

COLONEL JEAN-GUY BAVARD of the French Foreign Legion had a stock answer for what had brought him to enlist in the toughest, hardest-fighting and most disreputable outfit in all Europe.

"It is a long story."

It wasn't. But that gruff comment was enough to turn away all questions. That it was a long story was the time-honored evasion men of the French Foreign Legion used against prying reporters or too-curious temporary girlfriends.

Thus, no one ever learned that Colonel Bavard had joined the French Foreign Legion because of a gastrointestinal irregularity.

Cheese gave him gas. Not any common gas, but the most malodorous, ferocious gas imaginable. He had only to nibble a corner of Chevrotin, sometimes only inhale the pungency of Brie, when his bowels would churn and boil and begin venting.

It was acutely embarrassing. It drove off lonely women, lost children and hungry dogs. Even flies avoided Colonel Bavard when he was enveloped in a noxious cloud of his own making.

There were only two humane solutions. Give up cheese or join the French Foreign Legion, which would take anyone, no matter his sins or quirks. Colonel Bavard naturally chose the latter course of action.

After all, what self-respecting Frenchman could survive without cheeses? To dwell Brieless was unthinkable. And to be deprived of Rambol and Camembert? Not to mention the sublime La Vache qui Rit?

Colonel Bavard had served with distinction in Kuwait and Rwanda, and elsewhere in the French-speaking world. He had won countless medals for accepting surrenders. That some of those surrendering to Colonel Bavard were his own men was beside the point. Enemy surrenders far, far outnumbered comrades-in-arms who threw themselves gasping on the tender mercies of Colonel Jean-Guy Bavard.

So it was only natural that in their darkest hour, his fellow countrymen would turn to him.

"We have chosen you for this mission for a reason," the commander of the French Foreign Legion told him in his headquarters office.

Colonel Bavard saluted snappily. "I am prepared to die for my nation."

"We need an officer who can lead his men into the darkest quarter of hell."

"I have no fear."

"Your objective is the Blot."

"It is France's."

"It is already France's. Technically we own fifty-two percent. Or our unfortunate banks do."

"Then I will destroy it."

"We can accomplish that with an atomic bomb, and may we do so at a later point as a lesson to others who would inflict their inferior culture upon us."

Then they handed him a pair of goggles with the lenses crisscrossed by impenetrable black electrical tape.

"What is this for?"

"To protect your eyes."

"From what?"

"The terror of the Blot," they told him solemnly, and Colonel Bavard felt a slow chill creep up his stiff Gallic spine.

"But how will I lead if I am blind?"

"We will guide you by radio from a hovering command helicopter."

"What about my men?"

"They, too, will be similarly goggled."

"That is fine, but how will they follow me?"

His commander allowed himself a slow smile. "You have hit upon the very reason why you have been chosen for this mission, *mon Colonel.*"

And his commander handed Colonel Bavard a blue wedge of malodorous Roquefort.

"Excuse me," Colonel Bavard said, squeezing his cheeks together. Too late. The room was perfumed with the toil of his sensitive intestines.

"Bon appétit!" said his commander, clapping a respirator over his lower face.

WHEN HE EXPLAINED the mission to his men, Colonel Bavard told them it had an extremely low pucker factor.

In military parlance the world over, this meant that the mission was a low-danger one. The pucker factor being the degree to which the anal sphincter contracted with fear under combat conditions.

Normally low-pucker-factor missions were the most welcome.

Not in Colonel Bavard's unit of the French Foreign Legion. The higher the pucker factor, the easier the breathing.

"How low?" asked a lowly private during the premission briefing.

"The lowest possible."

The men looked stricken. Some, in anticipation of their immediate fate, stopped inhaling. Their red berets seemed almost to deflate in resignation.

"We expect to encounter poison gases?" a sergeant asked, unable to keep the hope out of his voice.

"No poison gases are expected."

"Should we not take our gas masks along just in case?" a private suggested eagerly.

"Gas masks are forbidden," Colonel Bavard said sternly. Some of his men, normally brave to a fault, actually quailed.

"You will don these." And he began handing out the taped goggles that sealed the eyes from bright lights.

The men examined the goggles doubtfully.

"If we are blind, how can we follow you into battle, *mon Colonel?*"

And to their utter horror, their colonel undid the flap of his blouse pocket and flung away the all-important roll of gas-absorbing charcoal tablets that Colonel Jean-Guy Bavard was never without.

"By your proud French noses," he told them.

WHEN THEY LEARNED that they were to assault Euro Beasley in an armored personnel carrier, the men under the command of Colonel Bavard almost deserted.

"Are you mice or are you Frenchmen?" Colonel Bavard demanded, chewing great gulps of cheese as the rear APC door gaped open. It was an AMX/10P APC, its fourteen tons looking like five due to the light desert camouflage streaking, and capable of conveying eleven men into battle.

"I will drive!" a chorus of voices volunteered.

"*I* will drive," said Colonel Bavard, to the relief of his men.

He sent the APC rolling through the French countryside of Averoigne, humming "La Marseillaise." In the back his men sang an old legion song. It covered the unsettlingly rude noises coming from the driver's compartment.

They barreled through the gates of Euro Beasley unchallenged, accelerated up Main Street, U.S.A., toward the redoubt itself. Still, no one challenged them.

"Goggles on!" Colonel Bavard cried when the drawbridge over the moat came into view. Bavard wore his own goggles high on his forehead and snapped them down. Holding the wheel steady, he bore down on the accelerator.

The asphalt under his wheels hummed. Then the sound became the rattle of rubber over wooden planking. Then a concrete zimming.

The AMX/10P slewed and pitched in response to the sudden pumping of the brakes. Grabbing up his MAT submachine gun, Colonel Bavard threw open the door.

"Out! Out! Out!"

The men tumbled out in confusion, utterly blind.

"This way, men of the legion," Colonel Bavard shouted.

There was a moment of indecision before the rude *blatt* his men knew too well cut the close air. They pivoted toward it. And when the awful odor found their nostrils, they charged toward it.

They charged, as history later recorded, toward disaster.

In his earpiece Colonel Bavard listened to the guidance of the spotters in the hovering Gazelle.

"You are seeking a niche directly north of the drawbridge," the control voice informed him.

"*Oui!*"

"In the niche there will be stairs."

"*Oui.*"

"The stairs lead to Utilicanard."

"For France and the legion!" Colonel Bavard cried, trailing a coil of cheesy odor from his backside.

When his combat boots rattled onto the top step of an aluminium spiral staircase, Colonel Jean-Guy Bavard paused heroically. He might have been posing for a recruitment poster.

And despite the blackout goggles covering his eyes, his entire world turned scarlet.

Later those who survived the massacre at Euro Beasley disagreed as to the exact hue that had brought about their downfall. Some said the color was scarlet, others crimson, still others swore that vermilion was the color of the horror.

For his part Colonel Jean-Guy Bavard saw red. It burned through the black electrical tape like laser light. It stabbed his retina with the force of a blow. His brain, receiving input from his eyes, filled with fire.

A great rage exploded in Colonel Bavard's breast. It was pure anger at the cruel fate that had made him, at middle age, wifeless, childless and without any family but for the Foreign Legion. In that instant, he hated the Foreign Legion and all it represented. Hated the very unit that had enabled him to hide from the more discriminating world that could not abide him.

Screaming his red fury, Colonel Bavard pivoted, firing from the hip.

He never heard the first 9 mm round leave the muzzle. He could not. His thick, rangy body was busy being whittled to kindling by the combined firepower of his men, who also saw the red light clearly, although some saw crimson, some scarlet and others vermilion.

None of them saw Colonel Bavard. But they smelled him, and years of pent-up anger came pouring out of their mouths in the form of colorful curses and out of their rifles in the form of hot steel-jacketed rounds.

Colonel Jean-Guy Bavard never knew what hit him. He went tumbling down the spiral aluminum staircase, shedding body parts that had been chopped from him by legion bullets.

In the Sorcerer's Chateau the remaining legionnaires, still seeing red, turned their weapons on one another, bespeaking minor faults, imagined slights and other infractions unspoken until the blood-red light of hell brought them out.

And under the castle, deep in the bowels of Utilicanard, Chief Concepteer Rod Cheatwood took his finger off the button labeled Optired.

"I can't keep this up forever," he muttered worriedly. "I'm running out of power."

18

Remo was dreaming of his mother before he awoke in the hospital bed.

He had never known his mother. But an apparition had materialized before him months ago, and he had recognized the face. Some buried glimmering of memory told him it was his mother. She had told him to seek out his father, but not who his father was.

In the dream his mother was trying to tell him something, but Remo couldn't hear her words. Her pale mouth moved, formed shapes and vowels, and as Remo strained to catch the fragmentary sounds, he awoke to bright light.

It was morning. It shouldn't be morning. His internal clock read a little after one in the afternoon. Even in sleep it kept track of the passing hours. Yet the sunlight streaming into the white-walled room where he awoke was morning bright.

Then he remembered.

Remo snapped himself up from his pillow—and the world reeled.

The door flew open with a crash, and Remo slapped his hands over his ears because they seemed suddenly as sensitive as the skin under his fingernails.

"Lazy slugabed! Get up. Get up."

"Chiun?"

The Master of Sinanju began tearing off sheets and bedclothes. "I have been up for hours. Why do you worry me without reason?"

Remo grabbed his head to make the white-walled room stop spinning before his eyes. "What happened?" he said thickly.

"You succumbed to vile sorcery."

"I did?"

"It is no shame."

"Wait a minute. What happened to you?"

"I rescued you, of course," Chiun said casually, as if dismissing a trifle.

Remo glared. "Chiun."

The Master of Sinanju turned his back on his pupil. Remo recognized the evasive set of his shoulders.

"Chiun, it got you, too, didn't it?"

"Why do you say that?" Chiun said aridly.

"Because if it didn't, you'd be telling me how you mounted Sam Beasley's head on a post somewhere."

"Do not speak that name to me."

"You talk to Smith?"

Chiun turned. "I have not had time."

A doctor entered. She carried a clipboard in one hand, and a stethoscope hung around her neck. She was fifty and wore her brown hair up in a bun. "Ah, I see you're awake."

Chiun blocked the way. "Lay not hands on my son."

"I'm his doctor."

"You are a woman. It is not proper."

"I examined you when they brought you in, too, you know," the doctor said.

Chiun blushed bright crimson, and if steam didn't exactly escape from his ears, he gave a good impression of an embarrassed boiler.

The doctor came over and inserted the earpieces of her stethoscope into her ears and laid the other end against Remo's chest. "I'm Dr. Jeffcoat. How are we feeling today?"

"What happened to us?" Remo inquired.

"You tell me. I couldn't get anything out of your friend."

Chiun snorted loudly. "I am not his friend. I am his father."

"Adopted," corrected Remo.

"Which one of you is the adopted one?"

"He is," Remo and Chiun said together.

Dr. Jeffcoat said, "Tell me the last thing you remember."

"Green."

"Green what?"

"Just green. It was a vicious green. I hated how green it was."

"It frightened you?" the doctor asked.

"Maybe," Remo admitted.

Chiun laid a palm over his purple-trimmed black velvet kimono. "He is fearless, but I am even more so."

"Didn't I see you run out of that truck like a bat out of hell?" Remo asked Chiun.

"You did not!"

Dr. Jeffcoat said, "You were found unconscious in your own vomit. Both of you."

Remo cracked a smile. "Good thing I was wearing clean underwear." Then, in a more serious tone, he asked, "Can you explain it?"

"Not from what you just told me. But something caused a massive convulsion of the vagus nerve."

"The what?"

"Vagus nerve. It's in the brain stem. You've heard of the fight-or-flight reaction?"

"Sure," said Remo. "People get scared. Some run, some fight. It depends on the person."

"Unless you train it out of him," Chiun grunted.

"Part of the fight-or-flight response involves an involuntary reaction of the part of the vagus nerve which terminates in the stomach," Dr. Jeffcoat explained. "It causes the stomach to contract with great violence. I guess that's so if you run from danger, you're carrying a lighter load and there's less chance of the stomach cramping if it's empty."

"I don't remember being scared."

"From what you described and the way they found you," the doctor said, unplugging her stethoscope, "you were scared green."

"Scared *by* green," Remo corrected.

"Have it your way." Dr. Jeffcoat started for the door. "By the way, I hope you're both covered by insurance."

"We have universal health care," said Chiun loftily.

"No one has that yet—if they ever will."

"Ask your President if you do not believe me."

"Cash okay?" Remo asked.

"Cash," Dr. Jeffcoat said, closing the door, "is king around these parts."

After she was gone, Remo said, "Time to call Smith."

Chiun rushed to Remo's bedside.

"Do not tell Emperor Smith of my embarrassment," he pleaded.

"What'll you give me?"

Chiun frowned. "What do you want?"

"How many thousand years do I have to cook dinner for you?"

"Three."

"Let's cut it to two, shall we?"

"Robber!"

And Remo laughed as he dialed. His stomach felt as if it had been boiled in carbolic acid. He couldn't remember the last time he had thrown up.

HAROLD SMITH SOUNDED as if he had been gargling with carbolic acid when Remo got him on the line. His voice was haggard.

"Remo?"

"Yeah. Who'd you think?"

"I have heard nothing from you for two days. I thought you were dead."

"Neither of us are dead."

"What happened?"

"We ran into Beasley. He was stage-managing everything, I guess."

"Where is he?"

"Search me. Chiun and I are in a hospital somewhere recuperating."

"One moment." The line hummed. "Remo, you are in the popular Spring Hospital."

"How'd you know that?"

"Telephone back-trace."

"Beasley got us with something green."

"What do you mean by something green?"

"A light or something. It was the ugliest green you ever saw, Smitty. It made me sick to my stomach. The doctor said my vagus nerve went crazy."

"Are you saying your flight-or-fight response was tripped by a green light?"

"I'm saying I pitched forward into my own puke and it's a day later."

"Two days."

Remo closed his eyes. "Fill me in, Smitty."

"The Beasley U.S.A. matter has been resolved. There is a truce. All combatants have agreed to stand down until the Virginia State Legislature has decided the disposition of the parcel of land adjoining Petersburg National Battlefield earmarked for sale to the Beasley Corporation."

"Then it's over."

"It has just begun. We have a problem in France."

"We always have a problem with France."

"This is different."

"Smitty, I'm not up to dealing with the French. Not on an empty stomach, anyway."

"Remo, listen to me. Two days ago French warplanes bombed Euro Beasley."

"Is that good or bad?"

"We have an international crisis brewing. The French have entirely surrounded Euro Beasley and are refusing to allow anyone to enter or leave."

"Is *that* good or bad?"

"The French National Assembly have rushed through emergency legislation forbidding the speaking of English within the borders of France."

"Huh?"

"American businessmen and tourists are being thrown out of the country. Our Senate has threatened retaliation. A U.S. mob was intercepted in boats near the Statue of Liberty. They were carrying acetylene torches. One confessed to a plan to dismantle Liberty and send her back to France in pieces. Someone blew up the French pavilion at Epcot Center. Quebec is in an uproar. We are on the verge of a war with France.''

"Over a theme park?"

"The specifics are difficult to determine. But you and Chiun must go to France and find out why Euro Beasley is under seige.''

"Probably the admission prices," muttered Remo. "What about Beasley?"

"Do you know where he is?"

"No," Remo admitted. "I only know where I am because you told me."

"We will deal with Beasley later," Harold Smith said in a biting tone of voice. "Right now I want you and Chiun in Paris as soon as possible.''

"I'm not up to this."

But Harold W. Smith had already disconnected.

Hanging up his phone, Remo turned to the Master of Sinanju and said, "We're going to Paris, Little Father."

"That dump," sniffed Chiun.

AT THE CUSTOMS STATION at Charles de Gaulle International Airport, Remo defenestrated a French customs officer for speaking French to him.

Remo had started to say "I don't speak French," when the customs officer inspecting his passport pulled a whistle from his uniform blouse and blew on it shrilly.

"Il ne parle pas français!" he cried.

"What'd he say?" Remo asked Chiun.

"You do not speak French," Chiun translated.

"I just said that."

"Il parle rebut américain!" the customs officer shouted.

"He said you speak junk American."

"Il faut qu'il se comportât."

"And must be deported," Chiun added.

"You're deporting me over your dead body," Remo told the customs man in English.

"Do you not mean over *my* dead body?" asked the customs officer, also in English.

"Exactly," Remo told him darkly.

Then, catching himself, the customs man clapped his hands over his own mouth. "I have been contaminated!"

Another customs officer strode up and arrested the first. They began arguing. In French.

"What's going on?" Remo asked Chiun.

"He has been arrested for speaking English," explained Chiun.

"Good."

Then a third customs officer tried to arrest Remo and Chiun for speaking English within the natural and eternal borders of the Republic of France.

That was the customs official whom Remo flung through the nearest plate-glass window. He screamed something that sounded inarticulate, but was probably just high-speed French. Both sounded the same to Remo.

Whistles blew shrilly, and airport security converged on Remo and Chiun. They were yelling excitedly in French, and since Remo didn't understand the language, he decided to put the worst possible construction on what they were trying to tell him and began resecting their frontal lobes with his index finger.

By some fluke he got a few speech centers, because the excited shouts stopped while the excited gesticulating continued as the airport security men decided to give the two English-speaking demons a wide birth.

Outside, Chiun hailed a waiting Mercedes cab in perfect French, which, he complained to Remo as they got into the back seat, was not perfect at all, but an abomination.

The cab driver, hearing English spoken in the back of his cab, which was technically French soil, brought the car to a screeching halt and ordered them out.

Since he gave the order in fluent French, Remo felt no obligation to obey and sat tight.

The Master of Sinanju, on the other hand, took immediate offense and hurled a long string of insults back in voluble French. The Frenchman hurled back as good as he got, and after a minute of shrieking cacophony Remo ended the argument by the simple expedient of giving the back of the driver's seat a sharp, sudden kick.

The driver flew out his own windshield, slid off the hood and onto the parking lot.

After Remo got behind the wheel, everything was fine except for the fact that the steering wheel was on the wrong side, and the wind blew back saltlike granules of shatterproof glass off the hood and into his face as he drove.

"So," Remo said as they entered highway traffic, "which way to Euro Beasley?"

"I do not know."

"Damn. That means we're going to have to ask directions from the locals."

They were already out of the city and into what appeared to be farmland dotted by small villages. So Remo pulled off the highway and asked a farmer.

"Euro Beasley?"

The farmer held his nose.

"You're a big help," said Remo, driving on. The next farmer spit when Remo repeated the name.

"How do you say 'Which way to Euro Beasley?'" Remo asked as they continued.

"*'Ou est Euro Beasley?'*" said Chiun.

"Say again?"

"*'Ou est Euro Beasley?'*"

"I don't suppose that's spelled the same way it's pronounced."

"Of course not. It is French."

When Remo repeated the fragment of French for a peasant woman, she picked up a roadside stone and bounced it off their back window. She was shaking a malletlike fist at them as they drove away.

"What'd I do wrong?"

"You mangled that woman's tongue."

"You ask me, her tongue was mangled by its inventors. You know, Little Father, I had three whole years of French at the orphanage."

"Yes?"

"Yeah. French I, French I and French I. After my third French I, the nuns gave up on me and speaking French. Latin, I could handle, though."

"French is to Latin what Pidgin English is to your mother tongue," said Chiun. "And the French spoken today is doggerel."

"Tell that to the French," said Remo. "Hold on, I see some police cars coming up on us fast."

"Excellent. We can ask directions of them."

"My thinking exactly," said Remo, slowing.

In the rearview mirror three caterwauling French police cars came barreling up, driving abreast of one another. They were tiny white Renaults, with flashing blue roof bubbles and rude sirens. The car in the middle dropped back while the two side machines surged forward.

When they had flanked Remo's taxi, one gendarme called out, *"Rendez-vous!"*

"Did he say rendezvous?" asked Remo.

"He is asking you to surrender."

"Ou est Euro Beasley?" Remo asked.

The gendarme flinched as if Remo had spit in his face.

"What'd I do wrong?" Remo said to Chiun.

"You told him 'He hears Euro Beasley.' "

"Oops. Maybe you should try."

But it was too late. Pistols came up out of police holsters, and Remo knew he had to act fast before their tires were shot out from under them. He accelerated, flung open his door and hit the brakes hard.

"Chiun!"

The Master of Sinanju copied his pupil's action.

The pursuing gendarmes were caught off guard. They hit their brakes too late and took off both taxi doors with a ripping of steel and the crash-bang of the doors smashing into their windshields.

When the third car caught up with them, Remo reached out and wrenched the passenger door off the pacing vehicle. Then he asked, *"Ou est Euro Beasley?"*

The driver pointed ahead. "Follow ze signs to A301."

"Did he say follow the signs?" Remo asked Chiun.

"Oui."

"Don't start speaking French to me. How do you say thank you?"

"Merci."

"Oh, right. *Merci*," Remo called, kicking out through the driver's side and catching the right front tire with the hard toe of his foot.

The spinning tire blew, sank and the police car went *falumphing* into a ditch. The driver got out and called *"Bonne chance!"* after them.

"He has wished us good fortune," Chiun translated.

Remo grinned. "Looks like clear sailing ahead."

19

Behind a basement door whose brass plate said White House Situation Room, the President of the United States conferred with his military advisers.

"Options, I want to hear options," he said.

"Do we have a policy?" asked the chairman of the Joint Chiefs of Staff.

The President looked to his national-security adviser, who glanced guiltily at the secretary of defense, who in turn threw the hairy eyeball back to the Chief Executive.

"Not yet," the President admitted. "I was kinda hoping you'd help us out with that."

"We have to retaliate, Mr. President," said the Joint Chiefs chairman in his musical East European accent.

"We do have to?" the President said unhappily.

"You did say you wanted to hear options," his national-security adviser said.

"Good options. Positive ones."

"I thought you meant military ones," the JCS chair said.

"Every time I send troops somewhere, my polls drop."

"We have to retaliate in kind," the secretary of defense said firmly. "American prestige is at stake."

"Damn."

"Look, the French have bombed Euro Beasley. Now they have it surrounded. We have one of two responses in kind available to us."

"I'm listening."

"One, we liberate Euro Beasley by inserting the Eighty-second Airborne. They'll hold it against further French incursions, wire it up good, slip out under cover of darkness and blow it to smithereens."

"Blow up Euro Beasley?"

"Mr. President, we can't let the French just march up and grab a symbol of American culture and prestige. And we can't exactly dismantle it and ship it back to the good ole U.S.A. in crates."

"What's option two?" the President asked.

"Option two is to retaliate in kind. They hit an American theme park. We hit a French theme park." The chair laid a map of greater Paris on the long conference table. "Here we have Paris. And this red spot thirty-two kilometers east is Euro Beasley."

"Right...."

"This is Parc Asterix. It's twenty-five kilometers north of Paris and both logistically and symbolically, it's a natural."

"How so?"

"It's based on some sissy French comic-strip character, so it has parity with Euro Beasley as a military target. You know, they hit Mongo, we clobber Asterix."

"What is the other red spot?"

"France Miniature. It's a theme park where the entire country is laid out in miniature. You can ride through it in a matter of an hour. Sort of a Lilliput kind of deal, I guess."

"Wouldn't that be a more logical target? It's more French."

"True. But it's an awfully small target. Hard to hit. The goddamn city of Paris they got there is no bigger than this room. Our satellites had a heck of a time getting a fix on the tiny Eiffel Tower, which we'd naturally designate ground zero."

The President rubbed his bulbous nose in indecision. "I don't like the idea of hitting a comic-strip-character park. It seems antibusiness and might turn the next generation of French children against us."

"It's tit for tat, sir."

"If it's tit for tat, shouldn't we strike a French theme park on American soil?"

The Joint Chiefs of Staff sat stunned for several ticks of the clock. They exchanged uncertain glances.

"Er, Mr. President," the defense secretary said, "the Pentagon has no intelligence on any French theme parks on U.S. soil."

"I don't think there are any," added the national-security adviser, reaching for his briefcase. Everyone reached for their briefcases and began digging through briefing papers and intelligence abstracts.

The President turned to the director of the Central Intelligence Agency, who had thus far sat through the meeting with his mouth shut and his hands folded.

"What do our ground assets in Paris tell us?" he asked.

"Nothing," the CIA director said morosely. "I regret to inform the President that they were rounded up the first day by the DGSE."

"Their covers were blown the first day of the crisis!"

"We have reason to believe their covers were blown the day they hit Paris."

The President looked his disbelief.

"I know how this looks, sir," the CIA director said helplessly. "But you have to understand, it's an exceedingly difficult language to learn. We drill and drill our people, but when they get into the field, they stumble over the words something fierce. Even the simple words. Like yes. It's pronounced 'we,' but there's no *w*. It's all goddamn vowels, not one of them an *e*."

The President said bitterly, "Obviously we've got another no-win Somalia-style situation on our hands."

"The Somalis speak French, too," the CIA director volunteered hopefully.

"Do you have any helpful suggestions?" asked the President.

"I have a scenario for introducing Valium into the French drinking-water supply."

"What good will that do?"

"Our people think if we can get the French calmed down, they might get off their high horses—or at least enunciate more slowly, thus putting our agents on a level playing field with their agents, linguistically speaking."

Everyone stared at the CIA director until the defense secretary said, "Got any Valium on you?"

"In my briefcase."

"Now would be an opportune time to indulge yourself."

While the CIA chief began rooting around, all eyes fell upon the President of the United Stated expectantly.

"I have the Vice President trying to reach the Beasley people on the net. Maybe they can shed some light on this."

"Shouldn't we explore all options?" the JCS chair pleaded.

"We *are* exploring all options. I have to be able to justify any military action I take to both the American people and the citizens of France. I can't justify tit for tat."

"Did I hear the word 'tit'?" a stern female voice called from the open door.

"Oh, hi dear," said the President sheepishly.

"Mrs. President," said the JCS chair.

"Don't call her that," the President whispered urgently.

"What have I told you uniforms about using sexist language in my house?" the First Lady snapped.

"Sorry, ma'am," mumbled the defense secretary.

"It was just an expression," added the national-security adviser.

"Yes, tit for tat."

The First Lady gave them all the benefit of her laser blue eyes. "How would you like it if the expression was 'dick for dock'?"

The JCS chairman looked away and played with his fingers. The President turned red. The CIA director popped his Valium.

"From now on, say 'an eye for an eye' or 'a tooth for a tooth.' Is that clear?"

"Yes, ma'am," the Joint Chiefs chairman and the President of the United States said in little-boy voices.

"At ease, boys," said the First Lady, coming over to her husband's end of the conference table and laying before him a single sheet of fanfold computer paper.

"This just came off the net," she whispered, glaring at the director of the CIA, who was trying to sneak a peak at the paper.

TAKE NO ACTION ON BEASLEY MATTER. AGENTS EN ROUTE. WILL REPORT AS DEVELOPMENTS WARRANT.

smith@cure.com

"We're adjourned," said the President of the United States, crumpling up the paper.

"What about our retaliatory response?" asked the secretary of defense.

"Our retaliatory response," said the President, "is about to hit the French the way that comet struck Jupiter."

The Joint Chiefs of Staff looked at one another with blank, vaguely fearful expression.

"But, Mr. President, we *are* your retaliatory response."

"Not for real situations," said the President, exiting the Situation Room with his wife.

Before the door slammed, the First Lady turned and showed the Joint Chiefs of Staff how pink her tongue was.

20

The first Euro Beasley sign they came to had a black X spray-painted over it. The second was desecrated by the slash-in-a-circle international symbol for no. The third had a *non!* scrawled over it.

"I think this is the way," Remo remarked dryly.

Remo recognized the exit off Route A301 that led to Euro Beasley because the sign, which was shaped like Mongo Mouse's head, was completely blacked out with paint.

He slid off the road, and the blue-and-cream Norman battlements of the Enchanted Village came into view.

Sleek helicopters buzzed its ramparts. A ring of desert camouflage AMX-30bis main battle tanks and APCs ringed the theme park.

"These guys look serious," said Remo.

They came upon a roadblock. Remo eased the car to a slow stop and stuck his head out the place where the window would have been had he not kicked the door off.

"Hey! Mind rolling aside for a couple of tourists?"

Green-bereted heads swiveled, and Gallic eyes widened in horror.

"Américain?"

"You bet," said Remo.

"Américain!"

The hated word ran up and down the ranks of the French army unit laying siege to the greatest theme park on the European continent.

A tank turret began rotating with a low, steady whine.

When the muzzle of the 105 mm howitzer was lined up with the taxi windshield, Remo said to Chiun, "I think we've hit a definite anti-American bloc."

They were out of the taxi before the shell coughed from the black muzzle and were accelerating to sixty miles per hour on foot when it struck.

The French taxicab took a direct hit and became the focal point for screaming shrapnel to ricochet in all directions.

When it settled back to the ground on puddling tires, it was a black frame of twisted steel in which flames crackled and danced.

While French army troops huddled behind their steel charges, waiting for the last bits of shrapnel to stop bouncing off, Remo and Chiun rendezvoused behind their siege line.

"That was easy," Remo said as they entered the park.

"These Gauls are very excitable, and therefore easily defeated by superior wits."

"I'll try and remember that," said Remo.

"I was thinking of my superior Korean wits, not your inferior white ones."

They walked down Main Street, U.S.A., unchallenged. Remo, who had been through Euro Beasley before, trying to locate Sam Beasley, was surprised how empty it was. Without the crowds who normally thronged the pavilions and attractions, there seemed to be no magic to the place.

Part of that may have had to do with the fact that most of the attractions had French-language names. Remo recognized the Swiss Family Robinson tree-house despite the sign saying, La Cabane Des Robinson, but what La Tanière du Dragon was, he had no idea.

"Last time I was here," Remo told the Master of Sinanju, "there was a way into Utiliduck—or whatever they call it here—through the castle."

"Therefore, we will not enter through the castle."

"I don't know any other entrance."

"Which only means that they will be expecting you to enter through the castle and will not be expecting us if we enter another way."

Turning a corner, they came upon red-bereted bodies around a grassy mound in the town square where Mongo's grinning face was reproduced in a varicolored flower pattern.

Everybody breathed, everyone's heart pumped, yet everyone lay facedown in a dried puddle of vomit, dead to the world.

"Looks like they got greened, too," Remo remarked.

Holding his nose, Chiun hurried on.

They passed an area called Parc Mésozoïque, and Remo said, "I don't remember that from last time. What's it mean?"

"Mésozoïque Park."

"That helps a lot," said Remo. "I thought you understood French."

"I understand the good tongue of the Franks, not this tongue-twisted patois."

The section of the park was walled off by a high bamboo fence, three times as tall as a man, lashed together with fibrous, ropelike vines. Remo tried to see through the chinks, but the spaces were caulked tight.

"Seems to me," Remo said, "something fenced off this tight might be important."

"I agree," said the Master of Sinanju, examining the fence carefully.

"Looks like something out of *King Kong*."

"We never worked for him," Chiun said vaguely, attacking the vines with his long, knifelike fingernails. They began parting with dry snaps, and a section of bamboo began to sag outward.

"Your turn," Chiun invited.

Remo made a spear with his right hand and began chopping. Bamboo splintered and crackled in surrender. When he got an opening, Remo stepped in.

CHIEF CONCEPTEER Rod Cheatwood watched the two strange intruders amble around the park curiously. They weren't French. Certainly the Asian wasn't. The white guy was dressed for shooting pool, so he couldn't be French, either. He looked as American as Bruce Springsteen. But he wasn't a tourist.

Rod stabbed console mike buttons trying to pick up shreds of their conversation, but they seemed to somehow sense the electrical fields surrounding the concealed mikes. They lowered their voices every time they came within audio range.

And when he moved the concealed security cameras, trying to track them, they seemed to sense those, too, always turning so their backs faced the lenses, as if to foil lip-readers. Not that Rod had that talent.

When they came to Parc Mésozoïque, Rod smiled slightly.

And when they began chopping away at the imported bamboo fence, he swallowed his smile and stabbed at console buttons.

It would be messy, but it was the best way. Since the French government had cut off all power to Euro Beasley, he didn't dare use the hypercolor eximer lasers unless he absolutely had to.

The things drank electricity the way a whale ingested water, and the Euro Beasley backup generators hadn't yet recharged from that French Foreign Legion incursion.

And his orders were to hold Euro Beasley at all costs until the cavalry came.

REMO DETECTED NO SOUNDS or scent of living things behind the bamboo wall so he entered Parc Mésozoïque with confidence, stepping into an impenetrable rain forest.

There were birds squatting on the trees, but they weren't real. They simply perched on branches and looked glassy-eyed. Animatronic. No doubt about it.

"Coast looks clear, Little Father," Remo called over his shoulder.

But Chiun had already entered. "This place is not real," he said, looking around with stern eyes.

"The trees are plastic," Remo explained.

"I do not like this place, where even the trees are not real."

"Hey, it's Beasleyland. Everything is plastic here. Come on, maybe we can find our way downstairs from here."

They melted into the plastic trees under the blind, watchful eyes of the jungle birds.

At the first earthshaking thud, Remo said, "What's that?"

"Something is coming this way."

The thud was followed by another. Foliage shook, and shook again. The thudding picked up.

"Something alive," Chiun added.

"If something living is coming this way, why don't I hear its heartbeat or lungs?" asked Remo.

"Perhaps it does not have any."

"Can't be animatronic. It's too big, whatever it is."

The trees continued to shake with each lumbering footfall, and branches snapped with a sound that was not right because the branches were not made of natural wood, but man-made polymers. They squealed and groaned instead of snapping and splintering as they should.

Remo hesitated.

"This is *really* starting to remind me of *King Kong.*"

Then the trees parted, and a leathery chocolate snout lined with countless ivory needle teeth dropped toward them.

"T-rex!" Remo shouted, breaking left. The Master of Sinanju stood his ground, staring up at the great behemoth, whose head waved back and forth like a serpent trying to fix its prey with its side-mounted lizard eyes.

Remo stopped, turned. "Chiun!"

"It is not living."

"It weighs as much as a truck and it has teeth. Move it."

The chocolate snout dropped lower. The mouth opened, and a mechanical roar issued from the sharklike mouth.

The Master of Sinanju cocked his head like a spaniel. "It is looking at me."

"It can't. It's a machine."

"Then someone is looking at me through it," said Chiun stubbornly.

"Now *that's* possible," said Remo, slipping up behind the full-size *Tyrannosaurus rex*.

DOWN IN UTILICANARD, Rod Cheatwood couldn't believe his eyes. Or the eyes of the T-rex, rather. The little old guy wasn't scared in the slightest. He looked back at the animatronic T-rex with a serene indifference that made the short hairs on Rod's bare forearms lift like spiders walking.

"The little guy sure has balls." And he pushed the traction lever that set the T-rex lumbering toward the old man.

The view through the T-rex's eyes jumped, then retreated. Something was wrong. It wasn't advancing. It was impossible. He had green lights all over the board.

Then one light turned red. It was a square panel and it was blinking so the red and black letters showed on and off. They read, "Overload."

Yanking the traction lever back, Rod rammed it forward again. Hard.

The T-rex lunged—and bounced back like a rubber band.

"What is wrong, dragon-beast?" the little Asian asked in a squeaky voice that reminded Rod of Dingbat Duck's cartoon voice. "Are you afraid to approach the Master of Sinanju? You, the master of a long-ago time?"

Rod didn't know what the Master of Sinanju was, but he hauled back on the traction control and, grabbing the head joystick, began twisting.

The T-rex head swung left, saw only jungle, then swung right. More jungle. Rod pushed it all the way, and the T-rex craned to see over its shoulder.

Directly behind, the white guy in the T-shirt and chinos was standing with his arms casually folded, one foot pressing down hard on the thick tail.

"How can this fucking be?" Rod gulped.

Then the white guy called out, "Show us the way down, or the lizard buys it."

Rod stabbed the Roar button. The T-rex roared its rage.

But the man with the foot of lead stayed put.

"Okay, if that's the way you want to play it," Rod said, deactivating the T-rex. "It's time to bring on the allosaur pack."

21

Dominique Parillaud might have had difficulty getting through U.S. customs at Richmond's Byrd International Airport except that U.S. customs was only too happy to eject any French nationals eager to return home before the conflict became hot.

"Au revoir," she told the customs man.

"Good riddance to bad rubbish," the man snarled.

When she came to the magnometer, it naturally beeped as she stepped through the sensitive metal frame.

"Empty your pockets," the security guard commanded.

"Qu'est-ce que c'est?" she said, wrinkling her smooth brow.

"I said, empty your pockets."

"Je ne comprends pas," she said.

"Damn. Another frog. *Parlez-vous anglais?"* he asked, flattening the lilt of the vowels and utterly demolishing the sweet consonants by actually pronouncing them.

"Non," she told him.

"Just keep going, Lewis-lover," the security guard said impatiently. "We don't want your kind here."

"Anglophone," Dominique muttered under her breath.

And so the greatest military secret since the hydrogen bomb sauntered past United States authorities and boarded an Air France jet bound for Paris, France, safely nestled between DGSE agent Dominique Parillaud's shapely legs.

When she crossed her legs, she winced. But the pain was exceedingly reassuring. It meant the Legion of Honor medal was hers.

Then she settled down to await the stewardess and the Air France meal that, although airplane food, true, was also French. And thus was exquisite even if the mussels simmered in white wine had cooled by the time the dish reached her.

The in-flight movie was a double feature, *Jerry Chez les Cinques* and *Doctor Jerry et Monsieur Love*. It was wonderful to see him in the original French.

Upon reaching de Gaulle Airport, Dominique had the taximan stop at a grocer while she purchased a warm, reassuring baguette of bread.

As the cab pulled away from the curb, she began tearing great chunks off with her bare teeth.

"U.S.A.?" The cab driver clucked sympathetically.

"Oui," Dominique said through a mouthful of cooked dough.

"I have seen strong men weep at the sight of a wheel of cheese hanging in a shop after spending a week in that awful land. But enough. You are home now. Where do you wish to go?"

"The DGSE. But not until I have finished this luscious bread."

"The Americans, they do not understand good bread."

"They do not understand good bread, fine wine or even cheese."

"Not to understand cheese. Unpardonable."

"But most of all, they do not understand French. Or speak it well."

"How can they? They are so gauche as to put junk into their mouths—how can anything but junk come out again?"

"Garbage in, garbage out," Dominique said, smiling as the taxi entered the gray city where a raging mob was sacking a Häagen-Dazs shop, tarring and feathering its manager with his own faux-European product.

It was delightful to be back in civilization again.

WHEN SHE WAS ANNOUNCED, the director of the DGSE flung open his office door and regarded Dominique with stark eyes.

"You live?"

"I have conquered. The secret of *l'affaire Beasley* is mine."

"Enter, enter, Agent Arlequin."

When the door shut behind her, Dominique Parillaud said *"Pardonnez-moi,"* and lifted her skirt to reveal her lack of underwear.

"This is the device that has unmanned our citizens," she said.

"I have always thought thus," said the DGSE director, looking away, not out of modesty but because a white string hung in plain view. He was squeamish about such womanly things.

To his consternation, he heard the squishy sound of a tampon being extracted and tossed onto his desk. It landed with a distinct click.

"Please . . ." he said.

"No, I mean what is inside that."

"Will you not do the honors?" he asked delicately.

Frowning, Dominique Parillaud picked the tube apart with her nails, exposing an object slightly larger than a child's marble from the cotton packing.

Gingerly the DGSE director picked it up. He saw that it was of machined steel.

"I do not understand. . . ."

"Turn it around."

The DGSE director did and, when the other side looked at him with a frosty gray glare, he all but dropped it.

"An eye?"

"An electronic eye. I think it is—how do you say—*cybernetique.*"

"Hush! That is now a forbidden word."

"Sorry," said Dominique. "I took this from the skull of a man the world has believed dead for many years."

"Oui?"

"A man made of machine parts. A man of evil. The mastermind behind the wicked terror of the Blot."

"Who is this evil one?"

"He is Uncle Sam Beasley himself."

The director of the DGSE blinked rapidly.

"Impossible!" he exploded.

"I do not know how this can be, but it is true."

Rapidly she explained her encounter with the American agents who seemed more than human but who fell before the pulsing lights from the cybernetic eyeball the DGSE director now rolled around between his nimble fingers.

"How did you best him?" the DGSE director added.

"Judo. He is part machine and, while stronger than I, very clumsy. I used that strength against him. While he was flat on his back, I took a rock to his skull, and as he lay insensate, his good eye rolled up in his head, while that abomination you now hold pulsed at me angrily. So I took it."

The DGSE director winced. "Did you employ a . . . knife?"

"No. I merely unplugged it."

"Just like that? Poof!"

"Just like that. Poof. Then I fled with my prize."

Eyebrows jumping up in astonishment, the DGSE director assayed a very Gallic shrug. "This is remarkable work, Arlequin."

"The light that compels men to do its bidding exists within that orb."

"What could it be?"

"I believe it is a laser."

The director of the DGSE hissed violently. "Do not say that word! It is a junk word. It, too, has been banned."

"I forgot. It is so hard. My brain is starved for true nourishment. I have been in America so horribly long."

"I sympathize. Just yesterday I caught myself using the word *waterbed* when I should have said *aqualit*."

"It is the horrid influence of American movies, all of which should have long ago been banned."

"Except for Jairy's, of course."

"It goes without saying," Dominique said carelessly.

The DGSE director held the orb up to the light, inspecting it curiously. "I wonder how you make this function?"

"There is an aperture in the back."

"Perhaps it will respond to electric stimuli," said the DGSE director, ripping the cord from his desk telephone and braiding the wire until it was small enough to be inserted into the hole.

"Is this wise?" Dominique asked.

"I will close my eyes. You say you are immune to its effects?"

"Oui."

"What color was its pulse?"

"How should I know? All I see are grays."

"Of course, of course."

"But it was not pink. Pink has a very positive effect, making even uncouth Americans positive and gentle in manner. The color that it pulsed made them vomit."

"What kind of color makes a man vomit?"

"For all I know, gray," said Dominique, shrugging her slim shoulders.

The director winced. "I will definitely close my eyes." And he did as he guided the copper wire into the eyeball that looked back at him like a disk of dirty ice.

The copper wire scratched around inside for a few seconds before a tiny spit of a sound triggered a faint click. The gray pupil brightened, and the black pupil seemed to explode.

That was what the DGSE director saw even through his closed eyes. An explosion of intense green. It stabbed like a thousand piercing jade daggers into his retina.

Then his stomach exploded out his throat.

WHEN THE DGSE DIRECTOR awoke a day later, he moaned, *"Vert..."*

"Eh?" a voice murmured.

"It was green. Green is the hue of vomit."

"Actually it was more yellowish."

"It was green..." he groaned.

"I myself cleaned the vomit off your face before you were brought here, *mon Directeur.*"

"I meant the color that makes men vomit," he murmured.

The DGSE director snapped open his eyes. They roamed around the room. He saw Dominique Parillaud's face hovering over his, looking cool and the epitome of Gallic sangfroid.

"I am hospitalized?"

"Under a false name, of course. But your vital signs are well."

"Brief me, Arlequin."

"The electronic eye pulsed, you puked and fell forward into your dinner. Escargot, if I am not mistaken."

"It was very good. And the light was very green. Hideous to behold."

"It has been analyzed. It is a laser."

"Shh."

"I mean a *rayon de l'énergie*. DGSE scientists have gotten it to emit pink, green, red and yellow. They have remarkable effects upon the nervous system."

"You do not have to tell me that, Arlequin," said the DGSE director, sitting up. "I am famished."

"Would you like a Bosc pear?"

"Merci." The director reached out to take it, saw that it was green, and began heaving into his pillow.

"What is wrong?"

"It is green. Take it away. It is green."

"I cannot tarry. I have been ordered into the Blot."

"Why?"

"American agents have been seen in that area. It is suspected they are the same ones I encountered in the Uncouth Nation. I am the only agent who is immune to the evil eye."

"Where is the awful *orbe?*"

"That, I am forbidden to reveal on the grounds of French national security."

"Say no more," said the director of the DGSE, burying his head under his pillow to keep out the sight of the ugly green pear that sat on the bed stand like an evil Buddha whose plump stomach reminded him how distressed his own was.

22

The allosaurs charged out of the brush like a stampede of angry plucked chickens running on pumping drumsticks. They were a vivid Purdue yellow.

"Now I know what this place is," Remo said to Chiun.

"What?"

"It's based on that hit movie they did a couple years back, *Mesozoic Park.*"

"What is a Mesozoic?"

"One of the big dinosaur eras millions of years ago."

"I prefer my era," Chiun sniffed. "And these beasts appear hungry."

"They're machines. They won't eat us. Probably just tear off chunks of flesh with their teeth and spit them out."

"A good idea," said Chiun, reaching up into the chest of the immobile chocolate brown tyrannosaur. One clawlike hand sunk its curved nails into the slick plastic skin and wrenched out a clot of machinery and wiring.

The Master of Sinanju reared back and, without seeming to take aim, let fly.

The tangle made a low and controlled *zizzing* arc

and, when it struck the lead allosaur in the pack, removed its head.

The allosaur kept up its birdlike hopping run, but blinded, it stumbled into the path of two others.

The resulting allosaur collision was nothing if not spectacular. No doubt real allosaurs were not subject to blind collisions, but these were mere machines. When they got their pistoning legs tangled, they kept running anyway.

Allosaur drumsticks wrenched loose with metallic screams, and three of the animatronic dinosaurs pitched snout first into the AstroTurf, trailing wiring and sparks.

Even lying legless on the ground, they fought to crawl forward. One took a bite out of another, and within seconds they fell into a cannibalization frenzy.

"Nice," said Remo, setting a foot onto the T-rex tail and stamping. The tail went flat where he stamped. Remo reached down and harvested the thin end with a quick twist.

Spinning in place like a discus thrower, he got the tail moving smartly, then stopped suddenly. He let go. The tail kept going.

Like chain shot out of a cannon, it flew, striking two of the remaining allosaurs across their throats. The heads snapped back, and while the bodies kept moving, they didn't get far.

That left one allosaur, which came on like a chicken gone amok.

"You wanna do the honors or shall I?" Remo asked Chiun.

"I vanquished three. You only accounted for two of the lizards."

"Actually they're birds."

"Chicken-lizards, then."

As they talked, the surviving allosaur roared and lunged low.

Remo took point, waved in a friendly manner even as the allosaur emitted a scream and lunged with gaping jaws for his head.

Remo stepped off to one side and stuck out his foot, catching a pebbled shin.

The allosaur stumbled, pitched its entire length and went sliding on its belly, whereupon the Master of Sinanju caved the crown of its skull in with a sandaled foot.

"So much for the superiority of dinosaurs over man," said Remo.

They went in search of a way down into the bowels of Utilicanard.

DOMINIQUE PARILLAUD watched the awesome battle through field glasses from her hovering Gazelle helicopter.

"It is they," she told the pilot. "Set me down."

"The park is alive with dinosaurs."

"*Zut!* They are but machines designed for the amusement of children."

"They are deadly machines. They could devour my helicopter."

And Dominique unshipped her 9 mm MAS pistol and showed the pilot its hard, merciless snout. "You will land for the good of France and for the sanctity of your living brain."

The pilot wrestled the Gazelle to the ground, cursing the DGSE and the Americans by turns. He did not come all the way to this hellish place to be devoured by

American-made dinosaurs, which, as everyone knew, were the junkiest dinosaurs ever constructed by man.

ROD CHEATWOOD SAT with his jaw hanging almost to his lap. He was alone in the main computerized control room of Utilicanard. He had been alone since the forced evacuation.

When the gas bombs had first dropped, he had been the one to relay the word to Vanaheim general HQ.

And the word back from Vanahein was, "You are sanctioned to self-destruct. Initiate countdown."

"I'm not dying for my job," Rod had snapped over the satellite uplink.

"If you're captured, they'll prosecute you under a zillion French laws. You invented the hypercolor laser."

"I didn't order it installed all over this white elephant! I was just following orders."

"Tell it to a French magistrate."

"I will, because I don't plan on dying."

"This is disloyalty and punishable by termination."

"Duck you. I just declined to commit suicide for the company. I'm not exactly about to change my mind to hold on to my job."

"That is not what we mean by termination."

"Blowing myself and Euro Beasley to smithereens is not in my job description."

"We pay excellent survivor benefits."

Rod sighed. "My cats will be delighted. Now, let's get real, shall we? What's plan B?"

"Defend our hypercolor technology at all costs. It must not fall into unfriendly hands. We have loose ends and damage control to do back here. Once we're done, we'll extract you."

"How do I know you're not hanging me out to dry?"

"You could implicate the company."

"True..." Rod said slowly. "Tell you what, you fax me a release on the TV remote finder, and I'll stick it out as long as I can."

"Robber," growled the voice of Bob Beasley.

"Takes one to know one," said Rod, who knew he had the company by its ratlike tail.

The fax arrived within fifteen minutes, and after he had read the fine print, Rod called Vanaheim back.

"It's a deal. Don't keep me waiting too long, okay?"

For twenty-four hours it had not been bad. The French had given up after the first two assaults. Every time they showed signs of advancing, Rod activated the low-power pink periphery lights. That made them grin and purr and try to lick the pink air as if it were cotton candy. It also forced the French field commanders to rotate their troops every few hours.

Now, according to the radio they had the park under what was being called cultural quarantine. It was a perfect standoff.

Then the two Americans showed up and made mincemeat of the Mesozoic Park population.

It was patently impossible. It was true that as dinosaurs went, the animatronic constructs weren't exactly perfect. They tended to stumble a lot, and the complex software that controlled their movements got their commands fouled up sometimes. Either that or some joker had deliberately installed a cannibalize program.

Still, they were several tons of mobile metal monster. They should have flattened the skinny white guy and the old Asian. Flattened them dead.

Unfortunately it had been the other way around. And now the unstoppable duo was creeping through Mesozoic Park, and Rod Cheatwood had a pretty damn good idea where they were headed.

The access tunnel to Utilicanard.

As the first droplets of cold sweat began popping out on his forehead, Rod Cheatwood went to check the generator.

There was enough power for a fast hypercolor pulse, he found. Maybe two or three if it wasn't juice-sucking Optired or Supergreen.

"Okay, let's see if you guys can take it as well as you can dish it out."

And Rod Cheatwood reached for a joystick that sat above a brass plate reading Supersaurus.

"UH-OH," SAID REMO, looking up through the trees. "More company."

The helicopter looked like a prehistoric dragonfly skimming low over the treetops. It circled, whipped up the plastic ferns and settled in a clear patch by a stagnant pool of plastic algae.

Out stepped the French agent they knew as Avril Mai. She advanced with her nose in the air and her cold green gaze fixing them.

"I see someone has wiped ze vomit from your sorry faces," she said haughtily.

"Have a care how you address the Master of Sinanju, Frankish wench," warned Chiun.

Avril Mai stopped dead in her tracks. The ice in her eyes seemed to shatter in shock.

"You are not—I mean, do you claim ze title of Master of Sinanju?"

"Does the sun claim to shine?" Chiun retorted coldly.

Avril Mai lost her color. Her face became slack. She made a red O with her mouth, and it began contorting into ovals and hoops of uncertainty. "Wha-what is your mission here?" she demanded at last.

"Tell us yours and we might tell you ours," said Remo casually.

"Nevair!"

"Suit yourself. C'mon, Little Father, we have things to do."

They started off. Avril Mai hurried to catch up. She wore a formfitting taupe unitard and a black balaclava rolled up on her head like a knit cap.

"I am coming with you," she said.

Remo noticed the balaclava. "Lose your beret?"

"Parisians do not wear berets except in stupid *Américain* cartoons. My beret was a disguise."

"Tell that to the troops camped outside the gates," said Remo.

"Zat is different. Zey are military men."

"And what are you?" demanded Chiun. *"Deuxième?"*

Avril Mai compressed her red mouth.

"We're with the CIA," said Remo.

"Moudi! I knew it. You are a CIA agent and because you are an incompetent *Américain* you 'ave hired ze House of Sinanju to assist you."

"Looks like you got our number," said Remo.

Abruptly Avril Mai got in front of the Master of Sinanju and paced him walking backward.

"Whatever ze *Américains* are paying you, France will double it. I vow zis."

"Their gold is very soft."

"Our gold is softer."

"Their gold ships on time. French gold is slow."

"Slow?"

"Yes, the gold of the Frankish kings was exceedingly slow. By the time it arrived in my village, the babies were being drowned in the cold gray waters of the bay."

"I 'ave not heard zis story."

"Slow gold is the bane of all French lieges. It is the reason my House has not served the House of Bourbon in many centuries."

"I offer speedy gold, gold zat moves with ze speed of light."

"Hey, isn't it illegal to speak English now?" said Remo.

"No. It is illegal to speak junk *Américain*. I am speaking the king's English."

"English is a serviceable language," Chiun admitted.

"Thanks to Guilliame le Conqueror, who gave it a certain insouciant flavor," said Avril.

"Guilliame le Conqueror?" said Remo.

"She means William the Conqueror," explained Chiun.

"After ze Battle of Hastings, Britain became a vassal of the Normans, and our language elevated ze true, good English. It is much like ze way your junk tongue debased our pure French, except in reverse."

"Le crap," said Remo.

They were walking along a footpath that meandered through the plastic ferns and other trees. From time to time a branch-dwelling bird would track them with dark, glassy eyes.

"We are being watched," Avril said.

"Your name really Avril Mai?"

"Non."

"Betcha I can make you tell...."

"Impossible."

"Her name is Dominique Parillaud," said the Master of Sinanju, striding along with his hands tucked into the sleeves of his kimono.

"Moudi! How'd you come by zis intelligence?"

"Very simply," said Chiun.

Dominique Parillaud gasped. "I am Agent Arlequin in all but ze most confidential files of ze DGSE. *Merde!* I 'ave given myself away."

And the Master of Sinanju separated his sleeves. Out came one ivory hand, a slim black leather wallet tucked between two fingers.

"I picked your pocket," he said. "Your true name was inscribed on a card."

"My driver's license!" Dominique said, snatching the wallet away.

Remo laughed. "Some agent."

Then he stopped laughing. They all stopped.

Not far away the branches were squealing and rustling.

"I don't hear any thudding," said Remo.

"What is zis zudding?" Dominique said.

"I said I don't hear any—"

"Ze word! What does ze word *zudding* mean?"

"Look it up sometime," said Remo, who fixed the sound with his ears and decided to climb a tree. "Under *z*."

He got to the top in about the time it would have taken a monkey to do it.

"Do you see anyzing?" Dominique asked anxiously.

"I think we're okay. It's just an apatosaur."

"What is zat?"

"Brontosaurus," said Remo.

And the head burst into view. It was gray and blunt and decorated with dark, soulful eyes. It hovered in the ferns like a disembodied python. The rest of its body was lost in the greenery.

"Oh, one of zose," said Dominique, lowering her MAS automatic.

Chiun's voice quavered. "Remo, is it alive?"

"You know better than that," said Remo, pushing the nudging brontosaurus head back. He made it look easy. It kept trying to knock him off his perch, but he held on with one arm while using his free hand to reverse the thrust of the stubborn head.

"For if it were alive, I would lay claim to its bones," Chiun said.

"Why would you want ze bones?" Dominique asked.

"Because dragon bones, mixed in a proper potion, prolong the life span."

"I can see why you would wish such a thing. You are very old."

"Thank you," said Chiun. "But I wish to see a greater age."

The bronto changed tactics. It began butting the trunk below Remo's feet. The plastic bole shook and shook.

Chiun called up, "Remo, stop playing with that ugly machine."

"I'm not playing with it. It's playing with me."

And Remo kicked down at the top of the beast's skull.

THE MONITOR PICTURE jiggled wildly before Rod Cheatwood's startled eyes. Again and again.

"What does it take to nail this guy?" he complained. "That's a damn supersaurus. The biggest radio-animatronic construct on the face of the earth."

But try as he might, he couldn't knock the guy off the tree or the tree out from under the guy. Every time he sent the head forward on its long gray neck, the guy batted it aside as if it were a garden hose.

Rod couldn't make the supersaurus advance. It was one hundred fifty feet long and stood on four truncated legs the size of redwood stumps. They were fixed in place. Not even Beasley animatronic science could make such a behemoth mobile. Only the head and tail moved.

Pulling back the neck-motor control, Rod positioned the head so it was looking at everyone.

Then he uncapped the lemon-yellow protective cap and laid his thumb on the button labeled Ultrayellow.

"Here's looking at you...."

REMO WAS STARING at the brontosaurus's head, thinking how much it reminded him of an elephant in the color and texture of its hide, when the dark, soulful eyes began strobing.

The first pulse of light seemed to stab Remo in the stomach with the kick of a lightning bolt. The second was hotter, more yellow, and if it lasted only a nanosecond, it was a nanosecond too long.

"Run, Little Father!" he shouted, letting go of the tree trunk.

"I am running," Chiun cried, his voice twisted.

When he hit the ground, Remo ran, too.

"Why are you running?" Dominique called after them.

"Look into its eyes and you'll find out!"

Dominique turned. The eyes of the brontosaurus were pulsing every second and a half. The light was quite bright. Very white from her perspective. It was not green or pink. They would appear gray.

"What color is zis?" she cried.

"Yellow," shouted Remo, not looking back.

"Yellow?"

"Sickeningly yellow," Remo said.

"Disgustingly yellow," said Chiun.

"Interesting," said Dominique Parillaud, reaching into a slash pocket of her unitard.

ROD CHEATWOOD COULDN'T figure out what the problem with the French girl was. She was actually staring the supersaurus down while the other two were tearing ass as if their shoes were on fire.

Rod was eating power he couldn't afford even if it was pulsed bursts of low-draw Ultrayellow. He was going to have to get serious.

One eye on the screen, he snaked his finger under the blue protect plate marked Contrablue while the French woman facing down the animatronic supersaurus lifted what looked like a tear-gas pen in both hands and aimed it upward.

When he had the button, Rod faced the screen and said, "This is going to hurt you a heck of a lot more than it hurts me."

Then the pen point flashed, the screen turned Supergreen and Rod Cheatwood was upchucking all over his console, which went bang when his unconscious forehead slammed into it.

23

In his office at Folcroft Sanitarium, Harold W. Smith was trying to pull the puzzle pieces together.

He thought he understood the objective in Virginia. The Sam Beasley Corporation, desperate to establish a new American theme park to offset the massive public-relations and financial losses of Euro Beasley, had set the stage for a public-relations coup by triggering a low-risk but high-impact media event significant enough to dominate the headlines but sufficiently isolated that it could be quelled before it raged out of control.

It had worked. Typically the press had run with the story, blowing it up bigger than it was. Even though the rebellion had been almost entirely limited to reenactors and civilians, it was being called by virtually every media personality the Second American Civil War.

Video footage of the pink Beasley-character balloons descending on the battlefield had been telecast nationwide. It was a propaganda bonanza for the Sam Beasley Corporation. They had already announced a multimedia product stream that included a TV miniseries, cartoons, comic books and a complete line of action toys dominated by America's latest overnight sensation, Colonel Dixie.

The participants in the Third Battle of the Crater were being signed up by every newspaper, magazine and TV talk show in the nation. Renewed interest in the Civil War and the steady stream of tourists already pouring into Petersburg had turned the tide of Virginia public opinion—already divided—toward allowing Beasley U.S.A. to go forward.

The Sam Beasley Corporation appeared to have won that campaign.

The Euro Beasley crisis was another matter. There was no question in Harold Smith's mind that Euro Beasley was the flashpoint for what the media was already calling the Great Franco-American Conflict.

But why? Why would the French air force bomb a theme park? Especially one that was technically owned by such institutions as Banc Frontenac and Credit Hollandaise?

Nothing was coming out of the corridors of the French government.

Nothing was coming out of the PR machinery of the Sam Beasley Corporation, either. After the first flush of victory in Petersburg, it had fallen silent.

Mickey Weisinger had dropped out of sight, as had Bob Beasley.

The whereabouts of Sam Beasley himself would be impossible to track. He had no more official existence than Remo Williams, whom the world also believed dead.

That was not true of the other Beasley officials, however.

Smith had to find them. He began calling up the airline passenger-reservations networks, beginning with Apollo. Punching in the names of Robert Beasley and Mickey Weisinger, he drew a blank at Continental Airlines.

Switching to Paz, Smith input both names. If they were moving by air, their names would pop up, and Harold Smith would find them.

The trouble was, their names were *not* popping up. And the airlines reservation system was overloaded with French nationals fleeing the United States and U.S. citizens evacuating an increasingly hostile France.

Determined to locate them, Harold Smith switched to the credit-card data banks. Beasley executives all had use of company credit cards. If they rented cars, purchased gasoline, ate in roadside restaurants and made any other purchases along their route, their names would surface and their courses could be plotted simply by electronically connecting the dots.

All Harold Smith had to do was locate enough dots.

24

Remo Williams caught up to the Master of Sinanju, who was tearing through the plasticky stink of Parc Mésozoïque. Side by side they zipped through ferns that flew apart at a touch of their scissorslike fingers.

"You scared?" Remo asked Chiun.

"A Master of Sinanju does not acknowledge fear."

"If he did, would you be as scared as I am right now?"

"You are a Master of Sinanju. You are not afraid, either."

"Then why are we running like two scared rabbits?"

"Do not underestimate the rabbit. In my village it is considered wise beyond all other creatures."

"If you're a rabbit, how come you look like a scared little rabbit, not a wise rabbit?"

"A wise rabbit knows when to embrace fear," Chiun snapped.

Remo started to look over his shoulder, then remembered how spine-chilling yellow the brontosaurus's eyes had been.

"How come we're scared of that yellow light here, and we weren't back at the Crater?"

"At the Crater we did not look directly into the awful eyes of the gray dragon."

"Good point, we only saw the back-glow, which wasn't so bad."

"This is no back-glow now," said Chiun.

"You want to stop and take a chance?"

"No."

"One of us should."

"I am not afraid, so you should."

"If you aren't afraid and I don't mind admitting that I am, why don't *you* stop?"

"Because I have conquered my fear, and you have yet to conquer yours. Therefore, you need to test your mettle against your fears."

"Nice try, Little Father. But no sale."

Eventually they ran out of park. The other side of the high bamboo stockade fence came rushing up.

"You stopping?" asked Remo.

"No."

"Then I'm not stopping, either."

They hit the wall in unison. Bamboo splinters flew in jagged chunks as they blew through the stockade.

They came to a halt only when they reached a lagoon that bore a sign saying *Vingt Mille Lieues Sous Les Mers De Jules Verne,* which Remo figured translated as Jules Verne's Twenty Thousand Leagues Under the Sea, but only because he recognized the submarine from the movie.

At the quietly lapping edge of the lagoon, they stopped and drank in the tranquil color of the water.

"Boy," said Remo, "that water is sure blue."

"Exceedingly blue," Chiun agreed.

"I love blue. Always have."

"It is a good color, perhaps not as good as gold, but good."

"I can never look at gold with the same eyes again. Too yellow for my tastes."

"Yellow is not gold, nor gold yellow."

"Gold is still too yellow for me. But man, I just love looking at this blue."

And as they stared deep into the placid, soul-calming blue waters, the deep blue turned indigo.

"Oh, shit."

"What is it, Remo?"

"Remember that soldier in the Crater? The one who saw a blue color when everyone else saw yellow?"

"Yes."

"I think that blue is catching up to me."

"I see it, too. It is like a burning in my eyes, except it burns deep blue and not a correct burning color."

"Damn," said Remo. "I feel awful."

"I, too, feel unhappy."

"Well, at least it's not yellow."

"It is not much of a blessing, but it is a blessing nonetheless," agreed the Master of Sinanju.

"Maybe if we blink up a storm, the blue will go away."

"It is worth a try."

When they had blinked the deep blue from their burned retinas, Remo and Chiun mustered up the courage to turn and face Parc Mésozoïque.

The stockade fence still held.

Remo licked his dry lips to wet them. "You up for going back in?" he asked.

"It is our duty."

"Then I guess we gotta, although between you and me, I feel more like going back on strike."

"It is a worthy idea. Worthy of Jool Phairne."

"Who?"

Chiun gestured over his shoulder. "That brilliant writer whose name adorns that sign."

"You means Jules Verne?"

"That is not how you pronounce it."

"You mean Jules Verne is pronounced 'Jool Phairne'?"

"Yes."

"No wonder these people keep getting conquered."

"It is part of their problem. From the Romans and Vikings to the Prussians and Germans, they have fallen before invader after invader. Perhaps it has given them an inferiority context."

"It's 'complex.' And you wouldn't know it to talk to a Frenchman. Or woman."

As they approached Parc Mésozoïque, the whine of a rotor disturbed the stillness of the park. A moment later a small French army helicopter lifted, canted west and droned out of sight.

"Damn, there goes that damn April May!"

They reached the spot where the helicopter had lifted off. There was no sign of anyone or anything.

Then the Master of Sinanju noticed the drag marks in the dirt at their feet.

"Behold, Remo. A man was dragged to the helicopter."

"Yeah. And these small footprints on either side belong to Dominique. She must have dragged someone away. The question is who?"

"Let us discover that."

They followed the footprint-decorated drag marks to an upthrust protuberance on the park grounds. It was a small volcano, as volcanoes go. Probably twenty feet high. The sides were molded of some kind of streaked red clay. When they climbed it, the skin crumbled under their feet, setting bits of clay rolling and bouncing down to the base.

At the lip of the crater, they looked down and saw a ladder disappearing into a very black hole.

"Looks like the back way in," muttered Remo.

"Come," said Chiun, swinging around so he could take hold of the ladder's rungs.

They climbed down into the darkness, which proved to be a flat plug of glassy obsidian.

"Dead end," said Remo.

The Master of Sinanju said nothing as he moved about the inner walls of the cone. It was rough but not terribly irregular. Except for a single knob of obsidian. Chiun took hold of it, pushing and pulling it experimentally until, with a jolt, the obsidian plug dropped two inches, then continued dropping with the smoothness of an elevator.

Black-and-yellow safety stripes appeared on the walls as Remo and Chiun rode past.

"How do we know this isn't a trap?" Remo asked.

"How could anyone trap a Master of Sinanju and his trusty badger?"

"That's 'gofer.'"

"Consider it a promotion to a higher order of animal," Chiun said magnanimously.

At the bottom of the cone, they found themselves standing before one end of a concrete tunnel with a great black mouse-head silhouette painted onto the floor.

Then they smelled a smell they knew very, very well.

"Death," said Chiun.

"A lot of death," said Remo.

There were a lot of dead, they discovered as they crept along the concrete tunnels and corridors of the French Utilicanard. People lying dead at their desks, in their dormlike rooms, even lying fallen over their maintenance brooms.

And every one of them clutched an amber lollipop shaped like the head of Mongo Mouse and smelling of almonds.

"Dead about two days," said Remo, touching a cool fallen body.

The dead all wore the jumpsuits they associated with Utiliduck workers except these weren't white as they were in the States but a very chic peach.

"Looks like a mass suicide," Remo said, straightening up. "When the French bombs started to hit, they must have decided to take the hard way out rather than risk capture."

"This is very sinister. Could à color have done this?"

"I dunno. In fact, I don't get this color stuff. How can colors affect us this way?"

"Colors are very powerful. The ancient Egyptians knew this. Pharaoh slept in a red room because it helped him to sleep. And when he died, he was entombed in a room of gold because this helped his body to retain its royalty throughout eternity. In my village it is well-known that scarlet wards off evil demons."

"I don't buy that superstitious bulldooky. Color is color. I don't even have a favorite color."

"Not even pink?"

"Well, maybe pink. Pink is good."

"Pink is exceedingly good."

And they both found themselves smiling at the thought of the color pink.

As they walked along, a sour smell assailed their sensitive nostrils. They followed it.

"Fresh," said Remo.

It was, they discovered when they entered a control room marked in French, *Defense D'Entrer.*

It was the master control room. There was no mistaking that. There were grids of video monitors showing every approach and attraction in the park. Control consoles literally ringed the room.

And on the main console was a still-dribbling splash of fresh vomit.

"Someone did not take their poison," said Chiun, looking about the empty room.

"No, but someone took him."

"I detect the faint perfume of the French woman."

"Yeah. Great. Now we're the only ones here with the entire French army laying siege outside. Time to call Smitty."

Remo picked up a satellite telephone and tried to dial Harold Smith in America. The trouble was Remo didn't know the country code for U.S.A. And when he finally got an operator speaking French, she hung up on him the minute he spoke two words, one of them "Please."

Sighing, Remo tossed the handset to the Master of Sinanju. "Just get me past the language barrier."

When Harold Smith came on the line, Chiun tossed the handset back to Remo.

"Smitty. We're not doing well here."

"One moment, Remo," said Smith absently. "This is very strange."

"What is?"

"I have unusual activity on Beasley company credit cards."

"Well, I can guarantee you the big spenders aren't over here in Euro Beasley."

"What makes you say that?"

"Because Chiun and I just penetrated their lower regions, and they're all dead."

"Dead. How dead? I mean, how long dead?"

"A day or two. They took poison."

"Cyanide," hissed Chiun.

"Chiun says cyanide. Looks like Jonestown, except with lollipops."

"Remo, this is very suggestive. Obviously Euro Beasley is not what it seems. It is much more than a theme park."

"So far, every Beasley theme park has been more than a theme park. But we missed one guy."

"You have a prisoner?"

"No, French Intelligence does. For all our troubles, we got yellowed."

"Remo, I think you are breaking up. Did you say yellow?"

"Yeah. The yellow light got us. I'll never look at a canary the same way again. Chiun and I took off for the hills when it hit."

"It is a wise rabbit which knows when to employ the ancient and honorable strategy of retreat," Chiun called out.

"By the time we got back," Remo continued, "that French agent had taken off with the one survivor. Whatever he knows, the French will have it by tomorrow is my guess."

Smith was silent a moment. "This is twice you have encountered mysterious colored lights."

"No," said Remo, "this is twice Chiun and I have been run over by these colored lights. I thought green was bad, but it was over quick. I never want to be yellowed again."

"Yet you enjoyed the pink light."

"Oh, yeah, that," said Remo, breaking into a pleasant smile at the memory. "I'd gladly walk through a football field lit by greens and yellows if there's some pink on the other side."

"Remo, listen carefully. These lights must represent some new technology the Beasley people have discovered. Look around for some sign of controls."

"Controls?"

"Yes, someone had to be controlling the yellow light."

"Hey, Chiun, check around the room. Smitty wants—"

"I have found many buttons with the names of strange colors on them," Chiun announced.

"Smitty, we found it."

"*I* have found it," Chiun said loudly.

"Remo, I am unable to locate any Beasley corporate officers. That means that man is our only lead. I want you to find him and extract from him what he knows. Only by determining the reason the French have seen fit to quarantine Euro Beasley can we get to the root of this conflict."

"Gotcha. How're things on the home front?"

"The Senate is debating a resolution outlawing the teaching of French in our major universities."

"That has my vote."

"The Modern Language Association has issued a strong statement condemning the French ministry of culture."

"You want my opinion, the only culture the French have belongs in a petri dish."

"They are calling for the expunging of all borrowed French words from American dictionaries. And the Academie Français has retaliated by demanding their French words back. They are also renaming Parisian streets named after Americans."

"How many of those can there be?"

"There are the Avenue du General Eisenhower, Avenue du Franklin Delano Roosevelt and Rue Lincoln, to name just three. Or were," Smith added.

"This is ridiculous," said Remo.

"This is a cultural war. But it threatens to escalate into the real thing. Remo, find that Beasley employee and get him out of French hands at all costs. No doubt he knows the secret behind this colored-light technology. I have a problem to solve."

"What problem?"

"Why the Beasley Corporation is sending scores of its employees to London."

"Good luck," said Remo, hanging up.

He turned just in time to see the Master of Sinanju bring a tiny ivory fist into contact with one of the control panels.

It shattered. Buttons flew upward to ricochet off the ceiling, and the smell of burning insulation curled up in smoky tentacles.

"What now?" asked Remo.

And when Chiun pointed to a now-broken bank of shielded buttons marked with names like Supergreen and Hotpink, Remo said, "Good job."

25

When he woke up, Rod Cheatwood knew he was in deep trouble.

The last thing he remembered was the green light coming back at his console video screen. It was Supergreen. No one had ever tried to project hypercolor by video. Technically it should not have worked. But it did. Rod had upchucked and blacked out. Splat.

When he woke up, he was on a hard bunk in a windowless concrete cell. The walls were nice, though. Teal. Very chic. Worrisomely chic, inasmuch as Rod had no idea where he was or who had him. But he did have his suspicions.

Rod glanced around the cell. There was a stainless-steel toilet, washbowl and a third plumbing fixture he realized with a sickening sensation was a bidet.

"I am definitely in deep," he muttered.

When they came for him, they wore black balaclavas pulled over their heads with only their eyes and mouths showing. They conducted him to a featureless room and sat him down on a hard wooden stool.

Something that looked like a dessert cart was wheeled up, but when he looked into the tray, Rod saw implements that made his empty stomach quail.

"You don't have to torture me," he said weakly.

"Parlez-vous français?"

Rod had picked up a little French during his stay, but only enough to get by. This was no time to stumble over shades of meaning. "No, I speak only English."

The eyes behind the balaclavas winced. They began whispering among themselves. Rod caught the gist of it. They were asking how they could be expected to interrogate an American who did not speak French if they faced a six-month jail sentence for speaking American. No one wanted to go to jail for six months. Not even in the service of his beloved country.

After conferring by telephone, the interrogators obtained some kind of a special dispensation from the ministry of culture and they brought out the crude electronic device resembling a toy railroad transformer with two wires and steely alligator clips at each end.

Rod instantly crossed his legs, thinking, *They're out to fry my balls.*

"I'll tell you anything you want!" he bleated.

"Tell us who is behind this outrage against our country."

"Sam Beasley."

"He is dead."

"I mean the Sam Beasley Corporation."

"Why did you not commit suicide like the others? Why are you so important?"

"I'm not important. Not that important."

"But you must be. You did not consume your suicide candy."

"What are you, nuts? I'm not dying for the fucking Sam Beasley Corporation. You have any idea how they treat their employees?"

"So many others did...."

"Well, I don't think they got screwed quite the way I did."

"How did you get screwed?" one interrogator asked, wincing at the ugliness of the junk word.

"I don't think I can tell you that," Rod said, thinking if he spilled the beans on the TV-remote finder, the French would leap to patent it. Never mind standing him in front of a firing squad for coming up with the hypercolor laser in the first place.

"Trade secret," he said.

That was when one of them approached with the alligator clips extended in each hand, looking like he intended to jump-start a Tonka truck.

"No, not my balls. Anything but my balls."

When he felt the clips dig into his earlobes with their serrated steel teeth, Rod Cheatwood almost laughed with relief.

A voice said, "Last chance to talk freely."

And then someone spun a crank.

The pain was so severe Rod Cheatwood saw sparks dance behind his clutched-tight eyelids and he began wishing the electric current would find another part—any part—of his body. Even his sensitive testicles.

THE TRANSCRIPT of the interrogation of Rod Cheatwood was faxed to French Minister of Culture Maurice Tourette within ten minutes of being transcribed.

He read it with quick sweeps of his eyes, a blue pencil poised over the document that was stamped *Secret-d'état*.

Finding a junk word, he crossed it out and inserted the correct form. Then he finished his perusal.

When Tourette was at last done, he called the president of France.

"Allô?"

"I have just read the transcript of the Beasley prisoner interrogation," he said.

"How can this be?" the president sputtered. "I myself have not yet received my fax copy."

"Please. Do not say 'fax.' It is an outlaw word."

"I will say what I please. I am *le Président.*"

"And I am the minister of culture. Do you wish to land in jail for six months?"

"What have you learned?" said the president wearily.

"They have developed a hypnotic *rayon de l'énergie* which bends those exposed to it to their will."

"Rayon de l'énergie. What is a *rayon de l'énergie?"*

"It is the word that has replaced *l-a-s-e-r,*" said the culture minister, spelling the junk word because he knew that he, too, could technically land in jail merely for enunciating it.

"I fail to grasp how a laser—I mean *rayon de l'énergie*—could hypnotize. Do they not cut things?"

"Oui. But this *rayon de l'énergie* uses tinted light. Pink pacifies. Red boils the blood—"

"Literally?"

"Non. Figuratively. Yellow makes the heart quail in fear, and green insults the brain and stomach so that one vomits and loses one's wits."

"What about blue?"

"Blue?"

"It is my favorite color. What does blue do?"

"Blue," said the culture minister, "depresses."

"Depresses? I have always believed that blue soothed. The sky is blue, *non?* And the oceans. They are very soothing to look upon."

"True. But you are forgetting that when you are sad, you feel blue. Forlorn music is called *le blues.*"

"Is that not a forbidden word?" the president asked pointedly.

"*Les bleus,* then," the culture minister said, adding it to his working copy of his dictionary of official terms.

"Proceed," said the president of France in a purring tone.

"They have installed pink lights all over that Blot. It creates a sense of well-being and receptivity. Like cotton candy for the eyes and the brain."

"It is no wonder that our poor citizens flock to the Blot."

"This is an indefensible provocation, an act of cultural imperialism. They have subverted our people, our culture, our way of life. What do you intend to do about it?"

"I must evaluate this fully."

"France cries out for strong action. Retaliation in kind."

"Do you propose that I have built a Parc Asterix on American soil and install pink *rayon de l'énergie* lights everywhere?"

"I meant military retaliation."

"I am not yet convinced this is the doing of Washington, but the lawless depredations of a private company. I will not be stampeded into—"

"'Stampeded' is a junk word. I do not wish to report this conversation to the High Committee for the Defense and Expansion of the French Language."

Unseen by the minister of culture, the French president rolled his eyes ceilingward. "What do you propose?" he asked through politely clenched teeth.

"We gave them the Statue of Liberty. Let us demand it back."

"Absurd!"

"Then let us destroy it."

"I understand that there are restive elements over there which have called for Liberty to be torn down and sold for scrap."

"That would be an act of war!" Maurice Tourette cried. "If they dare to harm Liberty, we should nuke them flat. Stamp out their junk culture and its uncouth language at one blow."

"I will have to speak with the minister of defense."

"He is on my side," Tourette said quickly.

"Have you spoken with him on this matter?"

"Not yet. But I know he is on my side. If you wish to ensure your political future," the culture minister said, "you should be on my side, as well."

"I will think about it," said the president of France, hanging up.

Then the expected fax entered the room, attached to the hand of an aide, and the president of France leaned back to read it over.

It was good, he considered, that the U.S. President was so indecisive. Between that and his own leisurely approach to this crisis, perhaps a solution would present itself before the minister of culture prodded both sides into something infinitely more dangerous than a war of words over words.

26

Harold Smith knew he was onto something when a computer check of the Beasley credit-card airline-flights purchases started concentrating in three states, Florida, California and Louisiana.

The first two he understood. Beasley employees. But there was no Beasley theme park in Louisiana. No corporate office, and no discernible connection to the Sam Beasley Corporation.

They were all going to London. Why were they going to London? It was not to catch connecting flights to Paris and thus Euro Beasley, Smith deduced.

First, no record of a massive block purchase of such connecting flights was showing up in any of the airline-reservations nets.

Secondly American citizens were being pointedly kept out of France as "undesirable aliens."

In fact, as Smith worked his keyboard, a bulletin told of the American ambassador to France being declared persona non grata and sent home for "conduct incompatible with his station."

This was diplomatic jargon used to describe illegal espionage activity. It was absurd. The U.S. ambassador had nothing to do with this matter—whatever it was.

Smith returned to his task.

Beasley employees were evacuating to France with the speed and single-minded fervor of lemmings seeking the water. Why?

"They can't be going to London," he murmured. "That would make no sense."

Then the truth struck Smith with the force of a blow.

Americans were persona non grata in France. But British citizens were still welcome—or as welcome as the French made any non-French-speaking people feel welcome.

Smith brought up a detailed map of the British Isles. He shrank it so the English Channel came into view, along with the northern coast of France.

Gatwick to de Gaulle or Orly was a matter of an hour's flying time. But any American attempting to land at either airport would certainly be intercepted by French customs. Even in overwhelming numbers, they could not get very far.

Smith considered the channel. Taking a ferry or landing craft was a possibility. But a sea invasion, even a small one, had a limited operational viability.

Frowning, he tapped a key that converted all English words and place-names to French in the wink of an eye.

The channel became La Manche, which was French for "the sleeve," and was the name the French had given what the rest of the world called the English Channel. There was nothing else provocative or helpful.

Smith was about to log off when his gaze alighted on an unfamiliar landmark that lay across the channel.

It was a red line.

And it had a label: Le Transmanche.

His weary gray eyes froze. Was there something he had missed before? Smith tapped the key that restored the English tags.

And on the map where Le Transmanche had been, appeared a new word. A word Smith instantly recognized. A word that made the skin prickle and crawl along the bumps of his spine.

The word was Chunnel.

BECAUSE THEY WORE no uniforms, they were not considered an army. An army comes wearing uniforms, bearing arms and marching to the threatening roll of drums.

The combined California Summer Vacation Musketeers, Florida Sunshine Guerrillas and Louisiana Costume Zouaves arrived in London, England, carrying American passports, their uniforms discreetly tucked away in their luggage.

And so they were considered tourists not soldiers.

When they showed up, in groups of two and three at London's Waterloo International railway station, they were carrying forged Canadian passports. They boarded the high-speed Eurostar trains as French-Canadian tourists and kept to themselves as the train rattled over the old track to Folkestone at a decorous eighty miles per hour because the brand of Louisiana Creole they spoke wouldn't exactly cut it in Paris.

Upon entering the special rapid track of the English Channel Tunnel they sped up to 186 miles per hour.

The combined forces kept their tongues still, although their hearts lifted with each mile that raced by.

French customs could be forgiven for not sounding the alarm. Who would expect an invasion force arriving by Le Transmanche, as the French called the Chunnel? It was the British who for centuries had resisted the link to Europe. It was they who feared invasion from the Continent, not the other way around.

Their passports were in order, their uniforms were neatly folded, blue and gray cottons nestled deep under their very British tweeds and linens.

And by the time they left Coquelles Terminal in Calais, bound for Paris, there was no stopping them.

For they bore no weapons recognizable as such.

And while it was unusual to bring personal universal TV remote-control units into a foreign country, it was not illegal.

AT FIRST Marc Moise welcomed the promotion to task force group leader.

"You will lead the Louisiana Costume Zouaves," he was told by no less than Bob Beasley himself. They were in a conference room in Sam Beasley World's underground Utiliduck, in Florida.

"Lead them where?"

And when Bob Beasley told him that the objective was to retake Euro Beasley to keep special technology out of French hands, Marc Moise swallowed very, very hard and said, "That sounds dangerous."

"It's for the good of the company."

"I understand that," said Marc hesitantly. "But—"

Then Bob Beasley fixed him with his crinkled father-figure eyes and whispered, "Uncle Sam asked for you by name. He said, 'I want Moose to spearhead this operation.' "

"It's Moise, sir."

"Eh?"

"Moise. Not Moose. It's French."

"That's another thing Uncle Sam told me. You speak the language and look just like one of those frogs. So what do you say? Will you come through for your Uncle Sam in his hour of need?"

Marc Moise felt a strange twinge deep in his stomach. He revered Uncle Sam. Had since he was knee-high to a muskrat. But the Uncle Sam he loved and the creature he had found regarding him with baleful gaze in the mobile communications van outside Petersburg, Virginia, were utterly different.

One was an avuncular charmer with a knowing twinkle in his eye who had occupied a special place in Marc's heart, not to mention his childhood TV.

The other was a creature whose left eye began pulsing a livid lizard green causing Marc to lose his lunch and his consciousness, awakening a day later in a Beasley infirmary.

In the end, it was fear not reverence that decided Marc Moise.

"I'll do it," he said.

Bob Beasley clapped him on the back and chuckled. "I knew you were our man, Moose."

"That's Moise, sir."

And as he was handed his plane tickets, Marc Moise asked, "You didn't mention what kind of a raise is involved in this."

"Consider your promotion as a raise," Bob Beasley said coldly. "All the others have."

BY THE TIME he got to London, Marc Moise was peeved. While speeding through the Chunnel, peeve had ignited a low, smoldering anger. And when the sleek Eurostar train pulled into Paris's Gare du Nord train station, three hours after leaving London, Marc was ready to kill.

But by that time he realized he was an enemy agent in a hostile nation with a dangerous mission to complete, and he swallowed his rage against his employer.

Besides, he had to keep these crazy Cajuns in line.

27

Dominique Parillaud felt proud. Remy Renard, director of the DGSE, had convened a high-level meeting of the directorate's Planning, Forecasting and Evaluation Group and had invited her.

"We would appreciate your input," he had said, then catching himself, corrected, "Your thoughts, Agent Arlequin."

"But of course."

Now in the somber room whose high windows were heavily curtained to keep out the incessant clangor of Parisian traffic and to foil observers, they sat about the long oak table on which the detached eye of Uncle Sam Beasley lay. It was still attached to the penlike activator DGSE technicians had hastily devised to enable it into a weapon.

"The heart of the device is a prism," a DGSE technician was saying. "As you know, white light passing through a prism has the property of scattering into rainbow hues. This orb emits light according to *cybernetique* command impulses, delivering the desired supercolor."

"Excellent summary," said the DGSE chief. "Now, of what use can this tool be to French national security?"

"Our agents, equipped with such devices, would be impossible to foil in the field," said Lamont Montgrande, head of the political police known as the Renseignements Généraux, who had been invited as a courtesy.

"Good, good, but there is the risk of losing the technology to an adversary nation."

"If this is American technology, as we suspect, it is as good as lost," said Fabian Rocard, the chief of Direction de la Surveillance du Territoire. "Our industrial-espionage bureau has been highly successful in acquiring American technologies, often, as you know, by procedures as simple as rooting in the unsecured garbage of aerospace companies."

"Still, if lost to others, it will be turned against our advantage," Renard said. "More thoughts, please."

There were several moments of quiet rumination as a scrumptious port wine, cheese and crackers made the rounds of the long table.

At length the minister of the interior and nominal overseer of the French Intelligence community spoke up. "Imagine this orb magnified greatly."

The table of Intelligence chiefs focused on the orb. In their minds it grew to great size. It was not difficult to envision. They understood that this object loomed very large in their nation's future.

"Now, further imagine this orb in orbit."

"In orbit?"

"*Oui.* In orbit circling the globe, the eye of France."

"A spy satellite?"

"No, the fearsome protective eye of France. Imagine the Germans nibbling away at our borders again."

This was not very hard to imagine, either.

"Then imagine as they marshal their foes to storm or invade, an irresistible pink radiance spilling down from the heavens to bathe them in its quelling radiations."

This vision was much more difficult to envision, but they put their concentration into it. Scowls came, as did facial contortions.

Eventually they saw the beauty of it.

"Or should the British become even more of a nuisance than they are already, bathe them in the awful green that causes the stomach to rebel."

"Their stomachs should already be in rebellion, with the unpalatable foods that they devour."

A combined roar of laughter floated toward the high ceiling.

It was the lowly Dominique Parillaud who had the best idea of all, however.

"Imagine," she said in a soft, conspiratorial voice, "bathing the U.S. with the yellow radiation that brings fear and consternation. They will never vex us again."

"We could keep them in thrall indefinitely," Remy crowed.

"Unless, of course, we require liberating again," said the minister of the interior. "Then we would naturally release them. Briefly. Until they have succored us once again with their industrial might and brave but foolhardy soldiers."

"Provisions, of course, will have to be made to scrupulously avoid infecting the habitation of Jairy, of course."

"Of course. This goes without saying."

"When is the next Ariane launch?" asked Remy Renard.

"Next week. A communications satellite, I believe it is."

"It is possible to substitute this?"

"*Non.* A larger package must be created using this technology."

"If we have the technology, how long can it take to recreate this larger package?"

No one knew, but everyone promised to get to work on the problem. For all understood they held a power, a force greater than the atomic bomb itself. One could not nuke another nation without incurring certain lamentable unpleasantries in return. Criticisms. Condemnations. Even unsympathetic retaliations.

But if the afflicted nation had no inkling that their distress was caused by colors emanating from outer space, who could criticize France?

As the meeting broke up, Dominique Parillaud decided to look in on the Beasley spy whom she had interrogated not an hour before.

The man had been asking for a television, which had been provided to him. Dominique was curious. What would a man in the difficult position of captured industrial spy want with a television set? Was there something he expected to see on it?

THE TAXI DRIVER a mile outside the Euro Beasley RER train stop didn't hear the rear doors open as he waited, drinking coffee, for a fare.

He barely heard them close. He should have felt the shifting of his rear springs because when he glanced up into his rear mirror, two men were sitting in back.

"*Mon Dieu!*"

"Take us to Paris," said the taller of the two, an obvious and unspeakable Anglo-American type. If not because of his gauche dress, certainly because of his painful pronunciation of the elegant name of Paris.

Pierre Perruche had been hauling unspeakable Americans and their unspeakable accents around Paris all his life. Many times he yearned to throw them bodily from his car when they announced their destinations with impossible words, but there were considerations other than his deep-seated desires. Namely income and the risk to tourism, which also impacted upon his income.

But with all American tourists ejected from France and their hideous accents also outlawed, Pierre Perruche saw no need to hold back any longer.

"Out!" he shouted.

"Look, we don't have time to argue. Just take us to Paris."

"It is pronounced 'Par-ee!' Out, impossible ones!"

Then the other man, the old Asian, spoke up. In perfect French that broke the heart and made Pierre Perruche, a lifelong Parisian, realize that his own speech was shamefully deficient, the Asian instructed him to go climb a tree.

"Va te faire pendre ailleurs!" he said haughtily.

And such was his pronunciation that Pierre relented. "You may stay," he said, tears starting. "The other, he must go. Now!"

What happened next was not entirely clear to Pierre Perruche, although he lived through the entire ordeal.

A steely hand took him by the back of his neck and impelled him to drive to Paris.

Pierre Perruche had no volition other than that which he received from the hateful American. He drove. When his head was turned like a horse, like a horse he drove obediently in that direction. He felt very much like a dumb beast.

From the back the old Asian spoke commands. Not to Pierre, but to the other. The other then compelled Pierre to drive that way or this way.

It was not the most efficient system but it worked quite smoothly, especially after they pulled onto the Ring Road and into Parisian traffic at its most frightful.

Pierre Perruche was astonished to find himself driving more skillfully than ever before in his life.

It was a strange feeling made ever stranger when he was forced to drive past DGSE headquarters on Boulevard Mortier.

There was no mistaking DGSE HQ. A hodgepodge compound of stone-and-brick buildings, it was isolated by a brown stone wall. A weathered sign prohibiting filming or the taking of photographs was the only outward indication of its sensitive nature. Its roof-mounted surveillance cameras followed every passing car, jogger and pigeon that chanced by its tracking lenses.

"That it?" asked the American of his Oriental companion.

"Yes."

And a thumb slipping up to squeeze one jaw muscle somehow caused Pierre's foot to depress the brake with the correct pressure to bring the cab to a smooth stop.

"The fare is—" he started to say.

"What fare? I did all the driving."

And before Pierre could protest, the American squeezed all awareness from his brain.

THE ROOF CAMERAS tracked them as they approached the DGSE HQ.

"Looks easy enough to crack," said Remo. "What say to climbing to the roof and dropping through the ceiling?"

Chiun regarded the ten-foot-high wall whose top was toothy with embedded bayonets to foil vaulters, and said, "Too obvious."

"I don't see a better way," said Remo.

"We will enter by the front door."

"Why is that not obvious?"

"Because they do not expect us."

Remo followed the Master of Sinanju up to a metallic beige door set in the wall. There was no knob, only an electric button.

Chiun pressed this, the door started to open and the Master of Sinanju bustled through and into the teeth of a DGSE security team.

One said, *"Arrêtez!"*

Remo asked, *"Parlez-vous franglais?"*

This was not well received, and when the Master of Sinanju showed every sign of breezing through the guards with a blithe disregard for decorum, one guard yanked up his MAT submachine gun and said, *"Allez-y! Dites-le!"*

Remo didn't need to draw upon his three years of French I to know the guard had just ordered his comrades to open fire.

He picked his target and started in, confident that the Master of Sinanju had already chosen his.

Chiun had. He pivoted in place and lifted one sandaled foot to the height of his own head.

It seemed only to brush two sets of jaws, but the jaws came off their hinges with a matched pair of cracks, hanging askew. The guards lost their weapons and went down trying to clutch their chins, which were no longer quite where they were accustomed to being.

Remo decided to offer up his own brand of professional courtesy and not kill anyone who was only defending his place of work.

Moving low, he let a stuttering Mat burst burn past one shoulder close enough that he felt the hot bullets pass. Then he popped up not an inch before the guard's comically astonished face.

Remo poked him in the eyes with two forked fingers, and the man recoiled, howling and clawing at his tearing eyes.

A second guard swung his stubby-snouted weapon on line with Remo but held his fire. Remo had grabbed the first guard by the back of his coat and held him between himself and the place where the bullets would come out.

The guard tried to angle his way around, the better to shoot Remo without harming his compatriot.

The blinded guard continued howling and dancing—not entirely of his own volition—while it soon became apparent that there was no shooting the intruder without also shooting his fellow DGSE agent.

Remo saw the subdued resignation creep over the guard's face and propelled the blind guard in his direction. They collided, knocking heads, and both collapsed, weaponless, to the floor.

Remo joined the Master of Sinanju as he swept into the main DGSE building unchallenged.

In the empty foyer Remo asked, "Which way?"

"Follow the sour trail," said Chiun.

And Remo smelled it, too. The faint scent of vomit. The man who had upchucked over the Beasley control console had passed this way, probably prior to being cleaned off.

They found the cell in the basement, and while they were getting ready to rip the blank door off its hinges, Dominique Parillaud stepped off an elevator.

She took one look at them, and her jaw dropped.

Remo was on her before her hands could make up their mind to stab the Door Close button or unship her pistol.

She did neither. When the elevator door closed, she was out of the car, her pistol in Remo's hand.

"How did you? How could you—" she sputtered.

"This place is a candy box," said Remo.

"You will never get what you 'ave come for."

Then the Master of Sinanju approached the door. Its hinges lay on the outside of the cell for obvious reasons, so he simply sheared them off with three quick slashes of one fingernail.

The door came out like a portrait from a frame.

"You will never take him away," Dominique insisted with less conviction than before.

"Wanna bet?" said Remo. "Come out, come out, wherever you are."

A blondish head poked out. The face under it was tanned and tentative.

"You Americans?" he asked.

"That's us. You the Beasley guy?"

"That's me."

"You're coming with us," said Remo.

"What about the you-know-what?"

Remo blinked. "We don't know what."

"The cybernetic hypercolor eximer laser eyeball."

Remo blinked. "Say that again in English? My French is real rusty."

"That *was* English. I'm talking about the eyeball the Beasley boys had me make. It was for some radio-animatronic project."

"It was for Sam Beasley," said Remo.

"Yeah. That's who I work for."

"No, I mean it was for Uncle Sam Beasley himself."

The tanned face looked doubtful. "But he's dead."

"I wish," said Remo as the Master of Sinanju pulled the prisoner from the cell by the front of his peach jumpsuit.

"Your name?" Remo asked.

"Rod Cheatwood."

"Make you a deal—you tell us everything you know, and we'll get you back to the good old U.S.A."

"EUD," hissed Dominique. "You must say EUD while in my country. It is the law."

"Stuff it," Remo told her. To Rod, he said, "How about it?"

"Done deal."

"That was quick. Whatever happened to company loyalty?"

"Are you kidding? You think I'd stick my neck out for those ducking bastards? They mugged me the minute I walked through their front door."

"Okay, let's go," said Remo.

"I wish you would have waited another hour," Rod said as they called for the elevator.

"Why?" asked Chiun.

"They're showing the finale of 'Star Trek: the Next Generation' this afternoon."

"You can catch that anytime," said Remo.

"I keep trying to, but it never happens."

"It would only be in French," said Remo. "Only Jerry Lewis movies work in French."

"Jairy *est Dieu*," sighed Dominique before being yanked bodily into the elevator.

28

Commander Luc Crocq of the French Foreign Legion forces surrounding Euro Beasley was confident in his men and matériel. They had encircled the park with a ring of steel. The tanks and APCs sat snout to rump and rump to snout all around the place of defilement. Commander Crocq considered it a defilement because although he had nothing against American culture in particular, he was a lifelong fan of Coulommiers cheese, which was made in this very area. That many of the farms that produced this cheese among cheeses were razed to prepare the land for the Euro Beasley park was in Commander Crocq's eyes the desecration of desecrations.

Secretly he hoped for word to roll in and raze Euro Beasley from the face of France.

But no such order had come. All was quiet since the last attempt to close the ring of steel had been met with a pinkish radiance that took the fighting piss out of his legionnaires.

There had been an altercation in which a French army helicopter had descended into the park, only to lift off again later. Nothing more was known about this operation, but Crocq suspected DGSE involvement.

All the commander understood was that he was to hold his ring of steel in place, tightly and without faltering, so that none could exit the hellish enclave of American junk culture.

He did not expect a wave of forces sneaking up from his rear to wash over his ring of steel and retake the park. The objective was not to defend Euro Beasley, Commander Crocq later pointed out to the military board of review. If they had wanted him to defend the park from external threats, as well, should that not have been included in his orders?

So pleaded Commander Crocq in vain before they court-martialed him.

There were many other reasons Commander Crocq was not responsible for what later transpired.

First there were crowds. They came by auto, by truck—even by metro line. The terminus of the A RER train line was called Parc Euro Beasley. Day-trippers who came to sample the place of cultural perfidy employed it. Although the park was under cultural quarantine, still they came to look, to gawk, perhaps to catch a glimpse of Mongo or Dingbat or one of the others who dwelled here no more.

It was a festive time, so when men dressed as soldiers of Napoleon III began to appear among the growing crowd, it was not a cause for concern, never mind interest. And since all attention was focused inward, not outward, just as his orders dictated, Commander Crocq was completely oblivious to the increasing preponderance of soldiers dressed in the fashion of a bygone century.

That is, until they attacked.

THEY CAME SCREAMING unintelligible sounds. Not curses, not imprecations, not defiance. Just sheer bloodcurdling noise.

This arrested the attention of all in the awkward moment when they came pouring over ring of steel in waves of blue and gray.

They carried no guns, no rifles, no pistols. To that, Commander Crocq swore to his dying day.

But when they poured under the ring of steel, the ring of steel lay helpless. Multiton tanks and APCs could not move as fast as a man. Not from a cold start. Not when parked snout to rump and vice versa.

"Defend your positions!" Commander Crocq cried. Too late. Their position had already been overrun. Soldiers of the past, including fez-hatted Zouaves not seen since the 1800s, poured into the gates of Euro Beasley.

"Fire at will!" Commander Crocq sputtered when he realized his line had been breached before he could respond to the insult.

That was when the horrible event transpired.

His men were chambering their weapons. Not a shot had been fired. Not by either side. That was the remarkable thing, the terrible thing.

The infiltrators turned, dropped into crouches and pulled masks of lead over their eyes. The peculiar quality to these masks was that they bore no eyeholes. The infiltrators were digging into defensive positions utterly blind.

Then they unleashed the terrible power of what looked from the near distance like universal remote controls.

There came flashes, pulses, strong lights. All hues and colors imaginable were represented. The lights bombarded Commander Crocq and his unflinching Foreign Legionnares like a light show with the kicking power of a thousand mules.

Some men ran for their lives, unhurt. Others lost their nerve and their consumed rations before succumbing to vivid green flashes. Still others, subjected to red, became beside themselves with anger, which they took out on their comrades-in-arms.

It was a horrible, unearthly thing. The ring of steel held strong, but the men manning it collapsed like paper dolls before a firestorm. A firestorm of rainbow colors.

For his part Commander Crocq, who sat high in the turret hatch of his tank, ducked down and pulled the hatch after him. He would later protest this was not an act of cowardice, but the reasonable response of a commander who needed to preserve his wits in order to marshal his forces.

For all the good it did him, Commander Crocq might as well have taken his medicine like a soldier of France.

The awful lights penetrated the tank's thick plate armor, showing the utter futility of France's engines of war before new technologies.

He received a simultaneous burst of pink and yellow.

Commander Crocq leaped from his tank and ran off into the scattering crowds of onlookers. He was very, very frightened by the yellow light that seemed to have deep-fried his brain in sizzling butter.

But under that mindless fear lay a peaceful feeling that all would be right once he got far away enough. It was a very peaceful feeling. And somehow it was pink.

MARC MOISE SAW the French defenders fall back in confusion and a wide spectrum of emotions. A few, pinked, actually came toward them. They were hued by cavalry who had control of the yellow universal units or by artillery, which had red.

They fell back, fighting among themselves.

When the commotion had died down, Marc led his Zouaves into the Sorcerer's Chateau and down into Utilicanard, while the California Summer Vacation Musketeers and the Florida Sunshine Guerrillas stood picketed at all approach roads.

The smell in Utilicanard was very ripe. Marc had to pink himself just to keep going. The Zouaves took it in stride. They had come for a fight, fresh from their triumph at the Third Battle of the Crater.

When Marc got to the main control room he found drying vomit and smashed hypercolor controls. Frowning, he got on the satellite phone and reported to the first person who answered.

"Cheatwood is gone. And someone smashed the controls."

"Any idea what happened?" a gruff, frosty voice demanded.

"No. But there's vomit. Could he have greened himself?"

"Not in his own control room. Check the video logs."

Marc replayed the tapes until he saw Rod Cheatwood succumb to his own video screen. The flash of green in the tape was enough to make Marc feel a little queasy, but he held down the food he'd last eaten. It wasn't hard. Although train fare, it was French.

"Looks like the French acquired the technology," he reported.

"Was it a woman?"

"Yeah, looks like."

"Damn her eyes. She must have figured out how to make the orb operate. Okay, hold the fort. We're coming in."

"Sir?" said Marc. But the line was already dead.

So Marc Moise sat down in the chair before the main viewer, trying to reconcile the crusty voice that had spoken to him with the childhood memory of Uncle Sam Beasley.

Uncle Sam was coming here. But why? That hadn't been in Marc's premission briefing.

FRENCH MINISTER of Culture Maurice Tourette was the first to hear of the rout at Euro Beasley.

"Who?" he sputtered. "Who is responsible for this outrage?"

"According to reports," the informant told him, "the attackers were dressed after the style of Napoleon III."

"Napoleon III?" Tourette chewed the leathery inside of his cheek as he processed that bit of intelligence. This was absurd; therefore it could not be. But it was. Therefore, it was an American absurdity. And checking the latest *Le Monde*, he saw the photographs of what the French press were calling *l'affaire Crater*.

The soldiers had come from America, he concluded. They had come to further insult the French Republic. And for that they would pay.

Picking up the telephone, he put in a call to the general of the air army.

"*Mon Général*, I have distressing news. But if you act in a timely manner, all might be saved. The cultural Chernobyl has been retaken. Perhaps this matter can be settled once and for all by turning it into a true Chernobyl. Do you, by chance, have any nuclear weapons at your disposal? Ah, you do. Very good. Now listen . . .''

THE HELICOPTER was jet black and skimmed low over the outlying farms and hills of Averoigne before settling into Euro Beasley.

Marc Moise watched it by manipulating the surveillance cameras. When the craft had settled, he was not surprised—but still it was a shock—to see Bob Beasley step out of the helicopter, look around and help Uncle Sam Beasley from his conveyance.

Uncle Sam Beasley wore a white uniform with gold trim and shaking gold-braid epaulets that made Marc Moise think of an Italian admiral of the fleet. Clumping along on his silver peg leg, he returned every salute thrown at him by the other regiments whose forage caps were decorated by black felt mouse ears.

It was a ridiculous sight, but it filled Marc Moise with foreboding.

At least, he saw, Uncle Sam wore a white eye-patch over the place where his left eye should be. Marc didn't think he could stare into that strobing steel organ ever again. . . .

WHEN DGSE DIRECTOR Remy Renard heard the door to the security room open even though he had buzzed no one in, he whirled around anxiously.

The door came bouncing in, its plate-glass window fracturing merrily.

Dominique Parillaud was thrust in along with the captive Beasley operative, Cheatwood.

After them came two of the strangest individuals ever to intrude upon DGSE preserves. One, American and therefore a bit of an oaf, and the other very old and very Oriental.

"He has come for the satellite," Dominique cried.

"Yeah, I've come for the satellite," said the white oaf. "Where is it?"

"You will never wrest it from us," Remy Renard said, placing his body between the interloper and the great vault door.

The white American approached the door, after first picking Remy up by squeezing his elbows to his hips and setting him off to one side like a coatrack.

Remy swallowed hard to keep down the ugly feeling in his stomach. He had never felt more helpless than at that moment. It was as if he were nothing to this man.

"That vault is eight inches thick," he sputtered. "The combination is known to but two men in this building and it requires two to open it. I am the only one with the combination here."

"It *is* thick," admitted the oafish American, scrutinizing the door with a perplexed expression.

"Then you realize the futility of even attempting to breach the vault door?"

"Yeah, it's too much for me," he agreed. "Wait here, Little Father." And he exited the room.

Remy Renard strove to relax. If he could just get through the coming moments, all would be well. Reinforcements would soon arrive. And there was no way these men could leave the building. Not unarmed as they so obviously were.

From down the hall came an awful cacophony of sounds. A punch press might have started the racket, but then a jackhammer sound blended in. Plaster groaned and lath screamed protestations. A metallic lamentation followed—awful, tortured, indescribable.

Then came a rattling series of sounds that, if Remy Renard had not known better, he would have vowed could only have been coming from inside the impregnable vault. But the vault was soundproofed to noise, and the great door, the only way in, was firmly sealed.

When it all ended, the white American appeared in the door, spanking plaster dust off his lean, bare forearms.

When he was done, he opened his right palm for all to see, and the supreme idiot said, "I couldn't find any satellite, but I did find this."

And Remy Renard could not contain his gasp of astonishment.

The American was holding the orb of many potent colors.

"*C'est impossible!*" Remy gasped.

"*C'est la biz, chéri,*" the idiot said, grinning.

"We are going now," the ancient Asian told him coldly. "But I leave you with your life and this warning, which may be more valuable than your life."

"What could be more valuable that my life?" Remy blurted.

"The knowledge that the Master of Sinanju works for the Eagle Throne of America and will treat any further aggravation harshly."

Remy Renard was strong of heart and spine. But he felt the blood drain from his sturdy legs and he realized the truth of the old Korean's warning.

For although Remy Renard was prepared to lose his life for France, he wasn't prepared to lose France herself.

And that was the gist of the Master of Sinanju's warning, which hung in the dusty air of the vault room long after the Master of Sinanju and his train had departed.

When he heard no sounds of shooting or commotion, Remy Renard knew it was safe to step out of the stagnant puddle of his own urine.

He immediately got on the telephone to the president of France. This was a far graver matter than defending French culture. National survival was at stake. The minister of culture could be of no value in such a war.

29

Outside DGSE HQ, Dominique Parillaud said, "You will never escape France."

"Don't say that," Remo said fervently. "I have to find a father I don't even know."

"I am serious. You will be shot."

"Beats being stuck here," said Remo, looking around for the cab. It was no longer in sight. He turned to Dominique. "Parked around here?"

"I will nevair reveal where."

"Never?"

"Nevair!"

Then a hand Dominique never saw drifted up to tweak one earlobe.

Dominique screamed. She thought she screamed so loudly that half of Paris must have heard her. But when she paused for breath, she realized she was emitting no noise, only pain. And when she realized that, she began nodding frantically, hoping that the unseen power that had inflicted such exquisite agony would release her.

"I think she's changed her mind, Little Father," said Remo to the unseen force.

Then the pain withdrew.

Clapping a hand over her throbbing earlobe, Dominique whirled to confront the force.

She caught a glimpse of the Master of Sinanju's long fingernails as his hands sought the black velvet tunnels of his closing kimono sleeves and understood.

"Now you know how it feels," Rod Cheatwood told her tauntingly.

"I am parked in ze garage," she admitted.

They walked down the street where she was pointing and came to the main garage door. It was closed, but there was a foot-wide space beside the door, completely unguarded and large enough to admit a thin person.

"Wait here," said Remo to Chiun, and guided Dominique into the garage.

Not a minute later the door rolled aside, and they came out in a diamond blue Citroën, stopped, and the car doors opened for the Master of Sinanju and Rod Cheatwood.

"Dominique agreed to drive us to the airport," said Remo.

"I 'ave no choice," Dominique said in a pouting voice.

"We take our agreements any way we can."

"I am confident we will nevair get to ze airport," Dominique said, slipping into traffic. She took her foot off the gas momentarily and touched a floor button that cut in the hidden microphones that would broadcast their conversation back to DGSE HQ. "We will be intercepted."

"We don't intercept easily," Remo said airily.

"I am certain ze airport will be surrounded by tanks and other vehicles. And soldiers."

"Won't be the first time," said Remo, noticing through the window that they were taking down a street sign that said Rue Edgar Allan Poe and replacing it with one which that said, Rue Auseuil.

The wail of French police sirens came all at once. It seemed to be all around them.

"Voila!" Dominique cried triumphantly. "Just as I 'ave told you. It is time you ended zis charade."

Remo took a sudden left up a street that was posted with a short white bar in a red circle.

"You idiot! That sign meant no entry."

"Sue me. I can't read French."

"That was not French. It was a sign. It is iconography."

"Can't read that, either," said Remo, leaning on the rude horn so the oncoming cars knew enough to get out of the way.

They emerged on a busy street and practically into a converging swarm of red-striped white police Renaults whose blue bubble-top lights flashed angrily.

"We're screwed!" Rod Cheatwood moaned.

Remo tapped the brake, sent the wheel turning right, then left, then right again. The car, responding, performed a seemingly impossible maneuver that caused it to spin in place.

Suddenly it was facing the other way and rocketing forward.

A long line of police cars was coming the other way. Remo warned, "Hang on," and prepared to hang a U-turn designed to bring the two converging groups of vehicles at one another.

But the approaching police cars suddenly turned off the boulevard and disappeared from sight.

Remo drove past, saying, "What was *that* all about?"

In the rearview mirror the pursuing cars also turned up that road. It was marked A4.

"Where does that road go?" Remo asked.

"It goes," Dominique said thinly, "to ze eastern suburbs."

"Euro Beasley lies that way, doesn't it?"

"It does," said Dominique.

"It was pretty quiet when we left it," Remo said.

A line of military helicopters skimming the low skyline also broke eastward.

"Something's up out there. Something big."

Remo turned on the dash radio.

He immediately got an excited crackle of French that didn't sound like a disk jockey speaking.

"What's he saying?" said Remo.

Dominique listened intently. Her face began to come apart like a house of cards.

From the rear Chiun spoke up. "He is saying that reactionaries have attacked Euro Beasley."

"Whose reactionaries?"

"The American reactionaries who fomented civil war."

"Reactionaries! You don't mean reenactors, do you?"

"It is possible I meant that."

"What the hell are Civil War reenactors doing attacking Euro Beasley?" shouted Remo.

When no one offered a ready answer, he pulled over to a pay phone and called America.

"Smitty, Remo. We got the Beasley guy, but something's up."

"I am receiving sketchy reports of soldiers dressed in the uniforms of the old French Second Empire

Army breaching the quarantine line surrounding Euro Beasley. What can you add?''

''Try Civil War reenactors.''

''What!''

''That's what the French radio is reporting.''

''It all fits,'' Smith said in a dull, barely comprehending voice.

''Not to me,'' said Remo.

''No, I mean the Beasley employees-transportation charges. They entered France via the Chunnel.''

''So what's their game? There's already a Beasley park over here.''

''Remo, my reports are the French forces were routed by very strong colored lights.''

''We wrecked those controls before we left.''

''*I* wrecked them,'' Chiun called from the car.

''The reenactors were obviously carrying their own devices,'' Smith said briskly. ''Remo, this has gone too far. The Beasley Corporation is controlling those Civil War units. I have no doubt of that. And what they have done is nothing less than an act of war.''

''Okay, but that's between Beasley and France, right?''

''I do not think that distinction can be made here. In the eyes of much of the world, the Beasley Corporation *is* America.''

''Every time that idiot Beasley launches a plan, he ends up dragging us to a hot war somewhere,'' Remo said bitterly.

''Remo, if you have to kill every Civil War reenactor at Euro Beasley, you will do this. Do you understand?''

Remo hesitated.

"Remo," Smith said, his voice like flint. "We cannot have a war with France over an entertainment company's mindless plans for global expansion. I want you to break their backs to the last man."

"All right."

"And if Uncle Sam Beasley is anywhere in that place, you will render him completely and totally immobile. Do you understand?"

"You want me to kill him."

"I want him destroyed to the last atom."

"Got it," said Remo, hanging up. He walked back to the car with his eyes strange, and when he got behind the wheel, his voice was thick.

"We've got our marching orders," he said, pulling away.

"Yes?" said Chiun.

"Waste the reenactors."

"Then we will waste the reenactors."

"And kill Uncle Sam Beasley forever," Remo added.

"That will be your task."

"Why me?"

"Because you are afraid to do this, and you can only conquer that fear by doing the very thing that you dread."

And as they drove toward Euro Beasley, Remo knew that was exactly what he was going to have to do.

He just wondered if he could do it. Years ago he had been one of Uncle Sam's biggest fans.

TASK FORCE GROUP LEADER Marc Moise moved among his Zouaves.

It was the beginning of the second hour of the retaking of Euro Beasley, and now that the French soldiers and the crowd had been scattered, they seized the ring of tanks and APCs that surrounded the park. In effect, they were expanding their sphere of control.

The tank-mounted howitzer and machine-gun barrels that had been pointing inward were rotated outward, covering all roads with overlapping fields of fire.

No one could approach without coming under annihilating fire. And if by chance a few did, his Zouaves would meet them with an irresistible rainbow of steel.

There was just one problem with all this. It was expressed to him in the form of a question as he moved among his charges.

"Do we wear our lead masks up on our foreheads or in front of our eyes?"

"Up on your foreheads, of course."

"And if we are attacked and must resort to showing our true colors?"

"Down before your eyes, of course."

The word was passed up and down the line. If attacked, the eye shields were to be worn on the forehead while defending with howitzer and machine gun. And if forced to pull back, the masks belonged in front of the eyes.

Marc Moise checked with every third man to be certain they understood their instructions. But in his heart he wondered about their willingness to kill. They were, after all, only Creole reenactors who had sided with the California Summer Vacation Musketeers back in Virginia because they had been offered reenactment jobs at Beasley U.S.A. Having closed ranks with the Corporation against the protesters, they had been hired on the spot.

And as they hung off the French military equipment—the first line of defense against attack—their fezzes askew, their manner excited, they looked for all the world like cannon fodder.

When the attack came, it arrived in a solitary diamond blue Citroën that coasted to a stop well short of the tank that squatted before the colorful entrance to Euro Beasley.

The doors popped open and four people got out.

They started toward the tank. They walked calmly and without fear. Except maybe for a blond guy who took up the rear. His knees were definitely knocking.

"GOD, IF THEY HUE US I hope they don't use Supergreen," said Rod Cheatwood in a nervous voice.

"Me, too," said Remo.

"Yellow, I think I could stand."

"Perhaps they will use pink," said the Master of Sinanju.

"I'd enjoy that," said Remo.

"Me, too," said Rod.

"You are all insane." Dominique Parillaud spit. "Zey 'ave machine guns and howitzers. Zey will annihilate us."

"I'd rather be annihilated than greened," said Remo.

"Or yellowed," said Chiun.

Dominique rolled her eyes. "I am not afraid of their gauche color. Only of French bullets."

"Bullets, we have covered," said Remo in a casually fearless tone.

They continued walking. Machine-gun barrels lined up on them, and excited words were shouted down.

"What're they saying?" asked Remo.

"I 'ave no idea," Dominique admitted. "It sounds like French, but no French zat I have ever heard before." She gasped. *"Mon Dieu! I think zey speak franglais!"*

No one fired, so they kept walking.

"No use to close our eyes," said Remo.

"How will closing your eyes protect you from bullets?" asked Dominique.

"I don't mean bullets. I mean the color stuff."

"Hypercolor," said Rod. "Too bad we don't have any lead masks," he added worriedly.

"Why do you say that?" asked Chiun.

"Lead is the only thing saturated color can't penetrate. It's too dense. When I used to work on the first hypercolor lasers, I'd wear a lead mask without any eyeholes to keep from getting hued."

" 'Hued'?"

"That's the technical term for it. Invented it myself."

"Little Father, do you see what I see up ahead?"

"I see clown soldiers wearing lead masks under their red fezzes."

"If we can get one or two of them, we're all set."

"If you wear masks without eyes, how can you fight?" demanded Dominique.

"We don't need eyes to fight with," said Remo.

"Yes," added Chiun. "We fight with our hands and our feet, not our eyes."

"You can be our eyes," said Rod.

"I will be no one's eyes," Dominique swore.

And suddenly, several 35- and 50-caliber machine guns pivoted in their direction, tipped downward, lining them up for slaughter.

Dominique Parillaud stopped dead in her tracks. Rod bumped into her and bounced back. Before the fear could overtake her, the two American agents surged forward.

They started walking calmly forward. Suddenly they shot ahead, leaping onto the main tank and breaking the machine guns with short, hard chops that looked ineffectual but caused steel gun barrels to snap and roll clanking off the armored side of the tank.

The Zouaves, seeing this, began recoiling in surprise and dug into their colorful sashes for black objects that looked to Dominique's eyes like TV remote-control clickers.

Before their weapons cleared, hands reached out to relieve them of their masks, which they were trying to simultaneously pull down over their eyes.

MARC MOISE WAS STANDING not six yards away when the strange pair appeared atop the main blocking tank. The way they broke the machine guns was awful to behold.

But the way they avoided being hued was incredible.

His Zouaves followed orders exactly. At the first sign of trouble, they simultaneously reached up for their lead masks and into their sashes for their clipped-on hypercolor lasers.

They got the weapons out in time to fire short bursts of pacifying pink.

The trouble was the Zouaves were quicker on the trigger than they were on the masks. Or perhaps it wasn't their fault, after all.

Zouave hands that reached up to their foreheads encountered only warm flesh, not cold lead shields.

When their first pink bursts came, the lead masks were firmly in place—over the eyes of the attackers.

The Zouaves reacted to the pink flashes in an entirely unexpected manner, although Marc understood it after the third burst.

Smiling, they brought their lasers up to their expectant faces, pinking themselves happily.

"Let de good times roll!" they murmured in Creole.

The pink reached Marc's brain through his open eyes—he had been so stunned by what he had witnessed that he had forgotten to yank down his own lead mask—relaxing him instantly.

Marc unclipped his laser, dialed up pink and hued himself in quarter-second bursts.

When the strange pair ran past him, he didn't care anymore. And why should he? He had been offered up as cannon fodder, and Sam Beasley didn't pay dick.

30

"We have a penetration, Director."

Uncle Sam Beasley turned to face the man who had spoken. Bob Beasley sat at the grid of video screens that monitored Euro Beasley.

"Are those damn Cajuns pinking themselves?" Uncle Sam barked.

"It seems so, Director."

"Damn. They're supposed to be our trip wire. They're no good to us now. Get the Florida regiment out there."

"Yes, Director."

Uncle Sam Beasley turned his attention back to the damaged control board where a Beasley technician was laboring.

"Aren't we back on-line yet?" he asked gruffly.

"The Hotpink button is enabled."

"I need offensive colors, damn it. What if the fucking Foreign Legion come parachuting back in?"

"Hotpink had the least damage."

"When I want excuses, I'll ask a vice president. Now, get to work."

"Yes, Director."

Bob Beasley spoke up. "Director, we have intruders on Main Street, U.S.A."

Uncle Sam Beasley moved to the screen in question. He saw two men walking calmly down the cobbled street, one white, the other Asian. Both wore lead masks over their eyes that didn't seem to slow them down.

"Those are the ones!" he howled.

"The ones who interfered at Third Crater?"

"Third Crater, my pink ass. They interfered at Second Bay of Pigs! Must work for the government. Order them empurpled."

"Uncle Sam—"

"Call me Director when we're on an operation."

"Director, you know how risky empurpling a subject can be. Purple combines the effects of red and blue. Anything could happen, especially with opponents as dangerous as them."

"Empurple their asses!"

"At once, Director." And snapping a switch, Bob Beasley leaned into a console mike and said, "Two intruders in Zone 12. Empurple them. Repeat, empurple them. And don't forget to mask first."

REMO WILLIAMS RAN THROUGH a world of darkness.

Although his sight was blocked by a lead shield, he was not by any means blind.

His nose detected scent molecules too faint for the ordinary human nose, his hearing picked up the steady pounding of the Master of Sinanju's heartbeat and pumping lungs beside him and his bare skin received a multiplicity of sensations—nearby body heat, draft eddies and the negative pressure of large, stationary buildings.

All of which combined to make Remo a running radar dish.

A wall of heartbeats converged on the unseen road ahead of him.

"Masks down, men!" a voice shouted.

"Here we go, Little Father."

And as they raced forward, their sensitive ears detected the tiny closing clicks of relays signifying hypercolor lasers were being brought to bear upon them.

Fixing the position of the forest of heartbeats, Remo calculated angles of attack. He went for the rotator cuffs, jamming them with stiffened fingers, puncturing flesh and muscle.

Men howled and gave way. The plastic clatter of hypercolor laser units dropping to the cobbles came distinctly. Remo and Chiun crushed them underfoot wherever they could.

The first wave of attackers fell back.

"THE FLORIDA SUNSHINE Guerrillas have been thrown back, Director," Bob Beasley shouted.

"Those pansies!" Uncle Sam Beasley scowled. "What's wrong with them?"

"Well, they *are* blind."

"So are those two pains-in-the-rear!"

"Being blind doesn't seem to bother them."

"Look at them turn tail like scared little mice. I expect more from my employees."

"They *were* complaining about the pay a while back."

"Don't they know they work for Sam Beasley, the greatest private company ever to export good old American fun?"

"We pound it into them at the monthly pep drills, but I don't think it motivates them as much as better wages would."

"Greedy bastards. Okay, turn out my elite musketeers."

"Director, as long as those two have their eyes shielded, we can't stop them with extraordinary means."

"Then shoot them!"

"We didn't bring any guns. Couldn't risk them not getting through French customs."

Uncle Sam Beasley stared up at the screen and saw the two people he most hated in the world approach the Sorcerer's Chateau, blind yet unchallenged and seemingly unstoppable. His exposed eye scrunched up like an agate in a fist.

"There's gotta be some way to kill 'em," he snarled.

"We could lead them into a trap."

"What traps do we have here?"

"Not much. All Beasley offensive capability is topside. We never planned for a Utilicanard penetration."

"Don't call it that. God, I hate these sissy French words. Where did they dredge them up?"

"Same place we did. From the Latin."

"I want solutions, you sycophant. Not language lessons."

"There *is* the LOX chamber."

"We have a deli down here?"

"Not that kind of LOX. Liquid Oxygen. We use it to create faux steam clouds for the Mesozoic Park volcanoes. It's nasty, subfreezing stuff. A cloud of it will cause your skin to crack off in sheets."

"Hey, I like that."

"We'll have to decoy them in."

Uncle Sam Beasley turned to address a trio of his loyal musketeers, who had entered the control room in Union blue, their mouse-eared forage caps carried respectfully in their hands.

"I need a volunteer. Hazardous duty. Who will stand up for his Uncle Sam?"

The California Summer Vacation Musketeers looked down at their boots and up at the ceiling— anywhere to avoid the cold gray stare of Uncle Sam's single exposed eye.

"I'll double the pay of the man who undertakes this mission."

No one responded.

"What's the matter, isn't double enough? Don't I pay you competitively?"

When no one answered, Uncle Sam Beasley snarled, "Draw straws if you're going to be that way. But I want a man ready for action before those two bust in."

Uncle Sam returned to the video grid. "What are those two doing to my best guerrillas?"

"Looks like the white one is just poking them in the shoulder area."

"Then why are they dropping like DDT'd flies?"

"Maybe there's a sensitive nerve center there," Bob Beasley said, stabbing buttons.

"What's the old gook doing?"

Bob Beasley craned up in his chair to see the screen in question.

"I think he's eviscerating them, Director."

"With what?"

"His fingernails, I suppose," Bob Beasley said in a thick voice.

"They're going to be in the chateau any second."

Bob Beasley reached for an insulated lever. "I'll raise the drawbridge."

"Don't bother. I want 'em where I can LOX 'em."

REMO KICKED a kneecap to pieces and stepped over the dropping foe. He paused, turning in place, to orient himself.

The wind was out of the northeast. There was a blockage of dead air in that direction, and only the Sorcerer's Castle was big enough to create it, Remo decided.

He turned, not seeing but sensing the Master of Sinanju.

"Chiun! Shake a leg. The castle is this way."

"I will be along," said Chiun, and the ugly crunch of human bone and brittle plastic came unmistakably. "These evil tools must be destroyed."

"You just don't want to have to deal with Beasley."

"Do not fall into the moat."

"Fat chance," said Remo, running toward the blockage. He smelled the water in the moat, and the scent of the wooden drawbridge, still damp from a recent rain, guided him over the moat and into the castle's cool, gaping maw.

There were no guards. No obstacles. Remo ran with all senses alert for any click, thud or electrical whirring of booby traps or snares.

Surprisingly there were none.

From the last time he had penetrated this place, Remo knew there was a spiral aluminum stairwell going down. From memory, he arrowed toward it. There was an updraft, cool and dank. That helped.

Pausing at the top step, Remo listened a moment. No traps. No human ones anyway.

Remo started down. His skin temperature began to cool in anticipation of what he had to do....

"DIRECTOR, hostile subject entering Utiliduck."

Uncle Sam Beasley turned to his waiting musketeers. "It's the moment of truth. Who's my brave volunteer?"

Feet shuffled and gazes were averted guiltily.

"Damn you slackers! You work for me!"

"Yeah," a musketeer returned, "but we aren't going up against that guy. Look what he did to the Florida Sunshine Guerrillas."

Uncle Sam made a fist of stainless steel and flexed it several times. It whirred like metallic butterfly wings. "It's not as bad as what I'll do to you bunch if I don't get my volunteers."

"How about we all volunteer?" one asked suddenly.

Uncle Sam blinked. "All?"

"Yeah. That way we'll have a better chance."

"All except the technician," Bob Beasley called over his shoulder. "We need him."

"Good luck, men," said Uncle Sam as the musketeers filed glumly from the room. When the door hissed shut, he turned to his nephew. "Punch up the corridor screens. I want to see this."

On the screen appeared the image of the skinny white guy with the thick wrists and high cheekbones walking down the white approach corridor, his arms swinging with deceptively casual ease.

"Doesn't look like much," muttered Bob Beasley.

"I don't know who he is, but his ass is mine."

At his console Bob Beasley swallowed hard.

"And here come my trusty musketeers," said Uncle Sam.

REMO WILLIAMS SENSED the footfalls of the approaching men. He counted six sets of feet.

They came around a bend in the corridor carefully, their hearts beating hard but not in the high pounding of a preattack rhythm. There was no residual gunpowder smell, so they carried no weapons Remo needed to worry about.

"Out of my way and nobody gets hurt," warned Remo, advancing on them.

"You looking for Uncle Sam Beasley?" a voice asked.

"That's right."

"Three doors down," said the voice.

"On the right," added another.

"Can't miss it," said a third.

"Who are you?"

"Ex-employees of the Sam Beasley Corporation."

"Since when?"

"Since we gave him up just now."

"How do I know it's not a trap?" asked Remo.

"We're supposed to lure you into a trap."

"What trap?"

"LOX room. Liquid oxygen. It's all the way at the end of the corridor."

"You guys are pretty free with information."

"You would be, too, if you worked for these cold corporate ducksuckers."

"Much obliged," said Remo, passing on.

"TRAITORS!" Sam Beasley screamed, stamping the floor with his stainless-steel peg leg. "What's wrong with them? I'm Uncle Sam. I practically raised those ungrateful brats!"

"They've been pretty unhappy since you froze cost-of-living raises companywide," Bob Beasley noted.

"Then why did they come all the way over here if they weren't behind this damn operation?"

"You promised not to fire anyone who signed on."

Uncle Sam Beasley rolled his eye down to the back of the head of his nephew. Stainless-steel fingers whirring, he snared a fistful of hair and yanked the head back sharply so he could glare down into Bob Beasley's upside-down face.

"Whose side are you on?"

"Yours, Uncle. You know that."

"Prove it."

"How?"

"You look a lot like me, you lucky stiff. You decoy him into the LOX room."

"But—but—"

Uncle Sam released the hair. "Do it!"

Shivering, Bob Beasley climbed out of his chair and backed out of the control room. "I won't fail you, Uncle."

"Not if you don't want those bratty kids of yours served up as cold cuts at the next company picnic."

The door opened and closed with a hiss, and Uncle Sam climbed into the seat his nephew had vacated.

"How's that control panel coming?" he snapped over his shoulder.

The hypercolor technician said, "I've raised orange."

"When you've got Supergreen, let me know. The French should be regrouping soon. I can't beat them back with pastels, you know."

"Yes, Director."

THE MASTER OF SINANJU stepped up to a pounding heartbeat that blocked his path and aimed at the point where he knew the man's belly would be. The nail of his smallest finger went in like a needle into butter, and a disembodied voice said, "Urrk."

The Master of Sinanju described the sign of Sinanju—a trapezoid bisected by a slash—in his abdominal wall and left the unseen foe lying in a heap of his own smoking bowels.

He moved on. The way to the castle was clear. He did not need anything other than the personal scent of his pupil to guide him.

But as he approached, a drone came from the north.

A nearby voice cried, "It is a bomber."

Chiun paused. "How do you know?"

"I know a French bomber when I see one," said Dominique Parillaud.

"What is it doing?"

"It can have only one purpose."

"Yes?"

"To bomb."

Then Dominique said, "Ze bomb bay doors are open. Somezing is coming down."

And the Master of Sinanju snared the wrist of the French woman agent and pulled her along.

"Hurry!"

"Are you mad? Zere is no escape."

And from above came a mushy *poom* of a sound that brought a squeal of fear from Dominique Parillaud's throat.

It was followed by a great fluttering as if a thousand origami wings had taken flight.

31

Remo moved down the corridor blind, but every other sense operating at peak efficiency.

A figure popped out of the third door on the right, paused and ran deeper into Utilicanard. The door hisscd shut.

A muffled voice said, "You'll never catch me." It sounded like Uncle Sam's voice.

Remo Williams heard the beating heart and laboring lungs and started after it.

But when Remo got to the door, he suddenly swerved and, holding the flat of his palm before him like a ram, broke it down.

The door screeched coming out of its grooves, and Remo was in.

There were two heartbeats, one fast and normal, the other unhurried, metronomic—the animatronic heart of Uncle Sam Beasley.

"Nice try," said Remo, facing the unnatural sound. "But no sale."

"I'm unarmed. I surrender peacefully," said Uncle Sam.

"It's not going to be that way."

"You're an American agent, right?"

"Right."

"So I'm surrendering to you. You have to take me alive."

"Who says?"

"It's the way the game is played. Don't kid me."

"Not my game," said Remo.

"What game is that?"

"Counterassassin."

"Counterassassin? What's a goddamn counter-assassin doing on my trail?"

"For special cases, we drop the prefix," said Remo.

Uncle Sam switched to a wheedling, ingratiating voice. "You wouldn't kill your old Uncle Sam? First time we crossed paths, you were going to. But you couldn't, could you?"

"You should have stayed in that padded cell," Remo said, adjusting to each shift of his opponent's body so he blocked the door.

"You couldn't do it because you remember those long-ago Sunday nights squatting before the old TV in your pj's, watching my TV show. Watching me."

"Stuff it. You aren't that Uncle Sam anymore. He died when you should have."

"You're pretty brave behind that mask. There's no hypercolor laser units here. Let's see if you can look me in the eye before you do it."

"Sorry. No time."

"Coward."

"Don't call me that."

"Uncle Sam is calling you a coward. Are you a man or a little mousie?"

Remo hesitated. "I don't have time for games."

"I'm not afraid to look into your eyes. Why are you afraid to look into mine? Only have the one, you know."

"No sale," said Remo, stepping up in the welcome darkness to do the job he had to do.

A whirring warned of the steel hydraulic fist coming up, seeking Remo's mask, but it was too slow by weeks.

Zeroing in on the regular pumping of the animatronic heart, Remo drove the hard heel of his fist toward the sound.

Uncle Sam tried to block the blow. Remo felt the initial pressure wave. But Uncle Sam might as well have been trying to block a steam shovel with a plastic drinking straw.

"Punk! I raised you! I raised you better than your own parents. And you know it. You can't kill me! You wouldn't dare."

"Shut up! You don't know anything about my parents."

"I know they mistreated you. Admit it. They tanned your helpless butt and left you to cry your little eyes out. And when you thought no one loved you, I was there. Me and Mongo and Dingbat. And if we'd asked you to shoot your folks back then, you'd have done it. Because we molded your mind, just as we molded the little minds of every American generation since the Depression. You think you can kill me? Don't make me laugh. We're family."

In the darkness of his mind, Remo was silent for half a minute. Then in a low, barely contained voice, he said, "Thanks. You just made it easy for me."

Remo's palm drove out, smacking Uncle Sam once over the mechanical heart, and it gulped twice. And with a gurgle it ceased all function.

Uncle Sam shuddered on his feet, a long hiss coming out of his slack mouth. He fell back, struck the console and slid to the floor.

He was still breathing, but with a dead heart that was just a matter of time.

Blindly, Remo turned to the other individual in the room. "Who're you?"

"Laser technician. I'm just here to do my job."

"Your job," Remo told him, "is over."

The flutter of skirts up the corridor brought Remo to the door.

"Chiun! I'm in here."

"Remo, Remo, look! Read this."

"Is it safe to take my mask off?"

"*Oui,*" said Dominique Parillaud.

"No," said Chiun.

"Well, which is it?"

"Look, look!"

Remo lifted the lead shield. Chiun thrust a white sheet of paper into his hand. Remo took it, glanced at the side with writing, frowned and turned it around. No matter how he turned it, he couldn't read it.

"French?"

"*Oui.* It is a warning from ze army air force. Zey say if all American nationals do not surrender within two hours, zis park will be—how you say?—*frappé.*"

"*Frappé?* You mean frapped?"

"*Non,* I mean, oh what is ze word for what you barbarians did to Hiroshima?"

"Nuked?"

"Oui."

"The French are willing to nuke Euro Beasley?"

"Zey are very angry over zis transgression. Besides, it is ours to bomb or not bomb as we see fit."

"We'd better check in," Remo told Chiun. "Come on."

They reentered the control room. Remo went to the satellite telephone and punched in the country code for the U.S.A. and then Smith's contact number.

"Smitty, we just did Beasley."

"You just did the fiend Beasley," said Chiun, hovering curiously over the slumped form of Uncle Sam Beasley, who stared ceilingward with his good eye and gurgled like a clogged sink drain. His chest rose and fell more and more slowly with each breath.

"And the French have just leafleted the park. They've given us two hours to surrender or they nuke it."

"Nuke?"

"Nuke."

"You say Beasley is dead?"

"Well, he's still breathing, but his heart is dead and his brain is sure to follow."

"Have you accounted for the Beasley operatives?"

"Not all of them."

"Remo, it would be best if there were no survivors to tell any tales."

"Hope that doesn't include Chiun and me."

"You have less than two hours to take care of business and evacuate the park."

"Gotcha. We're in motion."

Hanging up, Remo turned to the Master of Sinanju, who still regarded Uncle Sam Beasley curiously.

"He is not yet dead," said Chiun.

"He's got a mechanical heart. He's not going to die like an ordinary guy. Besides, I figure by stopping his heart, I'm not really killing him. I just broke a machine part. If that kills him, fine. He should have packed a spare."

"He looks so pitiful," Dominique said. "An old man."

"Don't let that fool you," warned Remo. "Now, let's get to work."

Remo started to turn away, his eyes clinging to the seamed features of Uncle Sam Beasley, once a hero of young America and now a broken travesty of himself.

"Finish me. . . ." Beasley croaked.

"Finish yourself," said Remo. His eyes were fixed on the one gray orb that was rolling up into the heavy lid, when from behind the white Mongo Mouse eye patch came a tiny click.

The warning was enough. Shutting his eyes, Remo started backing away, certain that Chiun would follow suit. Too late.

From behind the patch came a burst of Supergreen.

THE MASTER OF SINANJU heard the click, and while his pupil moved backward to protect himself from the unknown danger, he moved forward to meet it head on.

The seated figure was slumped against the console.

The Master of Sinanju, his right hand forming the sharp point of a spear, moved in for the kill. . . .

WHEN HE AWOKE, Remo first checked his internal clock. Over one hundred minutes had passed. Then he sat up and looked around.

The Master of Sinanju lay facedown. So did Dominique and the hypercolor technician. They had emptied their stomachs on the stainless-steel floor.

Uncle Sam Beasley sat slumped forward, his neck in his lap. The stump was red and raw and showed a cross section of sheared vertebrae and biological plumbing.

There was no sign of his head. But the hypercolor technician was dead. Lying facedown, he had choked on his own vomit.

Remo went to the Master of Sinanju and shook him gently awake. "Get up, Little Father. We were scammed."

Chiun blinked awake. He snapped to his feet like a tornado rearing up. "The fiend tricked us," Chiun said. "There was a false eye behind the patch."

"Yeah. We never suspected a spare."

"But he was too slow. I removed his head before the terrible color could whelm me."

"Well, he's dead for sure this time. And we have less than an hour to get the hell out of here before the bomb falls."

Chiun looked around worriedly.

"Where is the head?"

"Head?"

"Yes. I removed the fiend's head. Now it is nowhere to be seen."

"Forget the head," said Remo, lifting Dominique across his shoulders. "Let's save our behinds."

"The body is here, so the head must also be here."

"Look, you see the body. It's dead. So the head is dead. Now, let's shake a leg."

Reluctantly the Master of Sinanju followed his pupil from the control room.

"If we can get to the car, we might be able to outrun the blast," Remo said.

"The French would not destroy such a place as this."

"Don't count on it," said Remo.

They ran through the attractions, their legs carrying them in floating fashion that ate up the yards.

The drone of a bomber came distinctly. It grew. Its roar bounced off Big Rock Candy Mountain, the second-highest point on Euro Beasley, filling the park with thundering sound vibration.

"That's it," said Remo, not looking up because there was no time to waste. "We either make it or we don't."

"Run now, worry later," Chiun puffed.

They accelerated, becoming to the eye like a slow-motion film of two men running at high speed. It was as if the air offered no resistance to them, inertia ceased to exist and gravity was repealed.

They tore up Main Street, U.S.A., leaving their shoes and sandals behind because in the fractions of seconds they had, even those were an encumbrance.

The entrance gate with its iron scrollwork replica of the Beasley signature came into view. They ripped through that and into the parking area where French tanks and APCs stood sentinel.

Atop a tank was Rod Cheatwood, a hypercolor eximer laser in each hand. He pointed them up into the sky, shouting "Bastards! Bastards!" over and over again.

"Forget it! It's too high. You can't hit that bomber from this range. Run!"

"Bomber? I'm talking about the company. They stole my idea!"

On his way past, Remo reached out and snatched Rod Cheatwood up, tucking him under an arm.

"See this?" Rod complained. "I invented this. It's a remote-control finder. The ducking bastards ripped me off again!"

Out on the highway Remo bore down. The thunder of the bomber was bouncing all over the place. By his internal clock it was 118 minutes since the leaflets had been dropped.

"We're not going to make it, Little Father."

"Never give up!" Chiun growled tightly.

They heard the whistling, even though it was very high in the sky.

"Goodbye, Little Father," Remo whispered.

They were less than a mile from the Euro Beasley gate when the bomb struck Big Rock Candy Mountain, collapsing it.

The sound wasn't great. More on the order of a dull thud. There was no blast, no roar, and certainly no angry fist of atomic fire lifting up to spread horror and deadly radiation.

The shock wave was nonexistent.

"Do we stop?" Remo asked Chiun.

"It may yet go off."

"It takes an explosion to detonate a nuclear device. I think the explosive charges failed."

"We take no chances," Chiun snapped.

Five miles down the road, they finally stopped. Remo set Rod Cheatwood onto the side of the road and rolled Dominique off his shoulders.

He looked at Chiun, looked toward the Norman ramparts of Euro Beasley and back at Chiun again. "Guess it was a dud, huh?" said Remo.

Before Chiun could answer, the entire park suddenly erupted in a dozen synchronized balls of consuming flame. They dropped to the ground because there was nothing else they could do, and waited for the end.

A rolling wave of heat mixed with cinders and a napalmlike smell came up the road, and except for the sudden lack of oxygen, it was tolerable.

"Wonder what happened?" Remo said, getting to his feet.

"THE FRENCH never armed the bomb," said Harold W. Smith when Remo called him from a roadside telephone.

"It was a bluff?" asked Remo.

"We may never know. Whatever their intentions, the decision not to arm the device came very late in the event."

"Nonevent, you mean."

"We may have Jerry Lewis to thank for averting disaster."

"Jerry Lewis?"

"When the French minister of culture announced the deadline to surrender the park, Lewis issued a statement vowing never again to set foot in France should the French ultimatum be carried out."

"They backed down because a freaking comedian threatened to boycott them?" Remo exploded.

"Mr. Lewis is revered over there. Also, it appears that the president of France interceded."

"With whom?"

"With the minister of defense. Apparently there are elements there more loyal to the culture minister than the government itself. Those elements are being purged even as we speak."

"The culture minister ordered a nuking?"

" 'Inspired it,' might be the more precise term. He has been arrested."

"I would hope so. The guy tried to nuke his own country."

"Actually the charge was violating La Loi Tourette."

"Huh?"

"Er, it appears he personally wrote the ultimatum leaflet and used an outlawed word that had a French equivalent."

"What word is that?"

"Nuke."

"Let me get this straight. The French minister of culture was arrested for using the word *nuke*, not for trying to use a nuke?"

"It would appear so."

Remo squeezed the roadside telephone receiver for a long, strange moment.

"Ze French, zay are a fonny race," he muttered. "So what blew up Euro Beasley, if not the French?"

"You say you smelled napalm?"

"Yeah. I know that smell from Nam."

"Someone inside the park activated a self-destruct program. It is the only possible explanation."

"But who?"

"Remo, are you certain Sam Beasley is dead?"

"Decapitated. It's better than dead."

"Because a helicopter lifted off from Euro Beasley over an hour ago. French police helicopters gave chase but lost it."

"Could have been anyone."

"Spotters say a man resembling Uncle Sam was seen in the cockpit."

"Probably that nephew of his. What's his name? Roy?"

"Robert. I have no computer audit trail showing he has left the country, Remo."

"Uncle Sam is lying back there in the castle in two unequal parts. Trust me. Right, Little Father?"

"Except that we could not find the head."

"What was that?" asked Smith.

"Nothing."

"Was something said about Uncle Sam's head?"

"Chiun said he couldn't find Uncle Sam's head. We had him cornered and he greened us, but Chiun got him before we blacked out. When we woke up, he was sitting on the floor without his head."

"Did you look for it?"

"Who had time? We were about to be nuked."

"Remo, I want you to go back and be certain Uncle Sam Beasley is dead."

"Too late. The castle is ashes by now."

Smith sighed. "At least the technology was destroyed with it."

"What about this guy Cheatwood?"

"Who?"

"Rod Cheatwood. He invented the hypercolor laser. Said all he was trying to do was come up with a foolproof TV-remote-control finder, but the Beasley Corporation turned it into something else."

"There must be no repetition of this event."

"How about we just wipe out his memory?"

"Wipe out whose memory?" Rod Cheatwood asked from the side of the road.

"And get back as soon as you can," said Smith. "Americans are still persona non grata in France."

"I am Korean," said Chiun, "and welcome everywhere."

Remo hung up and walked over to Rod Cheatwood. He took the hypercolor lasers from his hands and squeezed them until they popped and imploded to shards of plastic and microchips.

"You didn't tell us you built a second cybernetic eyeball."

"Of course I built two. A radio-animatronic robot needs two, doesn't he?"

"Fair enough. You're not a bad guy, just foolish. So we're not going to kill you."

"I appreciate that," Rod said. "Really."

"We're going to wipe out your memory so you're not a danger to anyone's national security."

"Can you wipe it out back to 1986?"

"Why then?"

"So I can watch every episode of 'Star Trek: the Next Generation' all over again fresh."

Remo looked at Rod Cheatwood a long moment and said, "It's your memory." And while Rod Cheatwood closed his eyes, a goofy smile coming over his

face, Remo tapped him in the exact center of his forehead. Rod crumpled to the ground, and the Master of
Sinanju crouched down and began whispering into his
ear.

"You will forget you were ever born."

"Hey, that's not what I promised him!"

"That is why I am making certain this cretin troubles us no more with his idiocies."

When the Master of Sinanju was through, he stood
up and said, "What about her?"

"Might as well break the happy news." Remo knelt
down, lifted her head off the ground and massaged the
back of Dominique's neck.

Her eyes snapped open, and she found herself being held off the ground by a strong hand at the back
of her neck. She was looking into Remo's dark brown
eyes.

"Good news. We didn't get frapped."

"Non?"

"Jerry Lewis saved us."

"Jairy? Jairy is here! Where?"

"But he's gone back to America. He promised never
to darken your shore again if France didn't patch
things up with the U.S.A."

"EUD," Dominique corrected.

"It's my country. I'll call it whatever I want."

"And you are in my country and should observe our
cultural prerequisites."

Remo released her head. It went *bonk!* on the asphalt of the road. Dominique sat up holding her skull.

"We are going now," said Chiun. "You will remind your masters of my warning. Sinanju stands by

the throne of America. Let there be no further trouble between your emperor and mine.''

Dominique picked herself up off the road. ''I will do zis for Jerry. But only for Jerry.''

''Just as long as you do it right,'' said Remo, looking around for a car to borrow.

He spotted the Parc Euro Beasley RER train stop.

''You know, Little Father. I'll bet we can get to London by train faster than it would take us to book Air France out of here.''

''I have always enjoyed trains. Did I ever tell you about my first train ride? It was before you were born, of course.''

''Tell me about it on the train,'' said Remo.

And barefoot, they started off.

32

Two days later Remo answered the ringing telephone in his Massachusetts condo.

"Remo, Smith."

Remo glanced over to the Master of Sinanju, who sat on a reed mat in the far corner of the tower meditation room, writing on a parchment scroll held flat on the floor with jade beads at each corner. "What's the latest?" he asked.

"The President of the U.S. and his French counterpart have agreed to a summit to discuss outstanding Franco-American issues."

"I didn't know there were any left."

"There is tentative agreement that French will be more widely taught in U.S. secondary schools and universities."

"That's an awfully big concession. Think of all those poor kids repeating French I over and over again."

"In return, France has lifted all restrictions on English-speaking visitors to their country. Provided Euro Beasley is defanged and renamed Beasleyland Paris."

"Sounds like our side caved in—again."

"That is not important. All that matters is that the crisis is over, and with Uncle Sam Beasley dead, we

can only hope the Beasley Corporation goes back to
being nothing more than an entertainment industry.''

"Any news from that quarter?"

"There are rumors of an internal shake-up. CEO
Mickey Weisinger has been demoted, and Beasley
nephew Bob has assumed operational control in ac-
tuality, if not title."

"Just so long as Sam Beasley remains dead."

There was a long pause on the line.

"You have no ill feelings over having liquidated
him?"

"I didn't do it. Chiun decapitated him."

From across the room, a squeaky voice called out,
"You broke his heart. Therefore, you dispatched the
beloved Uncle Sam."

"He wasn't dead when you lopped off his head, so
you killed him."

Chiun's head snapped around, his hazel eyes hot.
"That is slander!"

"It's the truth, and you know it."

Chiun shook his goose-feather quill in the air, spat-
tering the walls with black droplets of ink. "The truth
is what is written in the true histories of the House of
Sinanju, not what actually happened."

"You'd better not be hanging Beasley's death on me
in your freaking scrolls," Remo warned.

"I am the victor. The victor writes the histories.
Therefore, I will write as I wish."

"Yeah? Well, I'm thinking of starting my own set
of scrolls."

"It does not matter what you write," Chiun sniffed.

"We'll see about that."

"Because you will write junk in junk American," cackled the Master of Sinanju. "And no descendant of yours or mine will be able to read such drivel."

"Why not?"

"Because in only a mere two or three thousand more years, yours will be a dead language."

"Did you hear that, Smith?" Remo called into the telephone.

But Harold W. Smith had already hung up.

So Remo hung up and walked over to the Master of Sinanju, determined that history tell his side of the story.

EPILOGUE

History recorded that the Franco-American Conflict of 1995 lasted but three days and both began and ended with the bombing by French warplanes of Euro Beasley.

The combatants, as combatants always did, patched up their differences at the cessation of hostilities, signed meaningless treaties, awarded chestfuls of medals to the deserving and undeserving alike, promised future cooperation and exchanged hostages.

No history book, however, recorded the fate of the instigator of the conflict. No history book ever knew his name.

Mickey Weisinger knew his name.

He walked into his office the morning after the last day of the conflict and noticed a workman scratching his name off the office door.

"What the hell's going on?"

"You're now the second-highest-paid ex-CEO in America," said an affable voice he knew only too well.

It was coming from inside his office. Mickey entered.

Bob Beasley was seated comfortably at his desk.

"Who gave you authority to take over?" Mickey shouted.

"Uncle Sam gave me the authority. I speak for Uncle Sam. Always have, always will."

"Uncle Sam! Isn't he dead? I mean, nothing's official, but I was monitoring the transmissions from France. And you came back alone."

"Not alone," drawled Bob Beasley, laying a hand on an insulated box resting on his desk—formerly Mickey Weisinger's desk. There was a small pressurized tank attached, and on it stenciled a word Mickey didn't normally associate with tanks: LOX.

"He's *not* dead?"

"Well, let's say he's not anything right at the moment."

"Say what?"

"Our medical people tell me I dipped him in liquid oxygen in time to prevent brain death. All we need is a suitable body to hook him up to, and the Sam Beasley Corporation will be back to business as usual."

And Bob Beasley turned the insulated box around, exposing a clear window on the other side. The window through which stared the frozen one-eyed head of Uncle Sam Beasley.

Behind him Mickey Weisinger heard the office door shut with a flat finality that meant no escape. None at all...

Gold Eagle presents a special three-book in-line continuity

THE ARMS TRILOGY

Beginning in March 1995, Gold Eagle brings you another action-packed three-book in-line continuity, THE ARMS TRILOGY.

In THE ARMS TRILOGY, the men of Stony Man Farm target Hayden Thone, powerful head of an illicit weapons empire. Thone, CEO of Fortress Arms, is orchestrating illegal arms deals and secretly directing the worldwide activities of terrorist groups for his own purposes.

Be sure to catch all the action featuring the ever-popular THE EXECUTIONER starting in March, continuing through to May.

Available at your favorite retail outlet, or order your copy now:

Book I:	March	SELECT FIRE	$3.50 U.S. ☐
		(The Executioner #195)	$3.99 CAN. ☐
Book II:	April	TRIBURST	$3.50 U.S. ☐
		(The Executioner #196)	$3.99 CAN. ☐
Book III:	May	ARMED FORCE	$3.50 U.S. ☐
		(The Executioner #197)	$3.99 CAN. ☐

Total amount	$_____
Plus 75¢ postage ($1.00 in Canada)	$_____
Canadian residents add applicable federal and provincial taxes	
Total payable	$_____

To order, please send this form, along with your name, address, zip or postal code, and a check or money order for the total above, payable to Gold Eagle Books, to:

In the U.S.
Gold Eagle Books
3010 Walden Avenue
P. O. Box 9077
Buffalo, NY 14269-9077

In Canada
Gold Eagle Books
P. O. Box 636
Fort Erie, Ontario
L2A 5X3

GOLD EAGLE®

AT95-2

TAKE 'EM FREE
4 action-packed novels plus a mystery bonus
NO RISK
NO OBLIGATION TO BUY

Adventure and suspense in the midst of the new reality

JAMES AXLER

DEATH LANDS®

Shadowfall

The nuclear conflagration that had nearly consumed the world generations ago stripped away most of its bounty. Amid the ruins of the Sunshine State, Ryan Cawdor comes to an agonizing crossroads, torn by a debt to the past and loyalty to the present.

Hope died in the Deathlands, but the will to live goes on.

Don't miss out on the action in these titles featuring
THE EXECUTIONER®, ABLE TEAM® and PHOENIX FORCE®!